AUTUMN
COLLECTION

AUTUMN
COLLECTION

Heather Horrocks
Stephanie Black
Heather B. Moore

Sarah M. Eden
Rachelle J. Christensen
Annette Lyon

Mirror Press

Copyright © 2014 by Mirror Press, LLC
Paperback edition
All rights reserved

No part of this book may be reproduced in any form whatsoever without prior written permission of the publisher, except in the case of brief passages embodied in critical reviews and articles.

This is a work of fiction. The characters, names, incidents, places, and dialogue are products of the authors' imagination and are not to be construed as real.

Original Cover Design by Christina Marcano
Paperback Cover Design by Rachael Anderson
Interior Design by Rachael Anderson
Edited by Annette Lyon & Cassidy Wadsworth

Published by Mirror Press, LLC
http://timelessromanceanthologies.blogspot.com

E-book edition released August 2013
Paperback edition released October 2014

ISBN-13: 978-1-941145-28-9

TABLE OF CONTENTS

A Hound Dog Named Elvis	1
Eye for an Eye	69
First Heist	133
Letter for Two	197
Silver Cascade Secrets	239
Chocolate Obsessed	305

OTHER TIMELESS ROMANCE ANTHOLOGIES

Winter Collection

Spring Vacation Collection

Summer Wedding Collection

European Collection

Love Letter Collection

Old West Collection

Summer in New York Collection

Silver Bells Collection

All Regency Collection

California Dreamin' Collection

A HOUND DOG NAMED ELVIS
A Chick Flick Clique Story

Heather Horrocks

To my naughty little dog, Gus, who is not a dachshund, but is every bit as cool as Elvis any day. And to Mark, even though he has never really been a dachshund or an ardent Elvis fan.

Other Works by Heather Horrocks

Pride and Precipitation

Regally Blonde

Bah, Humbug!

Kissing Santa

Snowed Inn

Inn the Doghouse

My Spare Lady

The Naughty List

1

The closest I ever came to getting married was just before I started singing. In fact, my first record saved my neck. — Elvis Presley

Autumn Festival, Aspen Grove, California ~ Friday, October 10th

"Could they have named this dog race anything sillier?" Kaitlin Hartley smiled at her friend as she opened the back door of her silver Jetta and unhooked her dachshund, Elvis, from the safety restraint. She attached his leash, set him on the ground, and bumped the door shut with her hip.

Kneeling, Lindsey Taylor rubbed Elvis behind his ears. Immediately, he flopped onto the ground in ecstasy and rolled over for his belly to be rubbed. She snorted. "It was my brother's idea. He's very proud of it."

"Figures." A couple of years older than Kaitlin and Lindsey, Jake was Aspen Grove's youngest mayor ever.

"But the First Annual Running of the Hallowieners? Seriously?"

"Halloween is only three weeks away." Lindsey gave Elvis one last pat, helped him upright, dusted him off, and stood. "We'd better get over to the starting line. Ethan said he'd be there too."

Ethan Peterson was Lindsey's on-again/off-again fiancé. Current status: Definitely on. Kaitlin used to double date with them back when she was still with . . . Oh, no. She was so not going there. Patting her dog's head, she said, "Let's go, Elvis."

She walked with Lindsey from the parking lot toward the entrance of Morrison Motorsports Park. The owners of the car and motorcycle race track had generously offered to host this particular Autumn Festival Race. Kaitlin had heard of dachshund races, but hadn't seen one until looking some up on YouTube a few nights ago. She'd decided to participate because it looked like it would be good, silly fun.

And, after the last year of intensive interior-designer training in New York, and the past week, when Kaitlin passed her certification test, she could use some good, silly fun.

Moving through the track entrance booths, Kaitlin signed in at the racers' table by the finish line. Checkered flags poked out of the top of a tall, round container—more to add comedy than realism, no doubt.

The young lady at the table, one of the teenage King twins, pointed to the row of large, bumpy plastic bags lined up behind her. "Inside is your dog's official racing uniform plus race buttons for the two people who will be at the starting and finish lines. Anyone else will need to stand along the sides of the track. You're assigned to lane four of the speedway."

"Thanks." Kaitlin handed Elvis's leash to Lindsey and

took one of the large bags. She peered inside, moved a few things around, and laughed. "A hot-dog costume? For a wiener-dog race? Are you kidding me?"

"No joke." The King girl shrugged. "It was the mayor's idea."

Kaitlin glanced at Lindsey, who put up her hands in protest. "Hey, I can't be held accountable for my brother. I'm just related to him."

Elvis wanted to sniff everything as they made their way the hundred feet or so from the table to the starting line. Chalk lines had been added to the car race track, marking a rectangle with the start and finish lines on each end, makeshift waist-high barriers along the longer sides, and lanes drawn up the middle. It made Kaitlin smile to think about the probability of the dogs actually staying in those pretty little lanes.

At the far end of the rectangle, she found lane four, Elvis's starting position, and glanced at her watch. Ten-ten. They still had twenty minutes until race time.

Elvis sat on his rump and looked up at her with soulful eyes. Unable to resist, she bent down and gave him a love. "You are the cutest dog ever."

"He is. And it is so good to see you back in town, Kaitlin Hartley."

Kaitlin turned and got out, "Candy!" before being swept into a hug.

Candy Kane owned Candy's Café, the place Kaitlin loved to hang out—and so did half the town. She reminded Kaitlin of Doris Day in her heyday, with streaked blonde hair curving gently about her face. She had to be in her mid-forties and probably weighed twenty or thirty pounds more than she had in her twenties, but she looked stylish.

"Have you seen Joshua yet?" Candy asked.

"Not yet," Kaitlin said, forcing a smile and changing the subject. "Do you have a dog in the race?"

Candy shook her head. "I'm looking for Sonnet Cassidy. She's the official photographer for the race."

"I haven't seen Sonnet in forever. I thought she was living with her parents."

"She's moved here, and her father is not happy about it." Candy smiled. "But your parents seemed to be happy with you being in New York for school. Even though they missed you. Are you done now?"

"Yup. Took my certification test last week."

"And you accepted the job at Kosta Architecture?"

Kaitlin nodded. "My dream design job."

"Be sure to bring some of your designs on over to the café, okay?"

Kaitlin said, "I will," and turned back to Elvis.

It took a few extra minutes for both Kaitlin and Lindsey to stuff his long body into the hot dog costume because of his excited wiggling and his wagging tail. Then they stood back to get a good look.

Pieces of bun ran along each flank, with Elvis's body being the actual hot dog portion of the costume, with a ribbon of ketchup squiggled along the top, which covered the triangle-shaped white marking on the fur of his dark brown back. As if he'd had enough excitement, he sat himself down again.

Kaitlin looked down on her little dog and crooned, "You're the cutest little hound dog ever."

"He looks more hang dog than hound dog," Lindsey teased and then spoke to the little dog. "But you look really handsome, Elvis. Really. You are definitely the manliest hot dog on this track." Lindsey looked over at Kaitlin. "Are you sure dachshunds are really hound dogs?"

"Yes, they are." Kaitlin nodded. "I don't think he likes the costume. He'd probably rather be in a sequined jumpsuit." Kaitlin scratched behind her dog's ears; he tipped his head and closed his eyes. "But you sure like *this*, don't you, boy?"

"Maybe he needs some blue suede shoes or something," Lindsey said, and then her voice rose. "Oh, no!"

"What?" Kaitlin looked up in surprise.

Lindsey pointed down the line. "*There! Double trouble!*"

Holding the end of Elvis's leash, Kaitlin stood and searched the crowd where her friend was pointing. What she saw at the far end of the starting line sucked her breath away. After a moment of stunned silence, she whispered, "Oh, no, no, no. Is that *Joshua*?"

"Worse—*Ethan*. The bum is *helping* Joshua! I don't believe this. I'll be back before the race starts. I'm going to go give him a piece of my mind. Maybe it's time for him to choose between me and Joshua." And Kaitlin's emotionally volatile friend shot off toward her unsuspecting boyfriend.

Kaitlin's heart pounded.

Joshua Moore.

The one man she didn't want to run into in Aspen Grove. Especially not when she'd only been back in town for one week. Give it a month or two—another *year*—and maybe she could handle it. Maybe. But not like this, not so unexpectedly.

Frozen in place, Kaitlin watched as Lindsey rounded on Ethan. She could hear their raised voices but couldn't make out the words through the sounds of the crowd—the same crowd that now watched the couple with interest. Kaitlin could see the angry sparks from here.

Lindsey pointed back toward Kaitlin, and both Ethan and Joshua looked her way. If Joshua's narrowed gaze and frown were any indication, he wasn't any happier to see her than she was to see him.

His gaze locked with hers, and warmth flooded her cheeks.

He was dressed in his trademark faded blue jeans and cowboy boots, his muscles sharply defined in a long-sleeved dark blue shirt. His dark hair was a little too long—just the length she liked to run her fingers through.

A familiar physical attraction flashed through her veins.

Appalled at her reaction, she turned, her hands trembling on the leash. Stop that! She wanted nothing to do with the man.

He'd broken her heart once.

She wasn't going to give him the chance to do it again.

2

Ambition is a dream with a V8 engine. —Elvis Presley

Kaitlin wanted to win this race.

She wanted Elvis to beat Joshua's matching dachshund, Priscilla, to the finish line.

Joshua stood behind the finish line in lane fifteen, Kaitlin in four. She had to force her gaze away from his magnetic pull. It infuriated her that she was still so attracted to him. That simply had to change.

At the starting line, Lindsey held Elvis's collar, and Ethan held Priscilla's—the matching purple collars they'd purchased in a former love life. Lindsey not only didn't mind looking at Ethan, she called out periodic insults. If it hadn't been so horrible, this day might actually be funny. Maybe in twenty years, she'd laugh about it.

The line of dachshunds in hot-dog costumes was genuinely funny, but Kaitlin wasn't in any mood to laugh at those, anyway. She just wanted to beat Joshua.

Over the loudspeaker, Mayor Jake Taylor said, "The race is about to begin, folks, so give your dog any last-minute instructions, and we'll begin the official countdown."

Lindsey stopped glaring at Ethan and knelt by Elvis—probably to tell him to forget the race and take Ethan down!

Jake continued with, "All right, friends. Welcome to the First Annual Running of the Hallowieners, the newest event in Aspen Grove's Autumn Festival, the race where the dogs are nearly as long as the track. We want to thank the fine folks of Morrison Motorsports Park for offering their award-winning race track for this special event." The owner of the track, the elder Mr. Morrison, spoke for a couple of minutes and handed the mic back to Jake.

Two men at the sidelines began waving the official racetrack starting flags, and Jake continued. "All right, hot doggers. Get ready to set your long dogs loose on the word *go*. Ready? All right. Here we . . . three . . . two . . . one . . . GO!"

As soon as the dogs were loosed, the track erupted in noise. The people at the starting line and along the sides cheered for their favorites, while everyone at the finish line called their dog to them, hoping to win the prize: the twenty bucks was short on cash but long on bragging rights over something silly, and sometimes that was its own reward.

Of the twenty or so hot-dog-costumed dachshunds, only three sprinted. One was Elvis, who bounded straight toward Kaitlin. "Good boy. Come on, Elvis!"

The other two were Priscilla and a dog Kaitlin didn't recognize. They weren't a worry, though, because Elvis was in the lead.

The rest of the dachshunds either strolled toward their owners, to someone at the side barriers, or stood there looking confused at all the noise. One little dog sat on its rump and howled.

Elvis and Priscilla and the third dog continued to race toward the finish line. "Come on, Elvis! You can do it! I love you, Priscilla, but you are going down."

Then, as if from a telepathic dog signal, Elvis and Priscilla stopped running and moved toward each other. It was the doggie version of those old movies with two people running in slow motion across the field. Or like watching cars spin out of a race.

"No, Elvis! You're supposed to beat Priscilla, not lick her face!"

But the two dogs, who had always loved each other dearly, rolled over each other, licked each other's faces, and in general showed that they'd missed each other terribly.

A cheer went up as the third sprinter jumped across the finish line and into its owner's arms, checkered flags waving. A few of the other dogs ambled across the finish line. The little dog still howled.

Elvis and Priscilla continued to play. Frolic. *Gambol.*

Their hot-dog costumes shifted on their bodies as they played, the buns sliding from the sides to the top and back.

Kaitlin took a deep, resigned breath and rose to her feet. She called Elvis's name again, and she heard Joshua calling to Priscilla, but the dogs ignored them in the midst of their little doggy reunion.

Lindsey shot her a disappointed frown. Kaitlin nodded at her friend. Then, deliberately not looking at Joshua, though she could see him in her peripheral vision, she walked toward the two dogs.

While Joshua and Kaitlin were dating, they'd decided it would be fun to get two matching dogs. When they'd found these, brother and sister, with identical triangle-shaped white markings on their back, they'd fallen in love with the little dogs. Joshua had good-naturedly let Kaitlin name them after her favorite singer and his wife. She loved both dogs.

When Kaitlin reached them, she knelt and petted them both. Both dogs jumped into her arms, sending her off balance just enough that she toppled over. She couldn't help laughing as she tried to avoid their eager tongues.

Forget Joshua—though she couldn't actually do that—she just let herself love on both dogs for a minute. When the dogs settled down, she gave them a last pat and pushed herself to her knees and to her feet. Only then did she look at Joshua.

Still frowning, he said, "When did you get back?"

"Last weekend," she answered, her voice icy. "Not that you care."

He shrugged casually. "I always cared."

"Oh, right." She glared back, thinking of the woman he'd chosen to date after she'd left town, Betty Branson. Kaitlin used her nickname. "Bitty? Really? Give me a break. Don't you have any class at all?"

"May I remind you that *you* left *me* behind?"

"You could have followed."

"And left my dream behind while you went for yours?" He looked away for a long moment. "I wanted you to stay."

She trembled with indignation. "I didn't come back to fight with you. I also want nothing to do with you."

"Fine." Without looking away from her hostile gaze, he clipped a leash onto Priscilla. "See you around, Katie."

"Don't you dare call me that! You are not authorized to use pet names for me anymore."

Without looking back, he put a hand in the air and then started walking away toward the parking lot.

Anger filling her, Kaitlin clipped the leash on Elvis. "Come on, boy. Let's go home."

3

I don't know anything about music. In my line you don't have to. —Elvis Presley

By the time they'd reached the car, Lindsey had caught up with Kaitlin and Elvis. "Oh, my gosh, I am *never* speaking to Ethan again. *Ever.*"

Kaitlin had heard that before and knew her friend would change her volatile mind in a few hours or days. She was like a flaming star—she always cooled back down.

"I hope I never have to speak to Joshua again either." Shivering in the cool October air, Kaitlin unlocked her Jetta, opened the back door, lifted Elvis onto the car's back seat, and put the safety harness on him. He settled himself on his cushion—specially made of blue suede, of course.

Lindsey flounced into the passenger seat and slapped on her seatbelt.

Kaitlin sighed and joined her, starting the car, hoping to get heat circulating. The gauge on the dash read fifty-three degrees outside. Downright chilly for the first dachshund race.

"I hate him," Lindsey said softly, staring straight ahead.

"No, you don't. You love him. You always have. You always will."

"I hate them both. Ethan and Joshua. They are such jerks."

Kaitlin didn't answer as she adjusted the vents to blow semi-warm air on her hands.

"You've always loved Joshua too. Why did he have to go and ruin everything by dating Bitty?" Lindsey spat out the name. Even Betty Branson referred to herself as Bitty, but she probably wouldn't approve of the way Lindsey said, "More like Bitty Brains. I hate her too!"

That made Kaitlin laugh. "Oh, Lindsey, I love you and your passionate nature. But you can't hate everyone."

Lindsey sent a glare in her direction. "I love you, too, Kaitlin, but you know it's dangerous to stop me mid-rant."

"I do." Kaitlin shifted the Jetta into drive and waited until a guy in a big truck paused to let her pull into the line of cars. She waved her thanks. Thank goodness other events were taking place here, or this would be a very slow drive back to town. A big chunk of the town had been at the race track.

"Joshua looked good." Kaitlin had to admit it. It was true.

"That's how they suck you back into their traps. Don't fall for it. They always look good—like a devil in disguise—right before they lower the boom."

Kaitlin sighed. "There was a time when all I wanted was to be married to Joshua. I used to practice writing *Mrs. Moore* over and over."

"Yeah, and I saw how you were looking at him today too. But remember how he started dating Bitty so soon after you left. Two weeks. Fourteen measly days. A fortnight." She laughed. "A fortnight is two weeks, right?"

"Yes. And don't worry. I do have regrets. After all, he broke my heart. But there are no old feelings for me."

Why was it so much easier to lie to other people than to herself? Kaitlin did still care for Joshua. Last year, she'd loved him with all her heart, and she was obviously still attracted to the man. But when her dream employer had offered to pay all her expenses for a year of specialized training and certification, including her living expenses, she couldn't turn down the chance to go for her dream.

She'd hoped he'd go with her.

But what had Joshua done? Had he gone with her? Or even waited for her? Her training was for just a year. Instead, he'd tried to keep her from going by proposing the night before she was supposed to leave. And then, a mere two weeks later, he'd proved his insincerity and disloyalty by beginning to date Bitty Branson.

"Don't forget how he tried to hold you back." Lindsey's voice softened, her rant fading already. "You should date someone else; that's what I always do."

"I'm not going to date anyone. I'm going to focus on my career and prove to Mr. Kosta that I'm worth the thousands of dollars he invested in my education. I am hereby officially forgetting all men."

Another lie. She couldn't forget Joshua. She hadn't been able to for the past year, and she couldn't get him out of her mind now.

She also could never forgive him. He hadn't really loved her, and she'd never get over that hurt.

Welcome to Heartbreak Hotel.

4

I'd just like to be treated like a regular customer. —Elvis Presley

Saturday, October 11th

The next day, Kaitlin took Candy up on her invitation to bring some designs to the café. She chose a notebook with her favorite designs, complete with fabric samples, sketches, and renderings. Her mother offered to drive, which gave Kaitlin time to flip through the sheet protectors. She loved her work. Using her talent and skills, she'd take fabrics, textures, colors, and furniture that, when combined, created a stunning room.

As she drove, Kaitlin's mother said, "Have you seen Joshua again?"

Kaitlin shook her head. "I'm making it a point of not seeing Josh."

"Too bad. I always thought you two made a wonderful couple. I guess I was hoping to see you back together."

When they reached Candy's Café, Kaitlin stopped first to put money in the jukebox and push the numbers for three

Elvis songs. "I'm All Shook Up" started to play.

With a delighted grin, Candy welcomed them. "You brought your designs to show us?"

Kaitlin nodded and held up her notebook.

"Bring it over to the counter, honey. Nobody's sitting there right now. Open it up and spread out the pages. Then everyone can come over and see them."

It took just a moment to line the pages up along the counter.

"They're beautiful," Candy said, looking them over one by one. When she reached the end of the counter, she looked up at Kaitlin. "Very elegant. You're an artist."

"Thanks. I worked hard on them."

Candy turned to the tables and called out, "Hey, everyone, come and see Kaitlin's designs. They're fantastic."

Her mother smiled. "Leave it to Candy to create some buzz."

Kaitlin looked around the café. Mid-afternoon found only four groups of customers.

At the first table sat Mayor Jake Taylor and a few of the employees of his thriving electronics store, An App a Day. Jake waved to Kaitlin.

A group of rowdy teenagers filled two adjacent booths.

At the next table sat Bitty Branson. Of course. Bitty glared at Kaitlin, tossed money on the table, and stormed out of the café, still pulling on her jacket as she pushed her way through the door.

Candy whispered to Kaitlin, "Don't worry about her, honey. She's just jealous."

"Thanks." Kaitlin nodded. She didn't have time to worry about Bitty's reaction, because at the table with the last group of diners was the other person besides Joshua whom

Kaitlin had been hoping to avoid for a while—Joshua's mother, Nina Moore—and two of her friends.

Kaitlin wasn't sure what kind of reception Nina would give her, but Kaitlin had always gotten along well with Joshua's parents. No matter what their son had done, she still had good feelings toward them. She just wasn't ready to socialize with someone who may be angry with her.

Her heartbeat quickened, and anxiety filled her, especially when Nina and her friends rose, picked up their purses and left a tip, and walked toward her. But Nina greeted her warmly, as did her friends. The three of them exclaimed over her designs and how creative they were, saying things like how they'd always known Kaitlin would be an artistic type after seeing her sketches when she was a little girl.

What a bittersweet moment for Kaitlin. She loved this woman as a second mother. How could she tell her heart to forget that? Things were a little *awkward* right now.

"Are you coming to our next Chick Flick Clique night, Kaitlin?" Candy wiped her hands on a dish towel and hung it back up. With a grin, she added, "If you do, we'll play an Elvis movie in your honor."

Kaitlin laughed. "You know me well, don't you?"

Candy nodded. "I bet you've played every Elvis song on my jukebox a hundred times."

Kaitlin's mother laughed. "Her father played them on every family trip we took."

Kaitlin nodded. "We were all *shook up* for days at a time."

"You certainly played Elvis at our house often enough," Nina said with a gentle smile. "Why don't you drop by our house tonight? Joshua will be stopping by, and we can play some games or something. I'll mix up some brownies. Your favorite."

Nina wanted to get her son and Kaitlin back together?

As the women around them grew silent and Kaitlin felt every eye on her, heat flushed her cheeks. What could she say? She'd loved Nina and Bob for years and had considered them family forever. What was the etiquette for dealing with the beloved parents of your previous faithless near-fiancé?

"That sounds delightful," Kaitlin finally said. "But I can't for at least a few weeks. I'll be spending most of my time trying to get up to speed at work. I have some big projects, and I need to get a handle on them."

Disappointment flashed through Nina's eyes, and Kaitlin felt horrible. Nina blinked and said, "Of course tonight wouldn't be a good night with you just back in town. And I know how much your new job means to you. Just know that the invitation stands when your workload lessens. We'd love to have you over. Any time."

Unexpectedly, Nina wrapped her arms around Kaitlin and whispered, "I love you, Kaitlin. Welcome home."

5

I didn't know that there were any radio stations in Nova Scotia. —Elvis Presley

Monday, October 13th

Wondering if everyone in town was hoping, along with their mothers, for her and Joshua to get back together, Kaitlin had come to a decision.

She wouldn't go outside of her parents' house for a week or two, not until things calmed down. Other than working at the office and walking Elvis, she'd keep away from people, avoid the café, and in general let the small-town busybodies find somebody else to talk about.

She didn't want to run into Joshua again. Or Bitty. And seeing Nina had shaken her more than she'd expected it to.

So after work and a delicious enchilada dinner fixed by her mother, she fed Elvis. As her parents left for a movie with some friends and Kaitlin washed the dishes, her cell phone rang. She wiped her hands. It was a blocked number. Hmmm. She answered it anyway, prepared to ask a telemarketer to place her number on the do-not-call list. "Hello?"

There was no response, and Kaitlin repeated, "Hello?"

The line disconnected. Wrong number, perhaps. One of those rude people who don't say they're sorry but just hang up.

As she slipped her phone back in her pocket, the doorbell rang.

Too bad other people didn't know of her decision. She didn't want to see anyone tonight. She debated whether to answer, but when the bell rang again, she sighed in resignation. It had better be Girl Scouts selling Thin Mints.

It wasn't a Girl Scout. It wasn't even a girl. No, it was a man. The most handsome man in Aspen Grove, California, and the one she most did not want to see. The one who still sent a thrill of attraction through her.

"Joshua?" At the sight of him standing on the porch, a gamut of emotions ran through Kaitlin. Surprise. Relief. Joy. Regret. *Anger.* "Did you just call me?"

He shook his head. "Hello to you, too."

Kaitlin looked beyond him at Priscilla, who looked up at her soulfully, then back at Joshua. "What are you doing here?"

"I'm bringing back your dog."

What was he trying to pull? "I have my dog."

"Actually, you have my dog." He shrugged. "We ended up with the wrong dogs after the race. When I realized our mistake, I figured I'd visit with Elvis until you noticed. But when you hadn't called in nearly three days, I decided I'd better bring him back. I'm here to pick up Priscilla."

"Whatever, Joshua. What is this? A cheap trick to see me again?"

"Elvis," Joshua said gently as he lifted the dog, "Meet Kaitlin."

Determined to call his bluff, Kaitlin stepped outside and closed the door to keep her dog—whichever one she had—inside the house until she could check out Josh's outlandish claim. If the dogs started playing together, she'd never know if he was telling the truth, not with their identical collars and markings.

When she petted his dog behind the ears, it dropped to the ground and rolled over, revealing definite boy-dog anatomy.

This *was* Elvis!

Elvis had left the building—with Joshua? And she hadn't even noticed? For three days?

How could she not notice she had the wrong dog? How was that even possible? What kind of awful dog mother was she anyway? Guilt-ridden, she looked into Joshua's eyes.

He shrugged and spoke gently. "It can happen to the best of us."

"But you noticed right away," she said with accusation in her voice.

"I've always been able to tell them apart."

He *had* always been able to—she remembered that now—where she'd usually had to put a bow on Priscilla's collar to help her know which was which. Still feeling cross, she asked, "Then why couldn't you tell them apart at the race?"

"Because their little backs were covered by a faux ketchup squiggle."

"Oh, yeah. That." A bird chirped in the tree in her yard. Grateful for an excuse to look away from Josh, she lifted her gaze to the tree. The bird chirped again then went silent.

"I can tell you're feeling guilty, but don't. You're great with the dogs. I know life is hectic for you right now. It's no wonder you didn't notice."

"So hectic I couldn't notice I didn't have my own dog?"

"Hey, easy on yourself. Priscilla used to be yours, too."

She opened the door to let Priscilla outside. Once again, the two little dogs began to dance around like they had at the race track. Watching them, she said, "They obviously enjoy being back together."

"They always loved spending time with each other. Maybe we should get them together once or twice a week. For a walk or something. For their mental health."

For a moment, she wondered if he was talking about the dogs—or them.

When she caught his gaze, he smiled innocently. "Shall we take them for a walk tomorrow night?"

She paused, hesitating. But the dogs were having so much fun, she couldn't say no. Torn, she finally said, "Okay. But only for a *short* walk."

"Great," he said. "Come on, Priscilla."

Both dogs followed him, and Kaitlin had to call out, "Elvis, come back, buddy."

Both dogs turned back toward her.

With a grin that made her knees weak, Joshua picked up Priscilla—maybe—and gave her a jaunty wave.

As she watched him saunter to his pickup, her heart caught. How could she go walking with him and hope to keep her emotional distance?

As Joshua gently secured the little dog in his truck, he glanced back at her and shot her a lop-sided grin.

Stop being attracted to the man!

As he drove away, she turned to her dog. "Oh, Elvis, what have I done?"

Elvis lifted a leg. She wasn't sure if he was commenting on her decision to walk with Joshua or her having been oblivious to his not being home, or if he was just proving his gender.

With the little hound dog's communication skills, it was hard to tell.

6

I was training to be an electrician. I suppose I got wired the wrong way 'round somewhere along the line. —Elvis Presley

Tuesday, October 14th

All morning long, as Kaitlin chose fabrics and color renderings and put them together with pictures of room furnishings, she'd been agitated. Usually she could lose herself for hours playing with colors and textures, especially as excited as she'd been to be assigned to the company's newest large project—an office building, Stafford House, halfway between Aspen Grove and Sacramento—but today she was on edge.

Why on earth had she agreed to walk with Joshua tonight? She didn't need to go. She should just hand him the leash and let him walk both dogs.

It was nearly noon, and Lindsey would be at the office shortly to take Kaitlin to lunch at a Chinese place that had opened while she'd been away. When she heard someone enter, she assumed it was Lindsay and looked up with a smile.

She was wrong. It was Mr. Kosta, her boss, walking into the back room and studying a color swatch sample she'd put together. Now even more nervous, she waited anxiously to see if he liked what she'd done.

Finally, he nodded with approval. "We're very happy with your work, Ms. Hartley. I was right to put that money into your further education. Welcome back."

"Thank you, Mr. Kosta. It was so generous of you to pay for my training." She'd had to sign a contract agreeing to work five years for Kosta Architecture in return, but she figured she'd gotten the better end of that deal. Easily. Especially since she'd love to work for Mr. Kosta forever.

He picked up one of her new business cards and read aloud, "Kaitlin Hartley, NCIDQ, Interior Designer, Kosta Architecture." He smiled at her. "I understand you passed the certification test with, pardon the pun, flying colors. You'll be a real asset to the company. I'm glad you have the dream of decorating."

"Thanks. I'll do my best." She'd been excited to follow her dream.

"Have you found a place to rent?"

Kaitlin shook her head. "I haven't really looked yet."

"My nephew Aaron just moved out of my rental on Quail Lane. It's being painted this week, but if you'd like, I'll give you first choice. You could start moving in next week. It's partially furnished. You'll need to get a new couch, though."

"I'd love to. I'll come by to see it."

"Good. I'll tell my wife to hold it for you. I'll even give you the family discount." He motioned toward the fabric hung around her space. The designers all loved fabrics, and it was amusing to walk through the design department, and see random fabrics hanging around the individual cubicles. Hers tended toward rich browns and blues—even one swatch of blue suede, of course. "This is more of an indicator that you are a *real* designer than your business card."

"Thank you for making it possible for me to go to New York." The year of study at the exclusive design house had been amazing and had opened doors to her that she could never have afforded on her own. Not without incredible sacrifice. "I'm hoping to have the rooms designed for the Stafford House by the end of the week."

"I know you'll work hard. I had an ulterior motive in sending you back to school. I wanted you to be the best designer in town—working for us. So, yes. Go make us proud." He nodded again. "I'm going out to lunch with my wife, and then she's dragging me to buy some clothes, so I may be late. I may never come back. I may die waiting for her to come out of the dressing room."

"I'll cross my fingers that you'll return safely."

He zipped up his jacket. "Enjoy your lunch. Someone needs to."

As he left, she happily got back to work and waited for Lindsey to arrive. She even forgot her nervousness about tonight's walk with Joshua.

When Lindsey called to say she'd be a few minutes late, Kaitlin continued playing with colors and textures. She was combining red, white, and yellow swatches for a dramatic entryway when one of the other designers came through the hallway. "Check this out," she said.

Kaitlin looked up. "What's up?"

With a huge smile, Lacey held out her left hand and waved it. "Ben proposed!"

Kaitlin examined the ring. "Wow! Is that the Rock of Gibraltar?"

Lacey giggled. "I know. Isn't it gorgeous?"

Kaitlin held Lacey's hand, adjusting it so she could see the ring more clearly. It was beautiful, with curving lines that would appeal to a designer. "That is so exciting. Have you set a date?"

"We're thinking February for Valentine's Day."

"And do you know where you'll honeymoon?"

"Oh, yeah." Lacey nodded. "We're gonna have fun in Acapulco."

Kaitlin squeezed Lacey's hand and released it. "I am thrilled for you guys."

And she was. But as she watched Lacey leave with her new ring, she couldn't ignore the hurt that squeezed her heart.

Joshua had offered her a ring last year. She could be wearing it right now. Except he'd only done it to keep her in town.

The lack of a relationship was driving her crazy.

If she couldn't have Joshua, maybe she should have a change of habit—take Lindsey's advice and start dating other guys. Try to find someone she could spend time with.

Someone who could help her live a little, love a little—and forget all about Joshua Moore.

7

I have no use for bodyguards, but I have very specific use for two highly trained certified public accountants.
—Elvis Presley

Kaitlin had spent the hours since work steeling herself for the moment when Joshua would show up at her parents' house. She was determined to stay detached and aloof. She was still considering just handing him the leash and letting him walk both dogs himself.

She was watching a movie with her parents in the family room, trying to relax and petting Elvis, when the doorbell rang.

Her parents shot her a look, and her mother smiled brightly. "Joshua's here. You'd better get the door, honey."

Dreading the confrontation—both with Joshua and her parents—when Joshua learned she wasn't going, she stood and carried Elvis, attaching his leash as she walked slowly toward the living room and the front door.

She paused a moment, and the doorbell rang again. She

set down the little dog, got ready to hand off the leash, and opened the door.

Joshua held Priscilla in one hand and three flowers in the other. "Hi."

"Hi." She stared at the yellow roses. His remembering her favorite flowers wouldn't do him any good at all. But her head and heart didn't agree, and she struggled to regain her earlier resolution to hand over the leash. It eluded her.

Looking up, she saw a slight smile on his face that didn't quite hide his nervousness.

She should hand over the leash, tell him they needed to not see each other again, but she looked at the roses. He was at least trying to be polite. After the roses, it would seem downright ungracious of her not to go. Plus, her mother adored him, and her father liked him. If she didn't go, she'd never hear the end of it from them.

"Come in while I put those in a vase."

She carried the flowers into the kitchen, found a vase, and, while it filled with water, trimmed the stalks. Placing the flowers in the water, she could hear her parents greet Joshua in the living room. Mom overdid it. Shocker.

Kaitlin lifted the vase and smelled the roses. Their beautiful scent softened her heart a little more. Setting down the vase, she steeled herself and rejoined the others.

They chatted for a few minutes, and then she found herself walking the wild streets of Aspen Grove with Joshua and her two favorite dogs.

The dogs were having so much fun together that they kept tangling the leashes. At one point, Joshua said, "Here, let me take both of them."

That made it easier to walk, with the dogs pulling out in front and Kaitlin next to Joshua.

"It's good to see Elvis and Priscilla back together," Joshua said.

That brought a laugh from Kaitlin. "Yeah."

"I've got a business trip to L.A. the week before Halloween. Is it okay if I leave Priscilla with you while I'm gone?"

"Sure," she said. "Elvis will be thrilled to have a playmate. Will you be back in time to trick-or-treat?"

"I should be. Thanks for keeping her." Joshua grinned. "And if Elvis and Priscilla ever had a puppy, we could name it Lisa Marie."

"Only if it were a girl puppy. But since they're siblings, and they've both been fixed, I'm kind of doubting that will ever happen."

"But if it did, wouldn't it be great?" His eyes brightened.

She laughed again. "It really would."

She could never stay aloof from Joshua. He was too nice, too fun, and too attractive. It took everything she had not to slip her arm through his like she used to, to run her fingers through his dark hair, to kiss him! Joshua was the epitome of "Love Me Tender."

She remembered how it was when she was allowed to kiss him whenever she wanted—and she wanted to right now. She reminded herself how close she was to safety. Only one more block. Which meant she only had a few more minutes to spend with Joshua.

She gave herself a mental shake and bent over, pretending to need to tie her shoelace, trying to give herself a moment to regain her composure. When she regained control of herself, she stood. She thought she could keep her hands—and lips—to herself now. She hoped.

Behind them, a woman called out, loudly, "Joshua! Kaitlin! Wait up!"

They turned.

No. It couldn't be. What were the odds? But it was.

Bitty Branson. Bleached-blonde hair curled down around her shoulders. Her too-tight jeans and jacket left nothing to the imagination. Good thing it was October and chilly; Kaitlin would hate to see the skin the woman exposed in the summer.

Why, oh why did *she* have to be here to ruin this pleasant evening?

As Bitty began to cross the street toward them, waving brightly and calling out, Kaitlin turned to Joshua. "I'll go ahead home. You two have a nice visit."

He started to protest but then sighed. "Okay." He held out one of the leashes.

She took it but then narrowed her eyes. Lifting up the dog he'd handed her, she checked the gender. Male. Now that she'd verified that she had Elvis, she was good to go.

Joshua smiled. "Let's go walking again in a few days."

Kaitlin didn't answer but instead started to walk Elvis toward her parents' house three lots down.

She could hear Bitty calling out to her, but she couldn't stand talking with the woman at the moment. It was already too hard being in this town where everyone knew she and Joshua had been together—only now they weren't, and any woman in town could make a move on him.

How could she have forgotten, even for an hour, what Joshua had done? A few flowers, a few teasing words, a few long glances, and her brain stopped working? Kaitlin was the bitty-brained one.

Sensing her desire to get home, Elvis sat his hind quarters on the sidewalk and stared back at the others.

"Come on, Elvis. I'll feed you a fried peanut butter and

banana sandwich when we get home. A peanut-butter dog biscuit, anyway." She picked him up and escaped into her parents' house.

"Where's Joshua?" asked her mother.

Perhaps *escape* wasn't the correct word.

8

Rhythm is something you either have or don't have, but when you have it, you have it all over.
—Elvis Presley

Joshua stared after Kaitlin, wishing Bitty were anywhere but five steps away and closing.

With Bitty so close, he forced his gaze away from Kaitlin. He still had feelings of guilt for dating Bitty when he'd had no romantic interest in her, but she'd apparently had some for him. After a month, he'd broken up with her as gently as he could. Now he always tried to be nice when he talked with her—nice and polite and firmly unavailable. But Bitty never seemed to take the hint.

She smiled up at him, flirting. "I didn't mean to interrupt. Are you two back together?"

How was he supposed to answer that? "Just friends." He wouldn't mention how freaking inconvenient it was that she'd shown up at this particular moment, when Kaitlin had finally been warming up to him.

Bitty reached out and ran her fingers down the sleeve of

his jacket. "I've missed you. When are you going to come over?"

Not again. Every time she saw him—and was it his imagination, or did her following him around have a stalkeresque quality?

Joshua took a step back, breaking her hold on his sleeve. "Bitty, I told you—"

"I know. I know. It's over. But it doesn't have to be." She sighed. "She doesn't want you back, you know. It's over between you two, as well."

Harsh words flowed through his mind, but he spoke softly, feeling sorry for Bitty, sensing her emotional fragility. "It's over between me and Kaitlin—and also between me and you."

She sighed again. "You know where I live. I'll see you around. Give your best to your parents."

He watched her walk away. Now there was one disturbed woman. It had been stupid of him to date anyone else just to make Kaitlin jealous—and doubly stupid to have chosen Bitty. They'd gone on five dates in one month, and he'd spent the next eleven months trying to convince her he wasn't the man for her.

As she turned the corner, he shook his head and looked where Kaitlin had disappeared into her parents' home.

He and Priscilla strolled to the Hartley home, and he drove them to his very empty house, which he'd bought after Kaitlin left him. He'd put a down payment on it before he'd proposed, because she'd fallen in love with the house, and he'd wanted to surprise her. Too bad she hadn't fallen as much in love with *him*. She hadn't taken the proposal well, so he'd never mentioned buying the place.

How had things gotten so turned around last year?

He'd only dated Bitty because Kaitlin had left him behind. He'd proposed, put his heart totally on the line, and she'd rejected him. She'd said she couldn't give up the chance at furthering her career. She'd expected him to follow her to New York.

But his career was here, in Aspen Grove, working with Stone Engineering. He'd gotten hired on at a great salary right after receiving his degree. If he'd left town for a year, Stone would have hired someone else to replace him. Joshua would probably have had to look outside of Aspen Grove for a job with the same income, and neither he nor Kaitlin had wanted to move. Not permanently.

Joshua would have taken care of Kaitlin. He'd told her he was willing to be the breadwinner after their marriage and let her do all the studying she wanted. Just not away from him.

But Kaitlin hadn't cared.

That had ticked him off.

And he'd been stupid, thinking to prove . . . *something* . . . by dating someone else. As if Kaitlin hadn't really hurt him. Or as if he was getting on with his life. And all he'd succeeded in doing was ruining his chances with Kaitlin now that she was back in town.

He wanted a second chance with Katie. And things had been going really, really well tonight—until Bitty showed up.

Bitty. The woman every girl in town hated. The perfect girl to make Kaitlin jealous. Only it had backfired on him. Now he'd hurt two women. The one he wanted didn't want anything to do with him, while the one he wanted nothing to do with kept showing up *coincidentally.*

If he could get a ring on Kaitlin's finger, maybe then Bitty would get it.

But how could he do that? What could he do to show Kaitlin how much he loved her?

He'd been an idiot. A year had seemed like forever back then, but he should have handled things differently. He should have waited.

He still wanted her for his wife.

It was time to reunite Elvis and Priscilla—permanently.

9

More than anything else, I want the folks back at home to think right of me.
—Elvis Presley

Saturday, October 18th

"I'll even keep Elvis here while you go," Kaitlin's mother said, five days after the dog-walking debacle. "I need to decorate for autumn, and I can't leave home until this fudge is done. It won't take you long. Please?"

"Thanksgiving is a month away, and Halloween is still two weeks away. Why do you have to start so early?"

"Early? Autumn officially started weeks ago. *Pretty please . . . ?*" Susan Hartley had a way of looking imploringly at her daughter that usually got Kaitlin to do whatever her mother wanted.

It worked this time too. Kaitlin sighed, and asked, "Does it have to be from the Pumpkin Patch?"

Her mother nodded. "Their pumpkins stay fresh much longer."

Trying not to roll her eyes, Kaitlin admitted defeat.

"Okay. Draw up a list of exactly what you want."

"I'll do better than that. I'll forward a picture my friend sent me from Pinterest."

As Kaitlin drove, she pondered. She remembered making this drive to the Pumpkin Patch two years ago, after her mother had pleaded, just like tonight. But unlike tonight, she'd gone with Joshua. And she'd gotten an awesome kiss from him there, in the backyard, surrounded by pumpkins.

That was the problem with Aspen Grove—powerful memories were hidden everywhere, memories of her and Joshua as a couple. A hug at Candy's Café. A cuddle under a blanket at the high school stadium during football games. A kiss at the Pumpkin Patch, at the Mexican restaurant, at . . . well, kisses pretty much everywhere, in far too many locales to count.

Joshua was a very good kisser.

So she might as well go to the Pumpkin Patch as anywhere. No matter where she went, she was either going to be assailed by her own memories or by other people's hopes and expectations.

Perhaps she'd made a mistake coming back home. But she'd had no choice. She was pretty much locked into Aspen Grove for the next five years while she fulfilled her obligation to Mr. Kosta.

The parking lot at the Pumpkin Patch, the most popular seasonal craft store in town, was crowded, with cars pulling out and others jockeying for the twenty or so parking spots. The store was full of people who would doubtless want to ask her how she was doing, if she was dating Joshua again, and if she was enjoying being back in town. So many questions, so few answers.

She parked her Jetta but didn't get out. Not yet. She

needed a few minutes to prepare herself. This was exactly why she'd wanted to hide out at home.

One of the four or five shoppers leaving the store was Candy, who was hefting a box with a pumpkin showing above the edge. She waved, set the box in the trunk of her car, and walked over.

Kaitlin rolled down her window and smiled. "Hi."

Candy leaned over and patted her arm. "Hiding out in your car isn't going to help. You need to pull up your big girl panties and go out in public. Everyone will get over the fact that you and Joshua aren't an item soon enough. About the time Ethan and Lindsey have another spectacular breakup, probably, which their current spat is leading up to."

Kaitlin laughed. "Is my hiding that obvious?"

"Just act as if you have the world by the tail—and pretty soon, you will." Candy motioned to the window. "Roll it up, get out, and grab hold of that tail, woman."

Kaitlin did. "Thanks. I needed that pep talk."

"Any time you need advice, you know where to find me." Candy motioned toward the store. "The best pumpkins are along the back wall."

She locked arms with Kaitlin, and they walked together until they reached Candy's car. After clicking her key fob, Candy opened the door. "See you around, sweetie."

"Maybe I'll come for that Chick Flick Clique Elvis movie after all."

"Great. I'll find a good one."

Kaitlin laughed. "They're all good."

"No they're not." Candy gave one last wave and climbed in her car. "Second Wednesday of each month."

Kaitlin entered the warmth of the small store, bypassing the displays of all things craftsy—from knitting needles and crochet hooks to beading and paint supplies—to follow the crowd outside through the rear doors, where the largest displays of yard decor were kept. The square, encircled by a chain link fence, was double the size of the building.

She turned the corner and, just as Candy had said, found tables covered with pretty pumpkins. She pulled out her cell phone and stared at the picture her mother had sent. Then, with a sigh, she started lifting pumpkins to find the perfect one her mother could use to *attempt* to make this Pinterest thing. She suspected it was going to be one of those *it's-supposed-to-look-like-this-but-it-doesn't* projects.

She chose one. People crowded the aisles inside, and she had to weave between them to get to the front of the store. Didn't these people know it was just autumn, not the holiday season yet? She supposed she was not exactly in a great holiday mood. Wait until the Christmas season. She'd be a Grinch by then.

Her phone buzzed, and she fished it out again. Another blocked number. What was up with that? "Hello?"

The sound of breathing was followed, after a moment, by a whispered, "Go back where you came from."

"What? Who is this?"

A click told her the person had hung up. Shaken, Kaitlin put her phone away with a trembling hand. Had she just been threatened? Or could it possibly have been a wrong number? She didn't have any enemies . . . *did she*?

She heard a voice that made her look over, and she saw a head of slightly too long dark hair. Joshua? What was he doing here? *And why does he keep showing up everywhere I go?*

Aspen Grove wasn't *that* small of a town! It had a university, even. There were people she didn't know, yet she kept running into *him*.

Surely he wasn't the one making the phone calls . . . *was he*?

Hands still trembling, she worked her way to another aisle and checkout so he wouldn't see her. Then she pulled up her jacket collar and pushed her hair under her knit hat. If she was lucky, she could get out of here without him catching sight of her.

She paid and, lifting her mother's newly purchased pumpkin, walked quickly out of the store. Halfway to her car, she looked back.

Joshua was watching her from just outside the door. Even from this distance, she could see the hurt etched on his face. He knew she'd left to avoid him.

She was furious—at herself, for feeling guilty. *She'd done nothing wrong.*

And, underneath her fury, lurked a vague unease. Who was it that wished her ill?

10

I think I have something tonight that's not quite correct for evening wear. Blue suede shoes.
—Elvis Presley

Saturday, October 25th

A week later, Kaitlin and her parents had moved nearly everything into her new, partially furnished rental. Her mom and dad had just a few more loads left to bring over.

Thanks to Mr. Kosta, she now had a great job and a cute little house he was giving to her for a steal. A quaint, old brick cottage with unique architecture, which intrigued her and may have been the reason he'd purchased it. The top of the front door made an oval shape instead of the usual corners, and a huge brass handle accented it beautifully. The little white fence was just tall enough to keep Elvis corralled inside. There were three bay windows—in the dining room, the living room, and the main bedroom—and he'd added a skylight that let in sunlight.

It was almost as wonderful as the house she'd fallen in

love with before everything had gone wrong. But she'd settle for this adorable house. It made her happy to drive up and know it was hers. For now, anyway.

She filled a box, taped it shut, and wrote *sheets & towels* with a marker.

The doorbell rang, startling her. Seated on one of his cushions, Elvis raised his head as if to ask if she planned on answering it.

She patted his head. "Yes, I am. You just sit right there," she commanded. Might as well command him to do what he was already doing—he was more apt to be obedient that way.

She pushed open the door, but no one was there. That was weird. Pushing open the screen door, she looked up the street both ways.

Nope. She'd apparently been doorbell ditched.

She started to close the door, when she caught sight of an envelope held in place on the porch with a rock. She fought the nervousness that hit her. It was probably an invitation to a wedding reception or something equally innocent. She pulled the envelope out from under the rock. It was sealed. A gust of October wind sent a chill through her.

Back inside, with the door securely locked behind her, she opened the envelope and pulled out an index card. Handwritten on it were the words: *Kaitlin Hartley, Go away. You're not wanted in Aspen Grove.*

This was getting ridiculous. It had to be a prank of some kind. She wasn't going to let it scare her. There was no one out to get her or scare her out of town. That was simply too far-fetched.

But she decided to take Elvis with her back to the new place. Surely he would bite anyone who dared threaten her in person. "You would, right, Elvis?"

He raised his chin.

"Good boy," she said and started loading more boxes into her car, then lifted Elvis onto his car cushion.

Driving from her parents' house to her new place, Kaitlin pulled into the driveway to find two forlorn figures slumped on her front steps. Joshua's shoulders were rounded, his arm around Priscilla, her head snuggled against his side. The sight touched her heart.

Feeling even guiltier over having avoided him at the Pumpkin Patch—*she had nothing to feel guilty for!*—Kaitlin unhooked Elvis from his safety restraint and set down his wriggling, excited body. He raced through the open gate toward the steps. Then Joshua had his arms around both dogs.

What was it about this man that could get under her skin and past her defenses? She thought she'd built enough angry barriers that no one could breach them, but he kept sweeping past them.

He and Priscilla both. She'd missed the little dog, too.

She tried to steel her heart. She couldn't afford to be vulnerable around Joshua. Stepping onto the walk, she latched the gate behind her. Joshua lifted his arm from around Priscilla, and the little dog ran straight to Kaitlin, prancing around and hoping to be petted.

"Hi, girl." Kaitlin knelt and reached for the dog's back. "At least, I'm assuming you're a girl."

"Yup. She's a girl." Joshua gave Elvis a big hug. "Hi, boy."

Kaitlin crossed her arms. "Do you know who might be leaving notes on my porch telling me I'm not wanted in town?"

He narrowed his eyes. "What? You're getting threats?"

His tone was indignant enough that it relieved her suspicion that he might be involved.

She nodded and told him what the note said. "It's like the UN-welcome wagon paid a visit."

"Did you call the police?"

"No. It's probably a prank of some kind."

"Or Bitty," he muttered.

"She's annoying, but I don't think she'd do something like this."

"Just be careful." He turned concerned eyes to her.

Locked in his gaze, she took a second too long before responding. "I will."

After a probing look, he nodded.

The dogs ran into the middle of Kaitlin's little yard and began to play. She shook her head. "They really do like being together."

Joshua pushed off the step and straightened his shoulders. "They should be."

For an instant, Kaitlin wasn't sure what Joshua meant by that. Was he going to propose again? What would she do if he did?

Her heart pounding, she realized she wanted to be with Joshua. Her foolish, foolish heart didn't know any better.

"I have one more box for you to take inside your new place." Joshua reached down for a medium-sized box from her porch.

"Like I don't have enough of those already, right?" she teased.

He didn't smile as he handed her the light-weight box. The flap was open, and she could see dog dishes, a dog bed, and a leash the same purple as Elvis's.

She looked up at him questioningly.

The sadness in his eyes almost had her dropping the box to hug him, but instead she clutched it to her.

"I know how much you love the dogs, and I can see how much they want to be together."

"I don't understand. You said you were leaving town next week and coming back for Halloween. Why are you bringing her over now?"

"I'm giving Priscilla back to you, Kaitlin. I have something to confess. When we were at the dog race and ended up with the wrong dogs, I knew I was taking Elvis. I can always tell them apart. I just wanted to see you again. I wanted to have the relationship we had before you left. But I blew it last year, and I can tell you haven't forgiven me. I'm so sorry." He drew in a ragged breath. "Maybe you can let me come take them for a walk occasionally. That would mean a lot."

As she struggled to come up with any sort of response, he gave her a quick kiss on the cheek. "Have a happy life, Kaitlin Hartley."

And he strode toward his pickup without a backward glance.

11

I've been getting some bad publicity—but you got to expect that.
—Elvis Presley

Stunned, Kaitlin continued to clutch the box of Priscilla's belongings as she watched Joshua drive away.

What just happened?

She knew how much he loved his dog. He loved both of them, as she did. He was actually a better dog parent than she was. He could tell them apart, while she hadn't even noticed when she'd had the wrong dog.

His words seared her. *I wanted to have the relationship we had before you left. But I blew it last year, and I can tell you haven't forgiven me. I'm so sorry.*

She wished she could believe him, but how could he say that when he'd been the one to start dating someone else immediately? She carried the box into the house, fed both dogs, and got them settled with a couple of chew toys. "I'll be back soon," she promised.

She had to talk with someone she could trust.

Her head still reeling, she drove toward her parents' house, but as she passed by Candy's Café and saw her mother's car there, she changed her mind. She parked on the street in front and pushed open the café door.

Candy looked up and smiled. "Nice to see you again, Kaitlin."

Her mother turned around, saw her, and laughed. "I'm just taking a little break. Really. I got tired of schlepping boxes."

"I know, Mom. That's not why I'm here."

The place was half full, keeping several waitresses busy, but the counter where her mother sat was mostly empty. Kaitlin took the stool beside her.

"Hot chocolate?" Candy asked, and sing-songed, "*On the house.*"

"That would be great, thanks." Kaitlin nodded. "Even more than that, I need some of that advice you promised."

Candy narrowed her eyes. "As in, advice to the lovelorn?"

"Something like that."

"Oh, honey, have you ever come to the right place." Candy poured a cup of steaming chocolate, added some whipped cream, and set it in front of Kaitlin. "Tell us what's wrong."

"Joshua just came over to my new place." She looked at her mother. "Did you give him the address?"

"When he came by this morning with cute little Priscilla, I told him you were moving. It's not a secret he couldn't get any other way."

"It's okay, Mom. I just wondered how he got it so fast."

Both women looked at her expectantly, and the silence grew heavy.

Kaitlin set down the mug. She wanted to tell them what he'd said, but she wasn't ready to address that yet. "Joshua came over and gave me Priscilla. As a gift. He loves that little dog. *Why would he do that?*"

Candy and her mother exchanged glances. Candy said, "You really don't know?"

Kaitlin shook her head.

"Honey, that man is in love with you. Smitten. Always has been."

"Then why did he try to keep me from going after my dream last year? That's not the act of a person in love." She blinked back sudden tears. "And why would he propose and then immediately start dating Bitty Branson?"

Her mother touched Kaitlin's arm. "Honey, I love you, but you never see anyone's side of the story except your own. There are always more points of view. Think about it from Joshua's perspective. You hurt him by leaving him behind. And why wouldn't Bitty want him? He's a nice guy. He's good looking. He's the most eligible bachelor in town. He's faithful—"

"Not true! Two weeks after he proposed to me, he started dating her."

"Are you kidding?" Candy leaned her arms on the counter. "Kaitlin, that man was heartbroken when you left. I talked to his mother. For two weeks all he did was sit in his room with that little dog. She was beginning to really worry about him."

"Oh yeah, heartbroken men go out and date someone else."

"Sometimes men who feel like they've been rejected and deserted do exactly that. To feel like they're desirable, even if it's to a woman who doesn't matter to them. From his perspective, you dumped him. When he proposed, you said no—not *later*, but a flat-out *no*. That was a horrible rejection."

Defensive, Kaitlin said, "Wasn't I supposed to get my training? It was an opportunity I couldn't turn down."

"I'm not saying he's perfect, darling. We're all human, and nobody's perfect. Even you. But there is *perfect for each other*." Candy snorted. "Besides, everyone with half a brain knows he only dated her to make you jealous. Even Bitty said as much to me. He probably thought you'd come running back home as soon as you heard."

"He wanted to make me jealous?" He *hadn't* just run off and started dating because he didn't care about her? The thought startled her. But she'd have to be blind not to have seen that.

"Not to keep you from your dream, but because he was so crazy in love that he didn't know how to live without you. You've both done some growing up in the past year." Candy stood back up. "I hope."

Her mother said, "I think maybe you shouldn't be hanging around with Lindsey so much right now."

"Why not? She's my friend."

"Because she has a suspicious mind. She takes offense too easily, and I think she helps you take offense too."

Remember, Lindsey had said. *Remember how he started dating Bitty so soon.*

"At least give him the benefit of the doubt." Candy waved to another person who came in the café. "And remember that it's easy for the rest of us to see, looking in from the outside, that the man is head over heels in love with you. Perhaps you could give him another chance."

Another chance with Joshua? She would love to have a second chance with him. "How?"

Candy smiled. "Tell him the truth."

"What, that I'm an idiot who didn't see the hurt I caused him?"

"That's a good place to start," Candy said and headed toward the jukebox.

Her mother sighed. "As long as we're telling the truth today . . . I called Joshua and told him you'd be at the Pumpkin Patch."

"Mom! Whose side are you on?"

"Yours, sweetheart. Definitely yours."

The jukebox started playing, and Elvis belted out "I'm Stuck on You."

Candy was smiling as she came back around the counter.

12

Some people tap their feet, some people snap their fingers, and some people sway back and forth. I just sorta do 'em all together, I guess.
—Elvis Presley

Kaitlin hugged first her mother and then Candy. "Thank you so much. I needed to hear that."

"Advice to the lovelorn is always on the house." Candy looked her in the eye. "You two will work this out. Now go, find Joshua. Have the talk you should have had last year, and be happy."

"I've always thought Joshua was a keeper." Her mother smiled. "I'll see you back at your place with the last of the boxes."

"Okay," Kaitlin said. "Thanks for helping me."

Still slightly stunned at what she'd learned, she stumbled out of the warm café and to her car. She drove home, latched the gate, and climbed the stairs to her new house then greeted the dogs—hers and Joshua's both. And could no longer hold back the tears.

If Joshua really loved her, she'd been a fool. They'd both been fools last year.

Until then, their relationship had been easy. This was much, much harder.

Sitting on her new blue-and-brown couch, with a dog snuggled on each side, she realized how much she still loved Joshua. She really did. She'd always loved him. And if she could believe Candy and her mother, Joshua still loved her.

If she could believe Joshua's own words.

She'd fooled herself for an entire year. Not about her feelings for him—she'd always known she loved him—but about his motives and his feelings. He hadn't been trying to hold her back; he just couldn't bear to let her go.

She *did* believe Joshua.

Now she had to figure out a way to win him back.

13

When I get married, it'll be no secret. —Elvis Presley

Halloween ~ Friday, October 31ˢᵗ

The last six days had been torture, having to put off her plans to win Joshua until he got back from his business trip. He'd said he'd be back on Halloween, so today was the day.

Kaitlin glanced out the front window. Both dogs were playing on the lawn. She'd need to let them back in soon, as it was another chilly day.

Kaitlin turned her attention back to her new plan just as Lindsey called. "What's up?"

Without waiting, Kaitlin said, "I think you ought to make up with Ethan."

"What, with that jerk?"

"And I'm going to make up with Joshua."

"You're kidding, right? Have you forgotten Bitty?"

"I'm serious. And no, he's not a jerk. He's a sweetheart. And so is Joshua. I took offense when I should have been looking at the fact that he's a good man. He was trying to make me jealous by dating Bitty. And Ethan's a good man, too. We should both make up with them."

There was a brief pause before Lindsey asked, "Have you started smoking dope?"

"No. And I've got to go. I challenge you to go kiss and make up with Ethan. I'm going to do the same with Joshua. It's time for us to be with the men we love."

"You're crazy." Lindsey laughed. "Okay, but only because I'm feeling lonesome today."

"Good. Now I've got to go. Call me tomorrow, and we'll exchange happy stories."

She hoped.

"Bye, crazy friend," Lindsey said.

Next Kaitlin called Joshua's number, hoping he'd answer when he saw it was her.

"Yes?" He sounded hesitant.

She was just relieved he'd picked up. "Are you home right now?"

"Yes." A pause.

"Stay there and break out the dog biscuits. The dogs want to come trick-or-treating at your parents' house."

"Okay to everything except my parents' home. I've moved out."

Surprised, she said, "Oh. All right. Give me your new address."

He read it off, and she wrote it down. The street name—Creole—sounded familiar.

She hung up. Time to put her plan into action. She glanced out the window and froze. *Bitty was in the yard, yanking Elvis by the collar.*

Her dog mother instincts coming to the surface, she sprinted out the door and yelled, "What are you doing?"

Bitty looked up and redoubled her efforts to get Elvis out the gate. Priscilla was jumping up on Bitty, probably wanting to play.

Bitty kicked her aside. Okay. That did it.

Bitty is going down.

She raced across the yard. In Bitty's eyes Kaitlin saw that Bitty wasn't going to leave without the dog. And Kaitlin was even more determined that Bitty wasn't leaving with him—and she was going to pay for kicking the other dog.

Kaitlin tackled her, and they rolled across the brittle maple leaves.

"Stop it, Bitty!"

"You can't have him back."

"I can too. He's my dog." Kaitlin worked the collar out of Bitty's hands and pinned her.

"Not your stupid dog. *Joshua.*" Bitty bucked Kaitlin aside and came for her. The fur on Elvis's back bristled in hostility. He growled, a sound Kaitlin never heard him make. Apparently he felt protective toward her too.

"It needs to stop," Kaitlin said. "The phone calls. The notes. The stealing. You could go to jail if you keep doing this."

"Joshua is mine! I need that dog!"

When Kaitlin reached up to keep Bitty from getting to Elvis, she punched out and grazed Kaitlin's head, making her pause.

That's when Elvis bit Bitty.

"Ow! Stupid dog!" Bitty held up her hand and glared at Kaitlin. "I'm going to sue you."

"Oh, this will look really good in court. You go right ahead and sue me."

"You can't prove anything," Bitty said, struggling to her feet and backing away.

Kaitlin's new next-door neighbor, Jack, a retired military gentleman in his fifties who had helped her move in, was leaning against the gate. "I saw most of what happened, and you'll be the one who gets in trouble, Ms. Branson."

He stepped into the yard and gave Kaitlin a hand. Elvis kept an eye on the man, but he was probably wondering if the man had his regular dog biscuits in his pocket.

"Thanks," Kaitlin said.

They both turned to look at Bitty, who started to cry.

Jack said, "Let me make some calls. I know a therapist who might be of help." He waved to his wife, who'd been watching out their window. She came out and, after a brief conversation, put her arm around Bitty's shoulder and helped her toward their house.

Jack said, "I'll call the police for you, if you'd like."

Feeling sorry for Bitty, Kaitlin nodded. "Thanks. That would be helpful. I've got to go for a while, though, so they'll have to speak with me in a few hours."

With Bitty in good hands, Kaitlin looked for Priscilla. Lucky for Bitty, Joshua's little dog was standing and looked okay. She came over and nuzzled Kaitlin's hand, and she gave Priscilla a hug. Elvis then wanted one as well.

After a moment of mushiness, she looked at the dogs. "Okay, lady and gentleman, I am now going to clean myself back up and then we are going to go win Joshua back. You will, of course, be on your best and most charming behavior. No biting, Elvis."

After pulling out pieces of leaves from her hair and brushing it, Kaitlin dressed the pair in the matching sequined cowboy and cowgirl outfits, which she'd purchased in Sacramento that morning. Definite gender definition was provided by the pink and blue. No mistaking them at all.

Except that she'd dressed Priscilla as the cowboy and Elvis as the cowgirl. This time she was playing the wrong-dog game. She couldn't tell them apart, but he'd said he could. She was counting on it.

"Okay, you guys look great. Now it's show time. Let's go win back your daddy."

They followed her to the Jetta, and she secured them both. She'd added a pink cushion for Priscilla. Of course, Elvis, the "cowgirl," sat on the pink one today, and Priscilla sat on his blue suede cushion.

She turned on the car. After uttering a little prayer, she said, "Okay, here goes nothing." Or everything.

She found the house number on the mailbox. *Their house*? The one they'd talked about buying? Surprised, she pulled into his driveway and set the dogs on the ground. "Okay, the show's on."

She held their leashes and turned toward the house.

It *was* their house! The one she'd fallen in love with; the one they'd talked about buying.

She'd been so intent on looking for the house number that she hadn't paid attention to the neighborhood or the house itself. But this *was* their house. Her heart melted entirely in that moment until it was a puddle of burning love.

After carrying the box of Priscilla's belongings to the beautiful wraparound porch, she set it on one of the two outdoor chairs and knocked on the door.

Joshua opened it and held it open wide as if welcoming her and the dogs. That was a good sign. She hoped. Screwing up her courage for what lay ahead, she smiled and said, "The dogs wanted me to tell you trick or treat."

He smiled and motioned them inside. The dogs jumped up, dancing for him to pick them up.

"Love the outfits," he teased, greeting the dogs and giving them each a biscuit—but keeping his attention squarely on Kaitlin. "What's up?"

Here it was. The moment she could either chicken out or say what she needed to. She was tired of being stupid and lonely and miserable. "It was incredibly generous of you to give Priscilla to me, but I can't, in good conscience, keep her." She went back outside, retrieved the box, and held it out to him.

Taking it, he raised an eyebrow. His voice was low and husky. "Are you sure?"

"It isn't fair to you or to Priscilla. She loves you. But I want to thank you, Joshua. It was very sweet of you." She leaned up and kissed his cheek like he'd kissed hers.

Handing Elvis's leash to Joshua, she called out, "Come on, Elvis," to Priscilla, leading her out the door.

Now to prove if he could really tell them apart.

She walked slowly and was only midway across his lawn when he followed her out and called out, "Wait."

She turned around.

He stood on the porch, his hands in his pockets, uncertainty in his eyes. "I've got the wrong dog."

"Oh?" Her voice came out little above a whisper. "I must have made a mistake."

He closed the distance between her, and Elvis followed right behind. "A mistake?"

"Yes." He stood so close, it took her breath away. She looked up six inches or so into his warm brown eyes and started the conversation they should have had last year. "Just like I made a mistake a year ago by not saying yes."

His eyes widened in surprise. When he spoke, his voice had a catch in it. "Do you mean—"

"Yes." Her heart fluttered as she waited for his response.

His voice was soft as he leaned in closer, his clean man smell reaching her nose. He stuffed his hands in his pockets again, as if he didn't trust what he'd do with them. "And I made a huge mistake in trying to make you jealous by asking out someone I didn't care about at all."

Kaitlin nodded solemnly. "Yes. Even though I have come to learn that Bitty is wackazoid. She requires a separate apology all by herself."

"How did you learn that?"

"She tried to steal Elvis right out of my yard."

"Oh, no, I'm sorry—"

"Don't worry about it. Elvis took care of it." She grinned. "He bit her."

"That somehow seems like the right thing to do." Joshua grinned back. "And just so you know, I've already made the apology *to* Bitty. But now I need to tell you how very sorry I am. I knew dating her would make you especially upset. I'm so sorry I hurt you like that. I just wanted you to come back to me."

She motioned toward the house. "You bought our place."

He nodded, studying the house for a moment before looking back into her eyes. "I bought it for you, for *us*, to make our home in. But I never had a chance to tell you about it."

She shot him a crooked smile. "I did something wrong, and then you did something wrong, and then I did something else stupid, and then you . . . well, you get the picture. What if we just split it down the middle and forgive each other?"

"I'd really like that." His voice was shaky, and he didn't

reach out for her, but he took his hands out of his pockets, and she could feel his desire to touch her. But she had one more thing to do first.

"Joshua?" She knelt on one knee the same way he had done with her last year. "Will you marry me?"

He pulled her up and wrapped her in his arms, the place where she felt most at home. He held her tight, his eyes suspiciously moist, his voice husky. "I love you so much, Kaitlin."

Wrapping her arms around his waist, she said, "I take it that's a yes?"

"Yes!" He spun her around once and set her down, keeping his arms around her, and turned to the dogs. "She wants us!"

Kaitlin smiled in joy. "Yes, she does."

He pulled her back to face him. "*Now* am I authorized to call you pet names?"

With a rueful laugh, she said, "Yes. You are hereby authorized."

He caressed her cheek. "I love you, my little Katie bug. I've never stopped loving you."

She pressed a hand against his heart. "I love you, too, my big, cuddly teddy bear. I can't help falling in love with you—all over again."

"So this is for real? We're going to get married?"

"I hope so."

"When?" He laughed happily. "And please bear in mind that I've already been waiting for a very long time."

"How about next month?"

"November? Your mom will kill me."

"She loves you, and she's been giving you advance notice of everything I do and everywhere I go." She pressed her cheek against his chest and drew in a happy breath. "She isn't the one who wants to marry you, but, okay, how about January?"

"No way. November sounds great. Do you still want to go to the same place for our honeymoon?"

"You've got it." She grinned at him. "Blue Hawaii, of course."

"Of course," he teased. "How did I not know that?"

And then they were making new memories of kissing in Aspen Grove.

14

I hope I didn't bore you too much with my life story. — Elvis Presley

One year later, at the Second Annual Running of the Hallowieners

Kneeling along the finish line, in lanes five and six, Lindsey and Kaitlin exchanged smiles. At the starting line, Ethan held Elvis's collar and Joshua held Priscilla's.

The crowd was even larger than last year—the silly new racing event was growing in popularity—and the racetrack was festively decorated with streamers hanging from poles along the sides.

The race track had passed out different costumes this year, so the starting line displayed a row of pirate dachshunds. No eye patches or aaarrrggghhhs, but a parrot perched on each of their very long backs. Hilarious.

So many things were the same as last year—but the year had brought so many changes to her life. And to others. Bitty even had a new boyfriend now—after months of therapy.

Kaitlin caught Joshua's gaze, and his warm smile sent tingles through her. She smiled back. He blew her a kiss. She caught it.

"You guys are making me sick," Lindsey said. "Stop being so happily married."

"Whatever. You and Ethan ought to try being happily *married* for a change."

The track owner, Mr. Morrison, said his few words and handed the mic back to Jake Taylor—still mayor—who again counted down: "Time for the Second Annual Running of the Hallowieners. This year's theme is Dachshunds of the Caribbean. Now get your long dogs ready. Aaarrrggghhh, maties. Let them fly on three . . . two . . . one . . . *go!*"

Elvis and Priscilla took off running down the field, sprinting side by side straight for Kaitlin, way ahead of the rest of the pirate pack. This time they kept running until they jumped into Kaitlin's outstretched arms together, bowling her over.

"We won!" Lindsey yelled.

Laughing, Kaitlin waited for the men to join them.

Joshua helped Kaitlin to her feet and hugged her. "We came in first!"

Jake's voice came over the loudspeaker. "We have a tie for first place. Interestingly enough, both dogs belong to the Moores, Joshua and Kaitlin. Glad your dogs are on the same team this year."

The crowd laughed and cheered.

"Come on up here. Bring those little pirates with you."

Joshua took Kaitlin's hand, and they walked the dogs up to where Jake was grinning. "We have a cash award for first place of one hundred dollars plus one hour of racecar stunt driving training offered here at Morrison Motorsports Park."

Kaitlin laughed. "I guess Joshua will use that."

"You bet I will," he said.

After all the hoopla ended, they found Ethan and Lindsey—who miraculously hadn't started a fight in their absence—and walked with the dogs toward the parking lot.

"And with that, ladies and gentlemen," Joshua said, "Elvis has left the building."

When they reached the Jetta, Joshua placed a protective hand on Kaitlin's belly.

"So what are you now?" Lindsey asked. "Two whole days along?"

"I went to the doctor yesterday. I'm officially *eight weeks* along. We had a good seven months after the wedding to get to know each other first."

"Like you needed it," Lindsey said. "You guys have known each other forever."

Kaitlin tipped her head. "Oh, like you guys haven't? When's the big day?"

"We don't have one yet," Ethan said. "Lindsey just took back my ring last week."

After another big fight that had lasted several months.

Lindsey winked at Kaitlin. "So if it's a girl, let me guess—you'll name her Lisa Marie."

Ethan said, "And if it's a boy, you can name him after Elvis's manager. Tom Parker."

"I have an even better idea." Kaitlin looked up into Joshua's eyes and took his hand. "If it's a boy, we'll name him after his daddy."

"Thank you." Joshua squeezed her hand. "Thank you very much."

ABOUT HEATHER HORROCKS

Heather Horrocks is the *USA Today* and Kindle bestselling author of fourteen books (*Who-Dun-Him Inn and Bad Mothers Club* mysteries, *Chick Flick Clique* and *Christmas Street* romantic comedies, and Women Who Knew inspirational books) plus an upcoming series for writers, sharing her unique character interview and her amazing book-in-a-day system developed by plotting over fifty books, each in one day, with her Conspiracy Group (Diane Darcy and Bruce Simpson are the *two or more people plotting together* with her). She is also the founder of Word Garden Press, a niche publisher of PG-rated fiction and nonfiction.

Raised overseas by her shop-til-you-drop mother and pay-for-the-purchases oilman father, avid mystery and romantic comedy lover Heather read her way through Columbia, Venezuela, London, Kuwait, and Iran—and later bought a video store so she could watch stories on the little screen, too.

When she learned that dachshunds are actually considered hound dogs, she knew she'd found her Elvis story. She is happy to report that she has now learned how to correctly spell *dachshund* and invites you to watch one of the hilarious long dog races on YouTube. She found the quotes by Elvis online, and the movie and song titles both online and in the LIFE book *Remembering Elvis 30 Years Later* (thanks for the lend, Millie Berry). She had a great time working them into the story.

She'd like to thank her readers: Diane Darcy, Kathleen Wright, Marie Barnhurst, A.N. Allan, Rangi Moleni, Dawn Duren, Janelle Fenn, Heidi Marsh, Anissa Wall, and Mindy Haltinner Horrocks (the newest addition to Heather's family and a talented designer, who also helped add authenticity to Kaitlin's dream job, certification, and, especially, the fabrics displayed in the design department).

She loves anyone who can make her laugh, which explains why she adores her witty husband, her funny friends, Anne George mysteries, Bill Cosby, grandbabies, and her cute little dog Gus (a Shih Tzu). She loves to cook for friends, siblings, and especially her children (yours, mine, ours, and some of theirs) and their families. She and her husband reside in Utah.

To be the first to learn of her new releases, or to see how many of the Elvis references you may have missed, go to www.BooksByHeatherHorrocks.com

To read her dog's outrageous claims, check out his blog:
GusTheGregariousGhostwritingDogBlog.blogspot.com
Twitter: @HeatherHorrocks
Facebook: Heather Horrocks Author

EYE FOR AN EYE

Stephanie Black

Other Works by Stephanie Black

Fool Me Twice

Methods of Madness

Shadowed

Rearview Mirror

Cold as Ice

The Witnesses

1

Startled, Mallory Ingram switched off the vacuum she'd been threading between cubicles and pulled her vibrating phone out of her hip pocket. A call at seven in the morning?

The display read *Michael Ross*, leaving Mallory puzzled. Uncle Mike never called—though if he *did* call, this was a reasonable time for him to do it, since he never slept in past six.

As she swiped the screen, she realized it was *not* seven in California like it was here in New York. It was *four*. Puzzlement escalated to apprehension. "Hello?"

"Nelson Sanders is dead," Mike said gruffly. "I figured you'd want to know."

"*What*?" Mallory stared dazedly at the row of windows showing the grayish glow of a cloudy October sunrise. "What happened to him?"

"Prison riot. Just saw it on the news when I got up to get some work done. A couple of gangs got in a fight, and

Nelson got mixed up in it."

"Nelson was in a prison gang?" Two images of Nelson muddled her mind: the wisecracking friend sitting across from her at a table in the library while they did more chatting than studying, and the desperate drug addict she'd seen running from her house, blood staining his T-shirt.

"News report didn't say he was in a gang, just that he was one of the casualties. Lot of prisoners got hurt. Two guards killed as well." He paused. "School going okay?"

"It's great," Mallory said numbly.

"Good girl. Keep at it." Mike hung up.

Mallory jammed her phone back in her pocket and gripped the handle of the vacuum. Nelson was dead? Maybe she should be happy about that. Scales of justice.

Tears filled her eyes.

Don't, Mallory. Not now. You need to finish your work. You need to study for your botany midterm. You need to work on that English essay.

She rubbed the tears out of eyes already burning from lack of sleep. From the other side of the expanse of empty cubicles, she heard the distant buzz of the lock. *Darien?* She'd never seen anyone else here this early. For the past couple of weeks, the hope of running into Darien Thomas had splashed a little fun into a dull predawn janitorial shift, but she didn't want to see him while she was crying. She'd make sure not to vacuum near his cubicle until she'd calmed down.

Oh, Nels. What had happened at the prison? She couldn't imagine Nelson as an aggressor in a prison fight. He'd probably been trying to stay out of the way, not wanting to hurt anyone—

Not wanting to hurt anyone.

Tears refilled her eyes. She wiped them away. Wanting

to know more about what had happened, she pulled her phone out of her pocket and tried to type Nelson's name and *Salinas Valley State Prison* into the search bar. Her fingers quivered, hitting the wrong letters.

Footsteps approached. Whoever had entered was heading toward her, not toward Darien's cubicle on the far left side of the room. Not wanting to be caught Googling and weeping when she was supposed to be cleaning, Mallory tried to stuff her phone back in her pocket but missed. The phone hit the floor.

She bent to pick it up. With the phone in her hand, she kept her face lowered and picked at a staple stuck in the carpet, hoping the intruder would ignore her as he or she passed by.

The footsteps stopped. "Good morning, Mallory."

Darien. "Morning," she said. With a quick movement, she used her shoulder to wipe a tear off her cheek then regretted it—when she'd dressed this morning, thinking of Darien, she'd put on a cute lime-green cardigan she'd found at Goodwill on Saturday. *And* she was wearing makeup, something she never would have done at work pre-Darien-crush. She'd probably just smeared mascara all over her new sweater.

"Dropped my phone." She tried to sound lighthearted as she rose to her feet, catching a blurry peripheral-vision view of big feet in brown leather shoes, long legs in khaki Dockers, and wide shoulders in a striped shirt. She focused on her phone screen, pretending to assess damage and hoping the next installment of tears would wait until Darien headed off to his cubicle.

"Not broken, I hope," he said.

"No worse than it was before." She ran her finger along

the crack in the lower right-hand corner of the screen. "So—you're here early again. Do you ever sleep?"

"At night I do. It's morning. The sun's even up."

"You're running late then," she joked. "You sound like my uncle."

"Mallory . . . are you okay?"

He could see her face; he knew she was crying. She had to look at him. Avoiding eye contact would make her look more upset. "Just . . . sleep-deprived. I'm fine."

He studied her with eyes that looked strikingly dark. Platinum hair, skin that looked like it never tanned, and eyes that were a deep brown tinted with green.

"I'd better get back to work. Good luck with your project." Mallory switched on the vacuum.

2

Darien Thomas sat in his cubicle, listening to the drone of the vacuum from the other side of the floor. What was Mallory upset about? He couldn't ask; he hardly knew her.

He'd probably made it way too obvious that he *wanted* to know her, showing up repeatedly at the Rains Building at the crack of dawn—or earlier—when he knew Mallory would be working, pretending that early mornings in his grad-student cubicle were great for productivity. Granted, there *were* advantages to being here instead of in his apartment—no sticky spots gluing his papers to the table, no smell of stale pizza, and no roommate snoring—but until this year, he'd come in the early mornings only when deadlines swamped him.

Ever since he'd shown up a few weeks ago to finish a presentation for the statistics class he was teaching and had seen the woman vacuuming cubicles and cleaning windows—that shiny dark hair curving around her chin, the sweet hazel eyes, the smile that made her whole face twinkle somehow, the sound of her voice when she slipped and started singing along with her iPod then stopped abruptly, realizing she was soloing without accompaniment—

He'd seen her twice more before he'd had the guts to introduce himself and ask her name, making sure *not* to show up unshaven and wearing a holey sweatshirt like he had the first time.

Maybe the button-down Oxford is over-the-top, he thought, surveying his striped shirt. *Go for it, champ. A six-foot-five-inch beanpole math geek with more bone than muscle, but wow, you can rock that business casual. Just ask her out. If she says no, at least you can start getting over her.*

She probably already had a boyfriend. But she'd said she didn't know many people in Birch Falls yet, that she was living with her sister and her brother-in-law. He also knew she was from California and hadn't started college right after high school—she'd blushed when he'd asked how long she'd been at Bowman and she'd said this was her first year—that she was a "geezer" in freshman-filled classes. He guessed she was in her early twenties.

Ever since he'd introduced himself, she would pause when passing his cubicle and switch off the vacuum to smile and ask how he was doing and what he was working on. She was a biology and secondary education major; surely the ramblings of a doctoral student in applied mathematics must bore her, but she always *acted* interested and asked thoughtful questions. Darien had started looking up biology facts on Wikipedia, wanting to make sure *he* sounded intelligent when she talked about the botany class she enjoyed.

Smart, beautiful—and tall. It was nice to chat with a

woman who actually came up to his shoulders. After a few minutes, when she moved away, continuing her work, Darien had to lock his jaw shut to keep himself from offering to vacuum for her or take over dusting some of the countless desks and shelves. Offering to help with a job she was paid to do would make him look like a weirdo *and* make it mortifyingly obvious that he was stalking Mallory.

But what was she crying about this morning? Plainly, she didn't want to confide in him, or she wouldn't have averted her eyes, made jokes, and turned away to vacuum an area where the spotless carpet told him she'd already been.

It's none of your business. If she wanted to tell you what the problem is, she would have. She doesn't need you to fix anything.

He reached for his computer and tried to work, but his thoughts were stuck on Mallory.

Get a grip. Just because she's friendly doesn't mean she wants you for a friend beyond a superficial acquaintance she talks to because you're the only person around at six or seven in the morning. What are you going to do, corner her while she's wiping classroom windows and pressure her to say what's wrong until she freaks out and never talks to you again?

Grimly, Darien put his fingers on the keyboard and forced himself to focus.

3

Sitting at her sister Eden's polished oak kitchen table, Mallory backspaced over a line and retyped it. The sentence still sounded like a stuck-up eight-year-old imitating a teacher, using words too complex for her to handle. Irritated, she backspaced again and thought wistfully of escaping to Gilroy and her job making chocolate shakes and mopping rocky road, strawberry, and garlic ice cream off the tile floor. She did that job well. But trying to access the part of her mind she'd shut down three years ago . . . No, *four* years ago; her senior year of high school had been a waste. If she went to class, she slept through it.

For the third time, she reworded the line. She *would not* fail at Bowman. She would *not* lose hold of the old goals she'd worked so hard to excavate from mountains of inertia. She'd always planned on college, had always been a good student—

She glared at the screen. She would *not* botch this assignment because she couldn't concentrate enough to write a persuasive essay about why science programs should receive more focus in elementary school curriculums. The more she worked on it, the more she regretted picking a topic that reminded her of her mother sitting at her desk, stressing about budget cuts, and grading piles of fifth-grade papers

In the two weeks since Mike's call, she'd felt so off balance, and she knew she was fueling the problem by dwelling on Nelson—reading news articles about the prison riot, re-reading articles about his arrest and trial four years ago, even dipping into old chat logs where she and Nelson had joked about homework or weekend plans . . .

Should she send his family a note of sympathy? She didn't know much about his mother except that she could punch hard enough to fracture Nelson's jaw. It was hard to imagine sending *her* a card. His sister, on the other hand . . .

When Nelson and Mallory were freshmen, Lori had been a senior. Mallory hadn't known her well, but school rumors said Lori was an expert at getting in trouble and getting out of trouble—and getting Nelson out of trouble. Lori's bossy, bullying attitude toward her brother appalled Mallory, but Nelson hero-worshipped her. He'd told Mallory stories of how Lori had protected him, cleverly fixed problems for him. Given how toxic their parents were, maybe Lori had become Nelson's lifeline, and Nelson Lori's.

Mallory had heard rumors that Lori was devastated when Nelson was arrested. Lori had to be crushed by grief now. Mallory should write to her. Lori probably hadn't received much sympathy after Nelson's death.

Would she want to hear from me? Mallory had no idea. She and Nelson's family had stayed away from each other after Nelson's arrest.

She pushed her computer back. Tomorrow, she'd call Uncle Mike to see if Lori was still in Gilroy. *Maybe that will help me get past this, by reaching out to her.*

She walked to Eden's fridge and refilled the stainless-steel water bottle with the faded logo of the dentist's office where their mother used to work. On the fridge was a dry-erase calendar filled with Eden's fastidious handwriting. She'd even added Mallory's class schedule for each day; organized Eden liked to know what each member of her household was doing. Mallory couldn't understand why Eden needed the calendar when she kept the same information on her phone.

Feeling better able to concentrate, Mallory sat at the table and reread her essay so far. It sounded decent—finally. She checked her outline and started on the next paragraph.

The sound of the front door opening indicated the return of Eden and Clint from an early dinner they'd attended with one of Clint's university colleagues. Mallory quickly closed her laptop and gathered her books. Clint and Eden had been generous in inviting her to live in their spare bedroom to help her save money, but Mallory didn't want to push her luck by being underfoot too often. She scanned the kitchen. Oops, there was a drop of chili on the counter near the microwave. She snatched the dishrag and wiped it up.

They walked into the kitchen. Eden's long dark hair was in a sleek French braid, and she wore a navy pencil skirt with a blue silk blouse. Blond Clint wore a navy blazer and gray slacks, and the blue stripes in his blue and red tie matched Eden's shirt—her choice, Mallory figured. Clint held a paper sack.

"Hey," Mallory said. "How was dinner?"

Neither of them smiled. "Fine," Clint said, his boyish face cold.

Mallory felt awkward. Had Clint and Eden had an argument? In the six weeks she'd been living with them, she hadn't witnessed any conflict worse than an impatient few words, but Clint was under immense pressure right now, worrying about the upcoming decision on his tenure.

"I'm going to go see if I can finish this English essay before I fall asleep on my keyboard," Mallory said lightly. She stacked her books on top of her laptop and picked everything up. "Good night."

"Mal? We need to talk." Eden's voice shook.

Mallory tried to think if she'd done something to upset Eden or Clint. Her sister was so meticulous, it was probably impossible to live in her house without doing something Eden viewed as disruptive, though she'd never complained to Mallory. "Sure. What about?"

"Have a seat," Clint said.

A sit-down conversation. Mallory tried not to look too apprehensive as she placed her belongings on the table and took her seat. Eden sat by her. Clint remained on his feet.

"Do you know anything about this?" Clint opened the paper bag and emptied it onto the table.

Mallory looked at the two small plastic bags that fell from the larger sack. One had a small amount of white powder. A handful of white, blue, and green pills was in the other.

Thoughts of Nelson, sobbing, rammed themselves into Mallory's mind.

"I'm really sorry, Mallory. I didn't mean to hurt her—my mind was shot. When she walked in on me, I just panicked."

Mallory swallowed. What was Clint doing with a sack of drugs—and why was he asking *her*—"I don't know anything about it at all. Where did you find that?"

"In my makeup drawer," Eden said. "When I was getting ready to go to dinner. And I didn't put it there."

"I didn't either," Mallory said.

Eden said nothing, but tears welled in her eyes.

"Eden! How can you think I'd—"

Eden brushed tears away without smearing her makeup. "I wasn't home when you were in high school, but Mom and I *did* talk."

Mallory's face burned forest-fire hot. "Okay, listen. I was stupid. But I never did drugs."

"Really? You hung out with your druggie friends—"

"They didn't start out that way! We'd been friends since elementary school. Yes, I know I was an idiot. I shouldn't have kept hanging out with them when they started doing that stuff—"

"Hosting them for a round of underage drinking, marijuana, cocaine, and who knows what else doesn't sound like you were *too* uncomfortable with what they were doing. Getting busted, getting Mom hit with a fine she could *not* afford . . ."

Mallory fought to keep herself calm. Eden had never mentioned any of this. She'd hoped Eden didn't know about that horrible night. "I didn't mean for the party to go that direction—I told them not to bring any of that garbage with them—"

"Oh, give me a break. You knew they would, and you wouldn't have invited them if you weren't okay with it. Mom had been worried about you for months."

Mallory clamped her hands around the sides of her computer and stared at the textbooks on top of it as though nailing her attention to evidence of her life now would keep her from toppling backward into the pain and guilt of the past. Did Eden blame her—

Of course she does. It's your fault.

Don't think about Mom. Just focus on what's happening right now and handle it.

"How long has this been going on—years?" Eden asked. "That was part of your problem after Mom died, wasn't it?"

"No."

"I thought you were getting yourself together. That's why I let you move in with us. But I won't put up with drugs in my house."

Mallory gestured at the baggies on the table, her hand trembling. "If that was mine, I wouldn't be dumb enough to put it in your drawer."

Clint picked up the two small bags and dropped them into the paper sack. "Unless you were too high to know what you were doing and meant to hide it with *your* stuff."

Mallory pictured Eden's drawer. The old bathrooms in this house had only pedestal sinks and little storage space, so Eden had put an antique dressing table in a nook at the end of the hallway. The top drawer on the left held Eden's hair and makeup supplies; the one below it held Mallory's.

"Look," Clint said. "We're not calling the police. But we're also not enabling this by giving you a cheap place to stay while you blow your money on drugs and wreck your life. You have one week to find a new place."

"*Those are not my drugs.* Who else has been here lately?"

"No one." Eden frowned at Mallory's metal water bottle as though contemplating opening it and sniffing to make sure it was water in there. "The drugs were put in my drawer sometime after I got ready for work this morning. Clint and I have been gone all day. No one else has been here unless you had visitors. Did you?"

Mallory shook her head. "Someone must have broken in."

"To *leave* drugs?" Clint snapped. "People on drugs break in to *steal* things. Not to leave them."

Mallory wanted to throw up. She removed her sweaty hands from her computer and wiped them on her jeans.

Eden, her face bloodless, was plainly thinking along the same lines as Mallory. "Clint, we know that," she said quietly.

"I'm sorry." Clint reddened. "I didn't mean to—"

"I didn't put the drugs there." Mallory drew a deep breath. "If you two didn't, someone else did." She held her hand out for the bag. "I'm taking this to the police. Maybe if they take fingerprints—"

"Clint and I both touched it," Eden said.

"There could still be other prints—"

Clint shook his head. "Let's not turn this into a charade. You're not taking it to the police. You just don't want to lose your next fix."

Flailing through a waterfall of anger and pain in search of rationality, Mallory said, "Let's buy one of those drug tests from the pharmacy. I can prove—"

"So I'm supposed to stand with my ear to the bathroom door and check to make sure you—" Eden looked disgusted. "We already know you're keeping drugs in our house. I'm not going to try to figure out if your high-school friends taught you how to cheat a drug test."

"*Fine.*" Mallory stood. "Clint, give me the drugs. If you don't believe I'm going to the police, come with me."

Clint looked disconcerted, and Mallory hoped her invitation had jarred him enough to get him listening instead of simply blaming. "Let's go," she said.

Clint folded the top of the bag. "If you show up and tell

them what happened, they'll think you're trying to cover for yourself because you're afraid we'll turn you in. You don't want to get convicted of possession. You'll get thrown out of school and go to jail."

Mallory stomped to the entryway and heard Clint and Eden following her. She grabbed her jacket and purse from the coat closet and yanked her keys out of her purse. "Give me the bag. If you think it's *mine* then give me back my 'property.' I'm taking it to the police."

"You'll only make things worse for yourself," Clint said. "Leave the police out of it. I'll get rid of it, but you have one week to move out. You're not bringing this . . . danger into our home."

Mallory clenched her keys, fighting the urge to leap forward and grab the bag from Clint. How dare he accuse her and not give her the opportunity to ask the police to investigate and figure out how the drugs *really* got here?

Because he was afraid of scandal. He was afraid of the police showing up, the neighbors gossiping, and word reaching the Computer Science Department at Bowman that Assistant Professor Clinton Westcott was involved in a drug investigation.

"Mal, please get help," Eden said. "My doctor can recommend—"

Mallory yanked the front door open and marched out. As she slammed it behind her, she saw a man towering on the porch—Darien Thomas, holding a bouquet of flowers and looking stunned at the way Mallory had thumped the door shut hard enough to bounce Eden's autumn apple wreath off the hook.

"Uh . . . hi, Mallory. Uh . . ."

Mortified, Mallory picked up the wooden wreath and

hung it on the door. One of the apples had a chip in the red paint. Great. She'd better find some paint to match it before Eden noticed.

"Uh . . . I . . . you've looked stressed at work the last couple of weeks, and I . . . wanted to say I hope . . . you're all right." Darien proffered the bouquet with a clumsy gesture. "Didn't mean to disturb you."

Mallory took the flowers. "Thank you. Um . . . I'm sorry about . . ." The humiliation of having Darien see her like this split another crack in her composure. Trying to hide the tears filling her eyes, she all but buried her face in red, orange, and yellow gerbera daisies, hoping Darien wouldn't wonder why she was so eager to smell flowers that didn't have much of a scent.

"I don't want to interrupt your evening; obviously you're on your way out," he said. "I just wanted to stop by quickly. I hope you don't mind that I looked up your address."

"Thank you for the flowers." She smiled at him, relieved that tears weren't running down her face. "They're beautiful."

"You're welcome." He stepped backward off the porch, not looking where he was going, and bumped into an urn of chrysanthemums.

"Oops, sorry." He grabbed the teetering urn. "I show up and almost wreck the place."

"Finishing what I started." Mallory glanced at the damaged wreath, and her tears escaped. She looked back down at the daisies and hoped tonight's chilly autumn wind would dry her face.

"Mallory . . ." His voice went from embarrassed to gentle. "I don't want to be a pest, but is there anything I can do?"

She shook her head. A couple of tears watered the daisies.

"Do you . . . want me to leave?" Darien sounded like he was floundering.

She didn't want him to see her bawling into a bouquet. But she didn't want to send him away either. She shook her head.

Darien waited as though hoping for a cue as to what to do next. Mallory struggled for composure, her forehead touching the flowers.

"Can I . . . take you somewhere?" he asked.

Mallory nodded.

Darien waited for a suggestion then said tentatively, "There's a chocolate shop near campus . . ."

Mallory laughed. Darien responded to tears by offering chocolate? He was brilliant. "Yes, chocolate," she said, lifting her head. "Let's go."

The porch light showed redness in his pale face as he held out a hand to help her step off the porch. Mallory clutched his fingers and didn't let go as he led her to his car, an old Toyota pickup. The cab was spotless and smelled like Tide.

As he drove to campus, Darien said, "Would you . . . feel better if you talked about it?"

She cradled the flowers, relieved that no new tears were forming. "It's crazy."

"I don't mind. What is it?"

He sounded so sympathetic, she surrendered to the urge to confide in him. She told him about the drugs and Clint's and Eden's certainty that they were hers. "They're not mine. I do not do drugs." Her tongue dry, she tugged at a flower petal, gently, so she didn't rip it loose. "My mother was killed by a drug addict."

"I'm so sorry." Darien touched her shoulder then put his hand back on the steering wheel. "When?"

"When I was seventeen, at the end of my junior year in high school." Mallory folded her arms around the stems and touched her chin to the edge of the cellophane wrapping. "I told Clint I was taking the drugs to the police, but he wouldn't let me. He's a professor at Bowman, and his tenure decision is coming up. I think he's afraid involving the police would be professionally embarrassing to him. Besides, he's so sure the drugs are mine that he doesn't see the point. I even offered to take a drug test, but Eden just made a snarky remark about me cheating it. And I guess all a test could prove is that I haven't done drugs *lately*, but that doesn't mean I'm innocent."

"Can't you turn the drugs over to the police even if your brother-in-law doesn't want you to?" Darien asked. "He doesn't have the right to keep you from doing that."

"He won't give them to me. He and Eden have made up their minds. I have one week to find a new place to live. When am I going to have time—or the money—to do that?"

Darien parked at the chocolate shop. "Do you think he might be trying to cover for himself? That the drugs are *his*?"

Mallory patted her fingertips along the petals of a yellow daisy. "That would be hard to believe. He's always seemed like a trustworthy guy. He was a jerk tonight, but it's hard to blame him if he thinks I brought drugs into his house. But I can't believe the drugs are Eden's, either. She's . . . so in control of herself, so organized, and drugs are so . . . chaotic."

"Besides *finding* the drugs, do your sister and her husband have any reason for thinking—" Darien went silent, looking out the windshield toward the brown and white awning over the entrance to the chocolate shop.

Mallory silently finished the question Darien had cut off. *Do your sister and her husband have any reason to think you are an addict?*

Mallory blushed. She wasn't offended that he'd asked—or almost asked—something so blunt; it was a logical question. Pretending she didn't know what he'd stopped himself from saying would flatten an honest conversation into a superficial one, and she didn't want that. But if she tried to explain, she'd start crying again.

Just keep it short.

"I . . . made some dumb decisions in high school, hung out with people I shouldn't have. I didn't do drugs, but my mother worried about me, and apparently she told Eden."

"So bad choices in friends from years ago? That's why she thinks you're guilty now?"

"It's not just that. I've . . . had a hard time for the past few years, since our mother died."

Darien unzipped the top of his jacket, and Mallory realized he was wearing a tie. Had he come from a dress-up event, or had he put the tie on for her? Even in her distress, the possibility of him dressing up for her glimmered in a warm thought.

He's adorable.

"I can't imagine *not* having a hard time after losing your mother like that," Darien said. "Was your father a support to you?"

"He was long gone. He left when I was six, remarried, then died of a stroke in his late forties. And Eden's eleven years older than I am. She was already out of the house, done with college, and working in New York City when Mom died."

"Is that when you moved in with her?" Darien asked.

"No. She didn't have room for me then; she was in a tiny studio apartment. My mother's brother Mike lived a few miles away. He took me in."

"Did that work out?"

"He's a good man, but his son was already grown, and his wife was dead. He . . ." Her voice trailed off. She didn't want to say anything critical of Mike. He'd done his best.

"He had no idea what to do with a grieving teenage girl?" Darien suggested.

She sighed. "I fell apart. I didn't care about anything. I still had a year of high school left, and I almost didn't graduate. If it hadn't been for a couple of teachers who dragged me through that last semester by the scruff of the neck, I wouldn't have finished."

"What did you do after that?"

"Nothing. *Almost* nothing. I worked part time at an ice-cream shop and spent the rest of the time sleeping or watching TV. I had no drive at all—no energy."

"That's more than grief," Darien said. "That sounds like clinical depression."

"Yeah." She pulled out the white envelope tucked between the flowers and the cellophane and looked at her name written on it. Darien's handwriting was narrow and a little sloppy. "Unfortunately, it took Uncle Mike and me a long time to figure that out. He finally hauled me to a doctor. When I started feeling better, I wanted to go to school, but it took me a while to get here. Eden was really supportive; she suggested applying to Bowman and offered to let me live with them my first year, but . . . Eden doesn't know me all that well. She's very focused, very motivated, and I think she has trouble understanding how I could have . . . stalled so badly, for so long. She wonders if drugs were part of the problem. But I swear, the only drugs I took were those my doctor prescribed, and I took them exactly as she told me to . . . You didn't want to know any of this, did you?" Why had she dumped all this on Darien?

He shows sympathy, and you start chucking all your baggage at him. Congratulations on scaring him away permanently.

"I *want* to know more about you," he said. "You don't need to be ashamed of your past."

"Let's get a couple of pieces of fudge, and you can take me home," she said wearily. "It still counts as home. I have a key, and Clint hasn't had time to change the locks."

"And he gave you a week, right?" Darien's long fingers curved around her shoulder with kind, comforting strength. "Let's look at this situation logically. If the drugs aren't yours and you don't think they're Clint's or Eden's, who else could have put them there?"

"Eden said no one else has been in the house during the window when they could have been stashed there."

"You mean she doesn't *know* of anyone who could have been there. How long have Clint and Eden lived there?"

"Two years."

"Were the locks rekeyed when they moved in?"

"I don't know."

"So someone else may have a key. Or someone could have broken in."

"But why would someone sneak in, stash drugs, and leave?"

"No idea," Darien said. "The first step is finding evidence that someone else was there. Motive is step two. Let's go get that chocolate. It'll help us think."

4

Several chocolate turtles and two hours later, when Darien dropped her at home and said goodnight with a quick, shy hug, Mallory still felt mentally sore, but not as panicky. She had concrete plans for tomorrow—small, probably ineffective plans, but at least they were a starting point. She'd check with neighbors to see if any of them had noticed someone approaching the house during the day. She'd try one more time to convince Clint that they should take the drugs to the police—if he hadn't already flushed them, which he probably had.

And she'd start looking for another place to live. She desperately wanted to find an outside explanation for the drugs, but the more she evaluated the situation, the more she had to acknowledge that the likely culprit was Clint or Eden, trying to hide behind Mallory.

The possibility that one of them could be cold enough to blame her for their issues rather than come clean with their spouse made her feel so isolated, so betrayed, that suspecting them felt like clutching a knife by the blade, evaluating the sharpness by letting it sink into her hand. Something else must be happening—a student angry at Clint for a failing grade, trying to stir trouble between Clint and his wife; a client from the bank Eden managed, angry at a rejected loan application, trying to hurt Eden.

Bracing herself, Mallory stepped into the house, hoping Eden and Clint had gone to bed early. The lights in the living room and kitchen were off, but the ones in the back of the house were on.

You don't have to say much to them tonight. Everyone will be calmer after a good night's sleep.

Mallory opened a kitchen cupboard and took out a vase. She filled it with water, unwrapped the flowers, and stuck them in the vase. The flowers were too tall, but she'd trim the stems tomorrow. Right now, even the basic task of making flowers proportionate to a vase sounded exhausting.

She opened Darien's card. Apparently, he hadn't been able to think of what to say in a message; he'd just signed his name. Smiling, she tucked the card between a red daisy and an orange one.

She headed down the hallway toward her bedroom. To her surprise, her bedroom light glowed. When she reached her doorway, she saw Eden pulling clothes out of dresser drawers. Clint stood in front of the open closet.

"What are you *doing*?" Mallory rushed into the room. "Get out of here!"

Eden glared at her. She wasn't crying, but her eyes were so puffy, she must have stopped not long before. She pointed angrily at the center of the dresser—at another small bag of white powder and two more bags of pills.

Horrified, Mallory gaped at the bags. "You found those in here?"

"We thought we'd better see what else you were hiding," Eden said. "And I can't believe you *stole* from me."

"Stole?" Was Eden admitting the drugs were hers?

"My emergency money in my dresser," Eden said. "Two hundred and fifteen dollars. It's gone."

"*What*? I didn't take it!" The calm, logical mindset she'd adopted from Darien tumbled away. "Those drugs aren't mine!"

"Mallory." Clint's voice was quiet. Apparently he'd had enough time to get over his initial anger and was now the calm professor. "Let's act like adults. No one came into your room and planted drugs."

"Yes, they *did*, because I *did not put them there*. And I didn't take Eden's money!"

"Please don't yell," Clint said. "The neighbors don't want to be part of this."

Trembling, Mallory looked at Eden. "Let's see what's in *your* room." She whirled and stalked down the hall. She expected one of them to protest, but they followed her silently.

Clint and Eden's normally spotless room was already a jumble.

"We looked here first," Eden said. "And we already searched the living room and the kitchen. Let's check your purse." She headed toward the living room.

Mallory followed her. "Keep away from—"

Clint stepped between Mallory and Eden. Mallory wanted to shove him aside, but if she turned this into physical confrontation, they'd take it as evidence that she was not only an addict, but a dangerous one.

Like Nelson.

Eden opened the coat closet and took out Mallory's purse.

"Fine, search it if you want," Mallory said. "There's nothing in there." But was she sure of that? Someone was planting things—setting her up. Clint? Eden? Who else could it be?

Eden rooted through the purse but only pulled out one thing: Mallory's keys. "I'll check her car."

"This is ridiculous." She started to step around Clint. With an outstretched arm, he blocked her while Eden exited.

"Sit down," he said.

"*Please* listen—"

"Cooperate, or I'll call the police."

"I *wanted* to go to the police earlier! You wouldn't let me!"

"I was wrong. I was thinking too much of gossip, not about how much you needed help. Do you want me to call them now? I will, if that's what you want."

Mallory's tongue was paralyzed. Did she want him to call the cops? And when Clint and Eden testified that Mallory's room was riddled with drugs, and that Eden's money was missing—

"Sit down," Clint repeated.

Mechanically, Mallory walked to the couch and sat.

"Give me your phone." Standing in front of her, Clint held out his hand.

"You have no right—"

"You don't *have* to give it to me. But if you don't, I'm calling the police."

Confusion deadened her brain. She couldn't face the police while she had no idea what was going on. The police wouldn't believe her. She'd get arrested. Sent to jail.

Why would Clint or Eden set her up like this? They wouldn't. She hadn't spent much time with Eden over the last decade, but Eden was her sister, and Mallory knew her well enough to know she wasn't a coldblooded devil. She'd gotten to know Clint little more than superficially since moving in, but she'd never seen any evidence that he wasn't a decent man. But weren't sociopaths good at fooling people?

I've lost my mind. Sleep deprivation. Stress. Weird flashbacks to Mom's death after what happened to Nels last week.

"Your phone," Clint said.

Anger flagging beneath humiliation and confusion, she pulled the phone out of her pocket and dropped it into his palm.

Clint stepped back and tapped the screen. Mallory assumed he was checking her texts, calls, and contacts. Looking for drug pushers?

The door opened, and Eden walked in. "Nothing," she said, to Mallory's surprise. Mallory had been almost sure Eden would come in brandishing another stash of drugs and saying she'd found it in Mallory's glove box.

My own sister? She wouldn't lie about me. Clint wouldn't either. But what other explanation makes sense?

No explanation makes sense.

I need to get out of here. She couldn't afford a hotel, but she'd drive to campus, sleep in her car—anything to get away from Clint and Eden.

Mallory moved to stand. It took a moment; she felt heavy, feeble. "Give me my phone. And I need my keys. I don't know what you two are doing to me, but I'm leaving."

"What *we're* doing?" Eden glanced at Clint.

"I didn't bring those drugs into the house," Mallory said.

"Are you saying *we* did?" Eden asked. "You think we'd

hide them in your room? Why?"

"I have no idea. Does one of you have a secret you want me blamed for?"

In silence, Clint and Eden both stared at her. Mallory realized how irrational she sounded. She had absolutely no reason to suspect either of them.

But *someone* had put the drugs there. Had Clint been using drugs to deal with work stress? Had Eden, to cope with the fact that no matter how hard she worked, she wasn't perfect?

"Mallory . . . how about you get some rest?" Clint said. "We'll talk in the morning."

"I'm leaving," Mallory said. "Give me—"

Clint stuffed her phone in his pocket while Eden stowed Mallory's keys.

"You can't hold me prisoner," Mallory snapped.

"You're not a prisoner," Clint said. "You can leave if you want, but if you go out that door tonight, I'm calling the police."

"I need my keys. I have to be to work at four."

"We know," Eden said. "We don't want you to lose your job. I'll take you there. But you're not going out tonight to . . . meet with anyone."

"Do I look like a druggie?" Mallory snarled then realized she probably looked anything but clean at the moment, with shadows of exhaustion under bloodshot, teary eyes, and her body shaking.

"We'll get you in to see my doctor tomorrow," Eden said. "We'll help you through this."

"What happened to kicking me out?"

"You can't live here, but that doesn't mean we're abandoning you," Eden said.

"I'm happy to go with you to the doctor. *They* can test me and prove that I *don't use drugs*. But I think one of you already knows that." She stumbled into her trashed bedroom and locked the door behind her.

Eden and Clint would surely be locking their door as well, to protect themselves from her. Not that the locks in this old house were worth anything. She slumped onto her bed, pushing a pile of papers to the floor, and closed her eyes, too stressed to think.

5

When Mallory rose at three o'clock to get ready for work, Eden got up as well. She gave Mallory her phone back, but not her keys. Mallory didn't bother to argue against the tacit implication that Eden was afraid Mallory would drive while impaired, nor did she bother avoiding Eden's searching looks as she scanned Mallory for any signs of drug use or withdrawal. After a sleepless night, she knew she looked glassy eyed and ill; whatever Eden was seeing, she'd regard as evidence.

They didn't speak as Eden drove her to campus until they arrived at the Rains Building and Eden said, "I'll call you as soon as I talk to the doctor."

Mallory nodded and exited the car. She wanted fervently to talk to Darien and get his perspective, but she'd have to wait a few hours. He'd planned to come in when she finished at eight to take her to breakfast. She couldn't call him now, waking him up, whimpering and accusing her own family of turning on her.

He showed up at seven forty-five as Mallory wheeled the vacuum into the janitorial closet, so tired it was hard not to steer the vacuum into the walls. He hurried toward her.

"I'm sorry," he said. "You look exhausted. I kept you up too late, didn't I?"

"It's not that," she said. "I couldn't sleep at all. Things are a disaster. Come talk to me while I clean the drinking fountains. Then I'm finished."

Darien followed. He took the cleaner and paper towels out of her hands and worked while she updated him.

"I feel like I'm losing my mind," she said after she finished her report on last night. "I can't believe I accused Clint and Eden—my own family—but who else could it be? I hardly know anyone in Birch Falls. I've only been here a month and a half! How could I have made an enemy like that?"

"You're certain *you're* the target?" Darien polished the handle of the fountain. "Maybe there are drugs throughout the house and the culprit wants *all* of you in trouble."

"They searched the whole house, or said they did. The only place they found drugs was in Eden's drawer—next to mine—and in my bedroom. There's no way to mistake my room for the master bedroom. Mine only has a twin bed."

"So you think Clint or Eden is the addict and is trying to keep from getting found out by blaming you," Darien said. "That maybe they're afraid their spouse saw the drugs, or now that the emergency money is gone, they need a way to explain where it went."

"I don't know. No, I don't believe that. I have no reason to believe it. But I don't know who else . . . They're good people . . . and it doesn't make sense. If one of them has an ongoing drug problem, there must be money besides Eden's emergency cash that's unaccounted for, but they didn't say anything about that. And Eden keeps such careful track of her money, she *would* have noticed anything missing. Maybe Clint is planning to claim there's been money missing from his wallet."

"Seems like he would have mentioned that last night," Darien said.

Mallory sighed. "Accusing one of them made more sense when they were just trying to throw me out, but after they found the drugs in my room, they took my keys, took my phone, and they warned me that if I left, they'd call the police. You'd think the guilty spouse would want me out of there fast rather than pretending they're worried about me. They both seem on board with taking me to the doctor, but if one of them is setting me up, they must know that the first thing I'll do is insist that the doctor give me whatever kind of drug test is most accurate, whatever kind there's no way I could fake, and that will prove I haven't—"

Feeling lightheaded, Mallory stopped. She'd assumed tests would exonerate her, but weren't there foods that could cause false positives? She often ate Eden's cooking—Eden loved cooking and always urged Mallory to join them if she was home and to eat leftovers if she wasn't. If Eden was trying to . . .

Are you kidding me? You think your sister would do that to you?

Mallory sat on the tile floor of the hall and pressed her burning eyes against her knees. She sensed Darien sit next to her and felt his hand on her shoulder. "Mallory?"

She kept her head lowered. "I'm crazy paranoid. I'm seriously losing it." *How can I suspect my own family?* But they suspected *her*. More than suspected—they were certain she was guilty.

But they had reason to doubt Mallory. What reason did Mallory have to doubt them?

"Hey, let's stick with the original plan, all right?" Darien's fingers pressed her shoulder, massaging it. His touch calmed her, and within a few moments, anxiety started to erode, washed out by sleepiness

"The fact that the situation is worse than we thought doesn't change how we approach it." Darien's hand shifted and began to rub the knotted muscles in her other shoulder. "We need to find out if anyone's been seen near your sister's house."

She didn't look up; a few more minutes of Darien's comforting touch and she'd conk out with her head on her knees. She wanted to ask him to reassure her that he believed the drugs weren't hers, but that wasn't a fair question. She and Darien had barely become friends. He didn't know her that well. To put him on the spot would be whiney and make him uncomfortable.

This was so pathetic. It had been so long since she'd been interested in a guy, and how did she start off? By making herself look like a needy, hysterical, possibly unstable, probably drug-addicted drama queen. Whatever smidgen of romantic interest he'd had in her when he brought her the flowers must have evaporated during this morning's rant about Clint and Eden.

Forget your silly crush. He was never going to get involved with an overage freshman. If he's still willing to be a friend, be grateful.

"You okay?" Darien asked.

She lifted her head and tried to smile. "Just really, really tired. And confused."

Darien drew his hand back. "Is there any other way

Eden or Clint could benefit from getting you in trouble—besides setting you up to hide their own issues?"

"Yes. If they can make it appear I died of a drug overdose, Eden inherits my share of the family jewels."

Darien grinned. "A solid motive at last."

"Sorry." She laughed weakly. "I'm not used to acting like a character in a PBS Mystery special. No, I don't have any money, or I wouldn't be working a four-in-the-morning janitorial job and taking out student loans to pay for school. We don't have any rich relatives. Our parents had more debts than assets. Uncle Mike doesn't have much money, and anything he does have would go to his son, not Eden or me. I don't own anything valuable. My car is sixteen years old and smells like Pine-Sol. I shop at thrift stores." She pointed to her Bowman University sweatshirt. "I bought this at Goodwill for six dollars."

"Could they be after something other than money?"

"Nothing." Too tired to sit up straight, she flopped her head back to her knees.

"What time is your first class?" he asked. "Do you have time for a nap?"

"Not until ten, but even if I did have my car, I wouldn't want to go home." *This is ridiculous. Eden's going to call me about a doctor appointment, and I have no idea what to tell her. I can't believe I don't trust my own family. And they don't trust me. What's wrong with us?*

6

Mindlessly, Darien exited his class with no idea what the discussion had been about. How could he help Mallory? He'd reviewed and analyzed everything she'd told him. He'd organized it all in a spreadsheet: what had happened, at what time, how Mallory interpreted each event, what Clint and Eden had said—as reported by Mallory—and his own thoughts.

He didn't have enough information.

He'd debated what to do and had finally decided that gathering possibly biased information was better than sitting in his cubicle, helplessly wishing he knew more. He might have made a colossal mistake that would destroy his friendship with Mallory, but he'd checked the faculty directory for Clints and found one: Clinton Westcott in the Computer Science Department. He'd called Clint, but gotten his voicemail, so he'd left a message, asking Clint to call him about Mallory.

His phone vibrated. Steeling himself, he pulled it out and saw a call from an unfamiliar number. "Hello, this is Darien."

"This is Clinton Westcott returning your message."

Darien's heart rate surged. "Thanks for calling me back. I'm a friend of your sister-in-law's, and I'm worried about—"

"Do you know where she is?" Clint interrupted. "My wife and I have been trying to get in touch with her."

Darien wasn't ready to share that he did know Mallory's location. "Sir, I'd like to talk to you about her, but could we meet in person?"

"I'm free right now. Come to my office. Number 450 in the Yarborough Center."

"On my way." *Good luck explaining to Mallory that you sought information from the guy accusing her.* "I'll be there in five minutes."

The sky was overcast, and wind ripped autumn leaves from the trees as Darien hurried across campus. Clint Westcott's office door was ajar, and he stood to welcome Darien.

"Thank you for contacting me. Please, have a seat."

Studying Clint's demeanor, Darien sat. Clint looked tense but not hostile. Tired, though not as exhausted as Mallory.

Clint sat behind his desk. "We're extremely concerned about Mallory. What led you to call me?"

"Last night and this morning, she told me some disturbing things." Darien was careful not to sound accusatory. "I'd like to hear your side of the story."

"What did she say?"

"I'd appreciate hearing your side of the story first, Dr. Westcott."

Clint frowned. "I take it you've come to defend her."

"I want to *help* her," Darien said. "But until I understand the situation completely, I have no idea how to do that."

"Good. If you want to help her, we're on the same page," Clint said. "What I'm telling you is completely confidential. I hope, for Mallory's sake, you'll keep it that way."

Darien nodded.

"Mallory has a drug problem," Clint said. "We just found out yesterday and tried to talk to her about it, but she was very defensive and hostile toward my wife and me."

Darien spoke neutrally. "What evidence did you find of drug use?"

"Drugs hidden in her room. And she's stolen money from Eden. Her sister. My wife."

"*She's* stolen money? Are you certain it was Mallory?"

Clint's eyes were keen, and Darien realized Clint was scrutinizing him the same way Darien was scrutinizing Clint. "During the period in which the money went missing, Mallory was the only one who could have taken it."

"You're sure?"

"Yes. Eden knows the money was there three days ago when she took out twenty dollars. No one has visited since then."

"How secure is your house?" Darien asked. "Do you have a security system? Deadbolts?"

"There was zero evidence of a break-in. Even if a thief managed to enter with no signs of a break-in, why would he leave jewelry and electronics behind and take the cash without disturbing anything else?"

"Fair enough," Darien said. "What evidence of drug

use—physical or emotional—have you seen in Mallory herself?"

"We don't see much of Mallory. As far as physical symptoms, she's been able to hide most of the signs. But there are bloodshot eyes, excessive tiredness, isolation, secretiveness, paranoia."

Excessive tiredness? She has to be to work at four AM; I'd look tired too on that schedule. "Secretiveness?" Darien asked.

"If she's home, she's in her room—or she heads there the instant I walk in the door. She seems intent on staying out of sight."

"What signs of paranoia does she show?"

"Making crazy accusations against her sister and me, accusing us of holding her prisoner, of trying to frame her."

"So this 'paranoia' manifested itself after you found the drugs? But not before?"

Silently, Clint reached forward and twiddled a framed picture on his desk. Darien couldn't see who was in the picture; he assumed it was Eden. "She also has a history," Clint said.

"Of drug use?"

"It's . . . not completely clear what she was involved in, but she hung with a bad crowd. Mr. Thomas, I realize that as her friend, you want to defend her, but denial isn't helping. If her drug use comes to the attention of the police and the university, she'll get arrested and expelled. Mallory has had enough trouble getting herself to this point. If you care about her, help us help her before she destroys her life."

"I want to help her," Darien said. "That's why I'm talking to you. But all of this evidence is circumstantial. I've never seen any signs in Mallory that she uses drugs. Until last night, all I've seen is . . ." He thought about his early morning chats with Mallory. "A woman who is hardworking, smart, friendly, funny, conscientious—"

"Then where did the drugs come from? She agreed to let Eden set up a doctor appointment for her, but now she's refusing to take Eden's calls. Why would she avoid seeing a doctor if she's clean?"

Darien scanned the bookshelves in Clint's office. It was easier to focus on the spines of textbooks on computational theory, JavaScript and MySQL than to look in Clint's eyes and see frustration and anxiety. Clint appeared and sounded completely rational. Concerned for Mallory.

Darien had left his sweatshirt with Mallory, but even in his short sleeves, he felt overheated, with sweat beginning to trickle down his back. He *wanted* to believe Mallory. But did he have any reason—any *rational* reason—for believing her over Clint Westcott? Incontestably, Clint's interpretation sounded far more rational than Mallory's frightened, confused insistence that she'd been set up.

"You said you've seen her today," Clint said. "How is she?"

Darien rallied. It was time to shove back harder and see how Clint reacted. "Scared to death, trying to figure out why someone would do this to her. Is there any possibility someone in your household is trying to cover up their own issues by blaming them on Mallory? Have there been problems before this? Other missing money, maybe from your bank account?"

"My wife would never do anything like this," Clint said wearily. "I would never do anything like this, and we never experienced any problems before Mallory arrived. Are *you* part of the problem? Her supplier, maybe? Are you the one who convinced her that drugs are a good way to deal with the stress of starting college?"

"No." Darien refused to let anger disrupt his concentration. He should have known Clint would be suspicious of him. "What about enemies you or your wife have? Maybe someone is trying to hurt you through Mallory."

"There's no one and nothing like that. And yes, Eden has checked with the neighbors to see if anyone has been seen around our house."

"She checked?"

"Yes. It was far-fetched, but do you think she *wants* to believe her sister is using drugs? If you care about Mallory, get her to talk to us and see a doctor instead of letting her manipulate you with crazy excuses. Do you know where she is right now? She skipped her class this afternoon."

Darien was silent. He knew she hadn't gone to her afternoon class. She'd been too worried that Eden or Clint would track her down there—which, apparently, had been an accurate fear, since Clint knew she hadn't attended. But the thought of skipping class had rattled her; she was terrified of backsliding into the trouble she'd had in high school. Realizing her stress and exhaustion had hit the point where she couldn't think clearly, Darien had coaxed her into taking a nap in a private place where no one would find her—the professor's office to which Darien had a key. Dr. Agosto was off in Chicago, presenting at a conference.

"I won't drag her to the police, or to a doctor," Clint said. "At least, not today. I just want to talk to her, but she's ignoring both my and Eden's calls. Will you help us get in touch with her? Or do you believe her accusations that we're evil and planting drugs in her room?"

"It's not really an accusation," Darien said. "Call it panicked brainstorming. She knows she has no reason to suspect you. She's just struggling to figure out what really happened."

"I can understand why she's having trouble facing this," Clint said. "Of course it's scary for her, and I'll admit, we were so upset last night that we were on the attack. If I could talk to her now, I may be able to calm things down between us."

Darien hesitated. *How can I best help Mallory? Not by helping her hide.*

"I'll talk to her," he said. "I know where she is. I'll do everything I can to convince her to meet with you and your wife. But let me approach her alone first. If I send you straight to her, she'll lose whatever trust she has in me—if she has any left—and that won't help any of us sort this out."

"Thank you." Clint rose to his feet and extended his hand. "Talk to her. Then call me."

Discouraged that the only thing he'd learned from the meeting was that Darien had no strong, logical reasons for believing Mallory, Darien reluctantly shook Clint's hand. "I will."

7

Sitting on the floor in Dr. Agosto's office, Mallory gripped her phone, her thumbs hovering over the screen as she tried to convince herself to answer Eden's texts. The messages had started out matter-of-fact, had turned to curt, and now sounded pleading.

Mallory couldn't decide what to do. She felt cornered. Bewildered. She wanted to collapse onto the carpeted floor, rest her head on Darien's folded sweatshirt, and go back to sleep.

Don't do it. Don't go there again.

She heard a key in the lock, and Darien stepped into the office. "Hey, you're awake," he said. "Feeling any better?"

Mallory nodded. Darien's hair was a mess, and his neck was red. She doubted the redness was from the wind that had styled his hair; it was blustery outside, but mild, unless the temperature had dropped rapidly in the few hours she'd been in here. Darien was nervous.

He sat on the floor next to her. "Ready for something to eat?"

She was hungry, but the thought of going anywhere scared her. She was sinking right back to where she'd been, unable to cope, mentally trapped. Skipping class, burrowing in an absent professor's office.

When she didn't say anything, Darien spoke quietly. "Mallory, listen. I . . . talked to your brother-in-law."

Jolted, she stared at him. "Clint contacted you? How did he know—"

"I contacted him," Darien said.

Dismay submerged Mallory. Even though there was no reason he should believe her, she'd hoped he did. "You . . . think I'm lying to you, don't you?"

"I went to Clint in hopes of getting information. Not because I think you're lying."

"What did he say?"

"Essentially the same things you told me. He interprets things differently, but you're sharing the same facts. He seems sincerely worried about you." Darien's dark eyes were anxious, sad, but intensely focused as he met her gaze. "I'll be honest with you. I have no idea what's going on here. I haven't made up my mind about anything—I don't have enough information. But I am your friend, and I want to help you. Clint wants to talk to you. I told him I'd try to convince you to do that."

She leaned against the wall, struggling not to panic at how isolated she felt. Darien had talked to Clint. Darien believed Clint. No. He hadn't said that. He'd said he didn't know what to think. She looked at the worry in Darien's face. "Thank you for telling me the truth."

"I'm sorry if you feel I betrayed you by talking to him."

She shook her head. "I want you to believe me. But if you *did* believe me without reservation, given the evidence, you'd be an idiot."

His platinum brows rose. "You're serious."

Mallory smiled bleakly. "If you knew me well and still doubted me, that would really hurt, but you don't. And if you're a guy who's so dim he'll keep blindly defending me even when all the evidence says I may be a toxic liar—that's not chivalrous; it's idiotic. What matters to me is that you're keeping your mind open and that you want to help me."

"I do." The relief in his smile was so evident that Mallory felt her trust in him growing. He'd gone to Clint because he cared about her. "I told Clint I'd never seen any signs of drug use in you," he said. "For a moment, let's assume you're innocent and that Clint and Eden are too. He claims she's already checked with the neighbors to see if they've seen anything, but they haven't."

Mallory wasn't sure if Eden really *had* checked, but the possibility made her feel a little more hopeful. "I did too," she said. "Before I napped. I looked up the phone numbers online. No one I talked to had seen anything. I left messages at the other houses."

"Okay, so we've done all we can do there for the moment." Darien opened his backpack and took out a bag of chocolate-covered pretzels he'd purchased at the chocolate shop the night before. "You must be hungry." He handed it to her.

"Thanks." Mallory unfastened the twist-tie around the bag. She should probably suggest that they get off the floor and sit in actual chairs. He didn't seem to mind the floor, though. He'd leaned against the wall next to her and stretched out his legs.

"Let's widen the range for brainstorming," he said. "You said you don't have any enemies here and that you don't even know anyone well enough to make an enemy. Maybe we need to look farther back. I apologize for bringing this up, but you told me a drug addict killed your mother. Is there anything related to that story that could lead someone to bother you now?"

"He's dead." A knot hurt Mallory's throat, and she set the pretzel bag down. "Just a few weeks ago. He was killed during a prison riot."

Darien studied her, and she could tell he was wondering how Nelson's death had affected her. "Did his death stir everything up—remind you of what he did to your mother?"

"Yes, but I also feel bad for *him*. He didn't mean to kill her, and he was absolutely devastated about it. He was a—a friend of mine. I was the one who—" Agony flamed, charring her with memories.

"Mallory?" Darien grasped her hand. "You were the one who what?"

Tears spilled down her face. "I was the one who made him think of my house as a target. It was at an awful party . . . I threw it when my mother was a couple of hours away, visiting a friend. Things happened at the party that I shouldn't have allowed. Nelson brought drugs; so did a few others. I should have thrown them out. Instead I joked about how my mom would never suspect, that she acted like she was living in rural 1910 and was the kind of person who hardly ever locked the doors or windows . . ." Her chest heaved; she fought to breathe steadily. The flames spread. Wildly, she wondered how to douse the memories, to change the subject.

Darien's arm enveloped her, his hand light on the side of her face, nudging her head to his shoulder. She slumped and let herself sob, her cheek pressed against his shirt. Spilling tears was a familiar sensation, but spilling them onto someone's shoulder was not, and the warmth of Darien's shoulder made it easy to release the rest of the story.

"He got desperate. That's why he chose our house—because he knew it would be easy to get in, and he knew my mother volunteered at the library on Wednesday nights and I always went with her to study there. But she'd stayed home that night to rest; she had a headache. The lights were off, and I had the car at the grocery store, so Nelson didn't realize anyone was home. She walked in on him when he was stuffing her laptop in his bag, and he panicked. Swung a lamp that hit her in the head. She fell. Died later that night of a brain hemorrhage. I came home just as Nelson was running away."

"I'm so sorry." Darien stroked her hair. "Mallory, what Nelson chose to do is not your fault."

"I know," she sobbed. "But I was stupid, and the result was . . . I'm sorry . . . I thought I was handling this. I did eventually go to counseling . . ."

"I doubt counseling comes with a guarantee that traumatic events will never hurt again," Darien said gently.

"But I'm not using illegal drugs to deal with this. Do you see why I would never—after what happened to Mom—"

Darien lifted his arm from around her and turned to face her, frowning. "This is going to be a painful question, and I apologize. But did Nelson's family know the details of what happened? How he came to choose your house?"

"Yes." Wiping her face, she tried to stop crying. "His lawyer mentioned it at the plea bargain, trying to make it sound like Nelson was a nice boy who'd been overwhelmed by irresistible temptation and deserved leniency. Things were pretty bad for him—he'd just turned eighteen, so he was an adult . . . the lawyer was using any tactic he could to convince the judge Nelson deserved a lesser sentence . . ."

"So the lawyer more or less made it sound like you'd lured Nelson there. Almost set him up?"

Mallory thought back. "Not quite. He tried not to sound like he was directly blaming me. Probably afraid of losing sympathy with the judge since my mother was dead."

Darien squeezed her hand. "But did Nelson's family blame you?"

"I have no idea. They never confronted me. We never talked. You're suggesting they could be the ones planting the drugs now, trying to get revenge on me by getting me in trouble?"

"Just a thought. If they felt like you set Nelson up, maybe they feel you deserve it."

Mallory tried to picture Nelson's family coming after her. "This happened four and a half years ago and two thousand miles away. If they blamed me, why wouldn't they have taken revenge at the time?"

"Maybe it took Nelson's death. What's his family like?" Darien knelt and reached toward Dr. Agosto's desk to grab a box of tissues.

"Serious problems," Mallory said, taking the tissues. "His mom was abusive. His dad was an addict; he's the one who got Nels hooked. He had one sister, Lori, who was . . . um . . . three years older. He worshipped her. Super smart, but she made a lot of dumb decisions. I can relate."

"Do you know where they are now?"

"His dad died of an overdose a few months after Nelson was arrested. His mother and Lori, I don't know." Mallory gave up trying to imagine Nelson's mother tracking her down, following her across the country, and sneaking into Clint and Eden's house. She wouldn't be patient enough for that. If she came after Mallory, it would be to scream at her and punch her.

But what about Lori?

"It's far-fetched, but so is everything else," Mallory said. "I'll call my uncle to see if he knows anything about what Lori Sanders is up to."

8

Clint waved Mallory and Darien into his office. "Thank you for coming."

Eden sprang to her feet then hesitated, as though not sure how to greet Mallory. She looked haggard, and Mallory realized she must have left work early to come here. Methodical Eden leaving work early?

"I'm sorry," Mallory said. "I should have answered your calls. I haven't handled this very well."

Eden took a halting step forward and wrapped her arms around Mallory. Mallory hugged her back, and to her surprise, Eden didn't let go, but cinched her arms so tightly, she all but deflated Mallory's lungs.

"Mal." Eden's voice broke. "I'm so sorry. I've been rotten to you for years."

"That's . . . not true."

Eden drew back and looked into Mallory's face, tears streaming from her eyes. "I hardly kept in touch with you after leaving home, and when Mom died, I left you to deal with it on your own. You were still a kid, and I didn't even bother to—"

Mallory felt her own tear-achy eyes fill again. "I didn't expect you to—you had a life away from—"

"You expected me to *abandon* you? Leave you with our old uncle who didn't have a clue?"

"Uncle Mike did his best—"

"He's a good man, but how long did it take him to figure out you were suffering from depression? How long did it take him to get you some help? And what did *I* do to help—text you maybe a few times a week to ask if you were getting out of the house or tell you to find some friends, or go to school, that you should just deal with everything?"

"Eden—"

"No wonder you don't trust me to help you now." She clamped her hands around Mallory's shoulders. "I *will* help you."

Clint put his arm around Eden's waist. "Let's sit down and hear what Mallory has to say."

Eden released her. Dazed by a love and concern more open than she'd ever experienced from Eden, Mallory sank into the nearest chair. Eden pulled a chair close and linked arms with Mallory so their shoulders touched. Mallory wondered if Eden wanted to comfort her or keep her from escaping, but the sisterly contact was soothing, so she didn't push Eden away.

"Darien, you're welcome to . . ." Clint gestured toward the only remaining chair in his office, his desk chair.

"Thank you, Dr. Westcott, but I'll stand."

Clint sat; Darien stood next to Mallory, who explained what she and Darien had discussed about the Sanders family. Clint leaned forward while he listened, arms on his desk, gaze sharp.

"I talked to Uncle Mike today," Mallory continued. "I told him what's been happening here and asked if he knew anything about what Lori Sanders is up to. He said he has no idea what Lori's doing, but admitted that a couple of days after Nelson's funeral, someone threw a rock through his window."

Eden gasped. "Through Uncle Mike's window? He didn't tell you this before?"

"You know Mike—the silent stoic who never says anything he doesn't have to. I asked why he didn't tell me, and he said because there was no point in worrying me. There was other vandalism too. Mom's grave."

Eden's fingernails speared Mallory's arm. "What happened to it?"

"Graffiti. Profanity, mainly. Mike wouldn't tell me exactly what it said; you know how he is about bad language, but the idea was that Mom deserved to die."

"Do the police think Lori Sanders is responsible?" Clint asked.

"Uncle Mike said they questioned her. She didn't admit to anything, and they didn't have any evidence against her. But a few days later, a friend of Mike's told him that Lori had quit work without warning and left town along with her newest loser boyfriend—who apparently has done time for drug dealing."

"What about Nelson's mother?" Eden asked.

"Mike said she moved to Wisconsin a couple of years ago. I don't think she's involved in this."

Clint tapped his fingers on his desk, lips pursed. "If thuggish vandalism is Lori's style, would she really have the patience to—"

"Maybe the thuggish stuff is her boyfriend's style,"

Mallory suggested. "Nelson used to tell me how clever Lori was. Devious. Maybe she wants more satisfaction than a broken window and junior-high-school dirty words on a gravestone."

"Getting you busted for possession, thrown out of school, and sent to jail?" Clint said. "If the police in Gilroy think Lori is on a vengeful rampage, it would have been nice of them to call to warn you."

"I wish they had. But it wasn't much of a rampage. Just two instances of vandalism. And she didn't make any threats against me. It probably didn't occur to them that she'd travel to the opposite coast to harass me."

Neither Clint nor Eden spoke, and Mallory wondered what they were thinking. *It probably didn't occur to them because it's a ludicrous idea.*

"I want to go to the Birch Falls police," Mallory said. "But I'm nervous doing that if I'll be asking them to investigate whether Lori Sanders is in town while you two insist the drugs you found are mine."

"We don't want to blame you for something you're innocent of," Clint said, his tone so cautious that Mallory knew he still thought she was at least as likely a suspect as Lori.

Eden turned in her chair and clung to Mallory's hand. "If there's another explanation for the drugs, we'd be grateful to find that out."

At least they were willing to question her guilt. That was the most she could hope for. "I'm calling the police," Mallory said.

9

The next day, Mallory had difficulty staying awake in class. The interviews with the police, and the officers' visit to the house, had kept her up late again, and at work this morning she'd been so tired she kept forgetting things, like how to switch the vacuum on, how to use her ID card to open doors, or which end of the mop went on the floor.

She had no idea what Eden, Clint, or Darien had said to Detective Jenny Ridley when she'd interviewed them last night, but the fact that Mallory wasn't in handcuffs by the end of the evening had to be a good sign. But if she was wrong about Lori Sanders—or if she was right, but the police couldn't prove anything, and they decided Darien and Mallory's theory was ridiculous—she could still up in prison.

By the time she reached her Wednesday evening class, she couldn't concentrate at all, only wonder foggily if Detective Ridley had learned anything, dream about how comfortable it would feel to rest her face on the desk and watch the darkening sky through the classroom window. For the first half of class, only sips of ice water from her mother's insulated metal water bottle kept her conscious.

For the second half of class, worry about Eden drove away the urge to sleep. Eden was home alone this evening, since Mallory had class until eight and Clint taught until nine. There was no reason to think Lori would dare show up when someone was home—if she wanted face-to-face revenge, she'd have confronted Mallory, not schemed offstage to get her in trouble. But Mallory got so nervous, she pulled her phone out and sent a text under the desk. Eden responded that she was fine, doing some cleaning. Mallory told her to lock the doors, which seemed like a futile instruction. When Lori had sneaked in before, the doors had been locked.

Stop being paranoid. If Lori's seen by anyone, she destroys her whole scheme. She won't come near an occupied house.

When she reached her car after class, Mallory found rain-wet leaves coating the windows. Anxious to get home, she rapidly cleared the leaves off by hand, not trusting her wimpy wiper blades. At least Eden had returned her car keys.

With her window cracked, so fresh, cool air would blow in her face, Mallory drove back to Clint and Eden's and parked in the driveway.

A whispery noise came from behind her seat, and a hand covered her mouth, pinning her to the headrest. Something cold poked the side of her neck.

"Don't make a sound." A male voice. "And don't move, or I'll cut your head off."

Shock slammed her. She contracted her muscles, ready to fight before things got worse, but the tip of the knife pressed harder against her neck. She stayed motionless, smelling beer on his breath.

"If you do everything I say, I won't hurt you," he said. "Don't make a sound." He removed his hand from her mouth.

This had to be Lori's boyfriend. If he'd come to kill her, what was he waiting for? For Lori to show up?

"Hold up your hand," he said. "Just hold it next to your shoulder. Got something for you."

Mallory lifted her hand and felt something light settle in her palm. She looked at what he'd given her. A capped hypodermic syringe and a strip of rubber.

"You're going to have a fun time," he said. "Roll up your sleeve."

Mallory stared at the syringe. If he wanted to drug her, why hadn't he stabbed her with the needle before she—

Because he wanted the needle mark to be one she could have made herself. Not a puncture in the back of the shoulder.

He and Lori were plotting something, and Mallory doubted the boyfriend would chuck the plans and cut Mallory's throat at her first whisper. She risked a comment. "The police know about Lori," she said. "And they know about you. They know you left Gilroy together."

He swore.

"If you leave now, they won't catch you," Mallory said.

"Roll up your sleeve."

"I don't know how to give myself an injection."

"It's not hard, college girl. I'll help you. If you miss the vein, that's okay—not as good of a rush, but it'll still get the stuff into your system. They'll see you're new at IVing. Looking for a bigger high."

"This won't convince—"

The knife poked harder. Mallory set the syringe and tourniquet on her knee and pushed ineffectually at the cuff of her left sleeve as though the baggy sweatshirt were too tight for her to get the cuff past her elbow. Looking through the windshield, she searched for Lori. The lights shone in the house. Eden was home.

He swore at her. "Quit stalling. It's eye-for-an-eye time."

An eye for an eye?

Mallory had taken Lori's brother—and he was dead. Chills whirled through Mallory, comprehension spinning into horror. *Eden.*

"Do it. Last chance, or I'll kill you."

Mallory slowly lifted the tourniquet. What was in this syringe? Not something deadly. Something to make her too high or too woozy to leave the scene of the crime, so Clint—and the police—would find her next to Eden's body with drugs in her bloodstream. She would be blamed for Eden's death. *That* was what the planted drugs had been about—making Clint suspicious of Mallory. Lori's revenge was Eden's death and Mallory's incarceration.

Lori had to be in there with Eden now.

Mallory clenched her first around the tourniquet and punched backward as hard as she could, praying she'd hit him in the face. Her knuckles slammed into something hard. Pain burst in her hand and neck, and the knife jerked backward. Mallory grabbed the door handle and flung the door open, but he caught the hood of her sweatshirt and yanked her back.

Screaming, Mallory swung her arm behind her, knocking the knife away. Pain blazed across the back of her hand. Twisting in her seat, she used her left hand to snatch the metal water bottle from the cup holder. The knife slashed her right sleeve. Mallory turned and slammed the bottle into his face as hard as she could. He reeled. She pounded twice more, and he collapsed against the seat, losing his grip on her sweatshirt.

Mallory lunged out of the car and sprinted toward the house. "Eden!" she screamed. She ripped the front door open; it wasn't locked. "Eden!"

"Mallory!" Eden's cry came from the back of the house. "Call the police!"

Mallory grabbed the nearest weapon she could find—Eden's big golf umbrella, which was leaning against the wall near the front door. "Leave her *alone*!" she screamed, racing down the hall.

"Mallory, *no*! Get away, she—" A thud made the floor vibrate. Eden screamed. Another thud. From Eden's bedroom.

Mallory hurtled through the door. The room was a mess, with Eden's jewelry all over the floor and her purse dumped. The nightstand lay on the floor, and Lori Sanders was holding Eden's heavy Waterford crystal lamp. Eden was on the floor, struggling to stand. Lori swooshed the lamp high and brought it down. Eden rolled to the side, and the lamp crashed into her arm. She screamed.

Mallory lunged forward with the umbrella ready to strike.

"She has a gun!" Eden yelled, just as Mallory saw the lamp drop and a gun come out of Lori's jacket pocket. Lori fired, but she hadn't aimed well; the bullet hit the wall. Mallory slammed the umbrella into Lori's hand, knocking the gun loose.

Staggering, Lori seized the end of the umbrella and

yanked, tearing it out of Mallory's grasp. Mallory dove for the gun. Lori hammered the umbrella across Mallory's shoulders, pounding her to the floor.

Mallory glimpsed Eden hurtling toward Lori. The umbrella crashed into Eden's arm. From the pain in Eden's scream as she stumbled sideways, Mallory knew Lori had struck the arm already wounded by the lamp. Mallory launched herself onto Lori, flattening her to the carpet.

"Eden, grab the gun!" Mallory shrieked, tearing the umbrella out of Lori's hand. "Her boyfriend has a knife, he'll be in here any second. I'm not sure if I knocked him out—"

"I have it." Eden stood and aimed the gun at the door. Mallory grabbed one of Lori's wrists and wrenched her arm up behind her back. Eden had a phone and was trying to tap the screen with a hand that clearly wasn't working right.

"We need help!" Eden yelled at the phone without lifting it to her mouth. "5834 McKinney Street."

A door banged, and an agitated male voice shouted, "Mallory! Eden!"

Darien?

"Back here!" Eden yelled.

"Watch out," Mallory hollered as footsteps thundered down the hall. "There's a guy with a knife—"

"Under control!" Darien raced through the door of the bedroom, the knife in *his* hand. Seeing Mallory on top of Lori, he jumped forward. "You're bleeding—"

"Grab something to tie her up, quick."

He grabbed one of Eden's belts from the mess on the floor. "I'll hold her hands; you tie them," he said. "The police are on their way."

"I called them too," Eden said, still aiming the gun at the door. Darien gripped Lori's wrists and pressed them together. Mallory wound the belt around them while Lori cursed her.

"Mallory—your neck—your arm—you have blood all over you—" Eden's voice trembled. "Your hand—"

"I'm fine. Everything works. I'm not bleeding to death." Mallory yanked the belt tight. Lori screeched profanity at someone named Jasper—must be her boyfriend. Heavy footsteps thumped from the front of the house, accompanied by a shout.

"Police!"

Mallory crawled off of Lori and collapsed into Darien's arms.

10

Wrapped in a fleece blanket, Mallory leaned against Darien and sleepily watched the flames in Eden's fireplace. Most of her ached, but as long as she held still, the pain didn't pierce through her fatigue. She kept falling asleep and waking up, driven repeatedly back to consciousness by her determination to wait for Clint and Eden to return from the hospital.

Darien kept both arms around her, his fingers interlocked. "You should go to bed," he said softly.

"I want to make sure she's all right."

"She's fine. Her arm won't even need surgery. Clint would call if anything changed."

"I know," Mallory murmured. "But I need to see her."

"I understand. Mallory . . . I'm sorry I was too slow to stop—"

"Quit it." He'd been blaming himself all evening. "You were the one perceptive enough to realize it wasn't likely that Lori would go to that much trouble then be satisfied with getting me convicted for possession."

"If I'd been perceptive a little earlier, instead of waiting until your class ended to come over here—"

"Shh. You tackled that thug with the knife. If he'd gotten inside before we had the gun, Eden and I would have been in serious trouble."

"I didn't do much. He was so dizzy from your clonking him, he could hardly walk. How did Lori know how to time this—when you'd be leaving campus, and that Clint wouldn't be home yet?"

"The calendar on the fridge, I think. Eden writes everything there. Lori must have seen it when she broke in earlier to leave the drugs." Mallory waited until a feeble resurgence of adrenaline faded before adding, "Darien . . . I'm . . . usually a pretty normal person. After the past couple of days, you must think I'm a disaster . . ."

He chuckled. "Am I giving you that impression right now?"

"No, but . . . you're a nice guy, good at comforting a friend."

His arms loosened, and he turned to look at her. The firelight showed apprehension in his face, but his voice was even. "Is friendship all you want from me? Whatever the facts are, I can deal with them, but I need to know the truth."

"Darien . . . I wore makeup at *four in the morning* for you."

"You did?"

"You didn't notice it, did you? Or the cute clothes? I give up. I'm sleeping in from now on."

He laughed. "You always look gorgeous. Even wearing—" He checked the clothing sticking out from the blanket. "Sweat pants, and . . . bandages and . . . I don't know what shirt you're wearing."

"An old Disneyland T-shirt that used to belong to my cousin." Mallory looked into Darien's eyes. He leaned toward her, and their lips touched. His kiss was tender, and Mallory reached to put her arms around him, but the movement sent stinging through the stitches in her hand and arm and made her bruises ache.

At the unsteadiness in her movements, Darien pulled back. "I'm sorry," he said. "You're hurting, and you're a little out of it from stress and sleep deprivation. Anything more than a handshake tonight is less than gentlemanly."

"I have six stitches in my hand, and my knuckles are bruised," she said. "I don't want a handshake."

He smiled and kissed her cheek. "Rest." He pulled the blanket back around her and drew her into his arms.

She leaned against his shoulder and closed her eyes.

ABOUT STEPHANIE BLACK

Stephanie Black is the author of five contemporary suspense novels, including *Shadowed*, and two dystopian thrillers, including *The Witnesses* (coming in October 2013). She has won four Whitney Awards for Best Mystery/Suspense, most recently for *Rearview Mirror* (2011).

She has five children, one cat, and a taste for her husband Brian's homemade pizza.

Visit her website at www.stephanieblack.net, or her blog, Black Ink, at www.stephanieblackink.blogspot.com.

FIRST HEIST
An Omar Zagouri Novella

Heather B. Moore

Other Works by Heather B. Moore

Esther the Queen

Finding Sheba

Beneath

The Aliso Creek Series

Heart of the Ocean

The Newport Ladies Book Club Series

The Fortune Café

1

Mia watched her contact from across the club, music pulsing through her body as her ears screamed for silence. But she had to be patient. She'd already been watching him for about an hour, and she wasn't sure she wanted to approach him yet.

She didn't care what her boss, Abram, had said. Even if Omar Zagouri was supposed to do the transfer, if she didn't think he was capable, she'd do the recovery mission herself.

Omar leaned toward a woman he'd been flirting with for the past twenty minutes. The long-legged blonde looked like she was falling for whatever lines he was feeding her. A second shot of vodka probably helped as well. Yes, Mia counted. Just like she noticed everything else going on in the room.

She'd counted thirty-eight people, twenty-three men and fifteen women. Most looked Israeli, with a couple of Europeans. Ironically, the club was free cover charge for ladies, which probably explained the number of men—outnumbered in hopes of taking home a date tonight.

Mia wasn't interested anymore in hookups, which may be thrilling for a few hours, but once the sun came up and the alarm went off, the man in bed next to her always became a nuisance.

The club had two exits—one by the restrooms and one in the miniscule kitchen behind the bar. There were twelve tables surrounding a dance floor and one long bar of gleaming wood. All fairly standard for a night club in downtown Jerusalem.

Mia's gaze floated back to Omar and the woman. What did the blonde see in him? She was probably a tourist from Sweden . . . If the lighting hadn't been so bad, Mia would be able to tell if the blonde had a dye job. Mia looked back to Omar and dissected his appearance. He wasn't that tall, maybe 5'9". As he took another swallow of beer, the muscles in his arms flexed. All right, so he was in great shape, but that likely came with his job requirements.

As an undercover agent, Omar would be trained in self-defense, counter-assault, and firearms. All well and good, but Mia wasn't about to trust the transfer to someone who was only capable physically. She needed someone who wouldn't back down from a challenge, no matter what. Her boss, Abram, had said this contact was high risk. Abram never said that lightly.

Omar was okay looking, in a swarthy sort of way. Dark, curly hair . . . no surprise there, as his father was Moroccan. Omar had olive skin and the faint beginnings of a goatee. The picture Mia had been sent of him showed a full mustache—which he wore when working undercover in Arab towns.

The blonde threw her head back in laughter. Omar smiled, but his gaze flicked away. *Interesting*, Mia thought.

He wasn't truly engrossed in the woman. Was he after a cheap one-night stand, or was he bored? Or maybe courteous? The blonde had approached him first, so perhaps listening to her was a polite thing.

Then Mia noticed Omar was looking right at her. Their eyes locked for a brief second, and she looked away, lifting her hand as if she were waving at someone across the room. She willed the heat to stay away from her cheeks. Omar knew she was watching him.

How had he known? She'd been careful. Omar must be more skilled than she'd first thought.

During the next few minutes, Mia plotted her escape. She could dance with someone, pretend to take a call and walk out of the club, or wait until he left first. Whatever she decided, she wouldn't initiate the transfer. Not tonight, not when he was half drunk. She couldn't afford to mess up her first assignment since her return to Jerusalem.

Mia blended in with the other clubbers with her fitted black dress and heels; she didn't want anyone paying attention to her. At least, not real attention. She wanted to be seen then quickly forgotten. Problem was, Omar had noticed her.

Mia pulled out her phone and texted her boss.

He's here but knows I'm watching him. He's already drunk. Aborting plan.

A reply came back from Abram. *Do the transfer.*

Not transferring the key to a drunk.

Omar's not drunk, Abram answered.

Mia exhaled. *How do you know? Are you sitting in this damn club, wearing a mini skirt too?*

Are you putting in your 2 weeks' notice?

Mia cursed under her breath, and before she could

translate that curse into a text, a hand touched her shoulder. She nearly jumped out of her chair, which made her want to curse again. She looked up into the dark eyes of Omar Zagouri.

2

Omar held out his hand. "Dance?"

Mia stared at his outstretched hand then she looked over at the bar. The blonde was gone. Mia rose to her feet, edgy and irritated all at once. She was petite, and most men towered over her, but in these heels she was almost eye level with Omar.

"All right." She could play his game. Her phone buzzed, but she ignored it. She'd be the one to decide if Omar got the transfer, and if he couldn't handle it, she'd transfer to another agent.

Mia slipped her hand in his and was surprised by the strength she felt there; his size was deceiving. He led her to the center of the dance floor and placed his hands loosely at her waist. She rested her hands on his shoulders—they were solid and muscled, confirming her first impression that he lifted weights or something, but that didn't mean he was the right contact.

Music throbbed about them, yet Omar kept a slow pace, as if dancing to an entirely different beat.

"Where's your friend?" Mia asked.

"Not sure," Omar said, drawing away a little, looking into her eyes. "You interested?"

"No." Mia kept her face blank; she wasn't going to let him goad her.

"Neither was I," he said, a slight smile on his face. "I've seen you around."

Mia's heart froze. "No you haven't." She hadn't been in Jerusalem in over four years, not since her mom had died in a car bombing. Mia had since worked mostly in Turkey, and only because of the delicate nature of this job did she agree to come back for a trial run.

His eyes stayed on hers, making her feel self-conscious, which was not easy to do.

"Maybe I should rephrase . . . I know who you are, and I know who you work for," Omar said. "And I've seen you in video surveillance from the Israeli Preservation Department, which I illegally confiscated."

Mia blinked. She'd never been speechless in her life. Apparently, there was a first time for everything.

He leaned closer, his mouth next to her ear. "What do you want, Mia Golding?"

Before she could answer, Omar released her with a push, hard enough to send her stumbling backwards. She caught her balance, furious at him, but before she could ask what his problem was, Omar had crouched to the ground.

A man swung at him, missing. Omar jumped up and drove his fist into the guy's face. The man went down, out cold.

A few clubbers screamed, and people backed out of the way. Omar didn't look flustered at all but simply knelt by the man, turned him over, and handcuffed him. The music was as loud as ever, drowning out excited conversation all around.

Since when did anyone carry handcuffs around? Apparently Omar did. Mia stared in disbelief as Omar rose and crossed to her. She said nothing as he grabbed her hand and pulled her toward the exit near the restrooms, leaving the cuffed man to writhe on the floor as he woke.

They stepped into a back alley, and the brisk fall air shuddered through Mia. Omar kept hold of her hand and walked quickly down the narrow street. He pulled something out of his pocket and turned it on.

"You have a flashlight?" Mia said.

"My phone," Omar said. "Shh."

Mia fell silent, letting this man lead her to the street, where they crossed together, moving away from the club and its music. Above, in one of the apartments, a woman sang off key in Hebrew.

Sirens sounded from a distance, and Omar slowed as they reached a parked black Mercedes. He pressed something on his phone, and the doors unlocked. Apparently they wouldn't be sticking around to find out if the sirens were heading to the club.

"Get in," he said, and Mia climbed into the passenger side of the two-seat sports car. It seemed Omar did well with bonuses.

He fiddled with something under the steering wheel.

"You're hotwiring it?" Mia asked, incredulous.

The engine started. "Yeah."

"I thought it was yours." Which of course was ridiculous now that she thought about it. This car must cost more than 100K. "How did you unlock the doors?"

"With a really cool app."

Mia stared at him as he pulled on to the street and sped down the road in the opposite direction of the sirens. "You're stealing this car?"

"I'm not going to hurt it." He flashed a smile. "The owner will have it back as soon as I figure out who's following you and why you were watching me tonight. Want me to guess?"

Mia folded her arms, shaking her head. The stories she'd heard about Omar's eccentricities came back to her now—apparently they were all true. "You had to steal a car to ask me a few questions?"

"No," Omar said, his tone amused. "I stole a car because I didn't bring one, and a car is the fastest way to leave a location unless you have access to a helicopter." He paused, his gaze sliding to hers with definite interest. "Do you have access to one?"

Mia didn't know whether to laugh or to punch him. "Why would you think that?"

"Because it seems that Abram thinks more of you than he does me. He sent you to check up on me, didn't he?" he asked. "So it's a natural conclusion that Abram would provide you with a helicopter, even though I've asked him for one for more than three years."

Mia wanted to laugh, but would it bring out the crazy even more? "I don't have a helicopter."

"Good," Omar said. "Or I'd really be mad." He looked at her, but she kept her gaze forward. He seemed to be studying her, and Mia was curious to know what he was thinking.

"I'm getting fired, aren't I?" he said.

Mia looked at him then, but his eyes were back on the road. "How would I know?"

"Because you're here, and I listened to your interview."

The more he talked, the more curious Mia became, but the best thing for her to do was get out of the car and report to her station. "I don't know anything about your job. Why don't you ask Abram?"

Omar scoffed. "Now there's the rub. Abram doesn't tell me anything, yet I see the signs. First he brings you into my city. Then he sends you to spy on me."

"I wasn't spying." This had gone on long enough. Mia was riding in a stolen car in the middle of the night with a man who was considered unstable . . . Now that she thought about it, he probably *was* on the chopping block. One thing was clear—he was smarter than she'd thought, and she'd give him the transfer, if only to get out of this car. "Okay, I was watching you, but it's because I have to give you the key."

Omar veered to the left and came to a stop in front of an empty shopping complex. Aside from a few security lights, it was completely dark. "I'm not taking it."

"Why not?"

"Because I'm the one who uncovered the trail to the stolen Olympian artifacts. The Greeks are already mad at me, so I put in hundreds of hours to make this recovery go right. The key is traceable . . . in fact, our contact is expecting it." He latched on his seatbelt. "By the way, we're being followed. You might want to put on your seatbelt."

Mia looked in the side-view mirror. A car crept around the corner, no lights on. She latched her seatbelt a half second before Omar peeled out and tore down the street. Mia gripped the armrests as she was thrown into her seat.

Omar didn't seem to notice her discomfort. "I'm so glad this Mercedes is an SLS. If it were an AMG, it wouldn't have nearly as much power."

"You *are* crazy," Mia said, staring at the side-view mirror. "Who's following us?"

"I thought you knew."

"No," Mia said, bracing herself as Omar whipped around a corner then drove straight through a red light.

"Do you have the key with you?" he asked, his voice calm.

Mia's breath was short as panic crept in. "How else would I make the transfer?"

Omar braked suddenly, throwing Mia forward. He backed into an alley then turned off the engine. "You should have established a pick-up location. They know it's on your person."

"Who?" She wanted to look around the corner to see if they were still being followed.

"Jamil's men, of course. The ones behind the stolen artifacts."

Mia was about to answer, but a car drove past, going about 80 kilometers an hour. It didn't even slow down. Mia exhaled with relief. They'd lost the car.

"Go ahead . . . verify with Abram," Omar said.

She pulled her phone out and texted her boss. Seconds later he replied. *Yes on Jamil. But he knows nothing. We have 48 hours.*

"What does Abram say?" Omar asked.

She looked over at him. "That Jamil knows nothing about this. Abram is giving you forty-eight hours to recover the Greek artifacts after you get the key."

Omar's hand clamped down on her arm. "Listen to me. It's a set-up. Abram knows it's too dangerous, and I told him so. Whichever agent goes in will be dead in minutes. The whole place is wired, and they're waiting for us to show up with the key." His grip relaxed.

Mia exhaled. "Abram said you'd try to push back, that

you refuse to do anything by protocol. This is too important to blow off Abram's instructions. The prime minister of Greece *resigned* because of this theft. If we restore the artifacts, it will buoy Greece's sagging economy."

But Omar shook his head, his eyes black and intense inside the dark car. "I owe Greece; I know that. But this isn't a typical recovery mission. Jamil's man followed you inside the club. He was there the entire time, watching you watching me."

"What, so Abram is setting me up now?"

"Abram is an idiot. He put you in the middle of something I've already handled," Omar said. "He has no faith in me, for whatever reason, since I've never failed at a job."

Mia had heard otherwise, but maybe Omar gauged failures differently than most people.

Omar inched the car forward and pulled onto the street when there was no sign of any other cars in either direction. "This is Abram's style," he continued. "Tells me to do a job, and when he thinks it's taking too long, he sends backup. Comes up with a plan like transferring a key that leaves a trail straight back to you and to me. Welcome to my life, Mia."

She stared at him, not knowing what to believe. Her boss had told her the job had gone south, and that if the recovery wasn't made within a couple of days, the entire mission would be compromised. But if she had been followed to the club, it already had been. She had no choice; she'd have to return to headquarters and report a failed mission.

"Ready?" Omar asked.

"For what?" She glanced over.

A smile played on his lips. "I just thought of a way to make the recovery tonight, without the key. You're coming with me."

3

"You're out of your mind," Mia said as they pulled onto the main boulevard. "If what you say is true, and Jamil knows about us, then we have to abort."

"Not necessarily," Omar said. "It just makes things more interesting. Like I said, I complete all my assignments, no matter what."

This guy was crazy for sure, but she was curious. "Tell me what happened in Athens."

Omar was quiet for a moment as he took the exit to Highway 1. "I was sent in to recover the Picasso and Mondrian paintings, which I did. Hadn't planned on getting lit on fire and burning up the Mondrian in the process." He lifted the right side of his shirt up to show a patch of mottled skin. "Still hurts."

Mia winced at the sight of the red and bumpy skin, but she wasn't there to commiserate with him. The paintings had been the beginning of Greece's struggle with the security of their museums. Soon after the paintings had been stolen, dozens of priceless items, including bronze, clay, and gold artifacts used by ancient athletes during the Games, were also stolen.

Those thefts pushed the country over the edge, bringing about the resignation of the culture minister. Omar had recovered the paintings, so to speak, but the Games artifacts were still at large. "Abram said you got too close to the source."

Omar barked a laugh. "He's just jealous. Big deal if I kissed the female security guard and it was caught on surveillance. She gave me pointers with a bonus thrown in. Since then, I've been more active in the surveillance department." He smiled, throwing her a wink. "Which is how I found out about you, so it's all good. Nothing has been wasted."

"Burning up a priceless painting isn't a waste?" Mia folded her arms.

"The value the free market dictates to citizens is ambiguous." Omar switched lanes, passing an Israeli bus, which traveled mostly empty. "Although the commission would have been nice, it's not like I was planning on buying a boat or anything."

Mia caught herself laughing then wondered if she should relax around an obviously unbalanced man.

Omar's gaze met hers. "So now that you know everything about me, tell me about you."

"Oh no," Mia said. "I want to know your plan . . . and why I should stay in this car with you."

He grinned. "You'll just have to trust me." Their eyes locked for a couple of seconds then Omar returned his attention to the road.

"I don't trust anyone," Mia said.

"Too bad." His gaze flicked to hers. "I'll admit that I do know some things about you, and I heard about what happened to your mother. I'm very sorry."

Mia exhaled. It had been four years since her mom's death, and the pain hadn't faded. Each morning it seemed to start fresh as the memories returned. She closed her eyes for a second and was surprised when Omar reached over and squeezed her hand. The touch showed a lot more than anything he could have said. Maybe he wasn't so crazy.

"There were never any official charges," Mia said in a hesitant voice. "But I believe it was connected to the assignment I was on at the time."

Omar remained silent, waiting for her to continue.

"Yeah, I know there were a lot of coincidences," she said, trying to steady the shakiness that had crept into her voice. "I mean, the bomb went off at the corner of my street at the exact moment my mother was walking by."

Mia shook her head, looking out the window as the nightscape sped by. "She was visiting for a few days, and she offered to go to the grocer's. We were out of cooking oil." She blew out a breath, remembering the sound of the explosion and the way her heart had stopped. She'd been in denial at first, but then her pulse raced like mad as she ran down the stairs and onto the street. It was like she knew . . . she knew her mother was gone. Everything inside her had turned dark, heavy, cold.

"Mia?" Omar's hand was on hers again, bringing her back to the present. "I read the report—everything that was connected with the case you were working on—and I agree. I think it was connected."

She sucked in her breath. No one had ever agreed with her, and now that someone did, the pain sharpened like a knife.

"I'm sorry. That's probably not what you want to hear," he said, his voice soft and totally lucid. This was a different Omar than a few minutes before.

"I'm glad someone agrees with me." She paused. "But it scares me too. I'm used to people discrediting my theories."

Omar turned on the blinker. "After we get through with this job, I can go over my theories with you."

Mia glanced at him, her heart thudding. He couldn't know how much that meant to her—to have someone believe her—to have someone want to help. "All right."

Omar took an exit Mia wasn't familiar with. She straightened in her seat. "Where are we headed?"

He checked the rearview mirror before replying. "A place that used to be a military compound."

Moments later, he pulled into a neighborhood, drove through several streets, then slowed near a rundown collection of stores. He pulled around behind them and parked next to a group of trees. "We walk from here," he said, popping his door open.

"Wait," Mia said, licking lips that suddenly felt dry. "If it's not safe to use the key, what's your plan?"

"It's better that you don't know, in case you get caught."

"What about you getting caught?"

"Then it would still be better if you don't know anything." Omar held her gaze. "Can you trust me?"

It was the second time he'd asked that, but this time, something inside her softened. "All right. For now I'll trust you."

They met at the front of the car, and Omar led her through the trees, out into the back parking lot of the buildings.

"Where's the compound?" Mia whispered.

"We won't get there until morning, but that van over there is our way in."

Mia looked where he'd pointed, at a beat-up van parked behind one of the shops.

"Every morning it delivers pastries to the compound. Tomorrow it will deliver a lot more than that."

Mia slowed her step. "We're going to be the delivery guys?"

"Too transparent. We wouldn't get past the gate." He opened the rear door of the van.

Mia peered inside the mostly dark vehicle. A shelving rack was welded to one side. Otherwise, just a few cardboard boxes lay scattered around.

Omar climbed in and held out his hand.

"What are we doing?" she asked.

"Hiding back here until the delivery route starts."

Mia looked from Omar to the night sky. "That's hours away."

He gave a shrug. "It's the best chance we have."

Still, she hesitated. "So we're going to wait in this van for hours until someone shows up. Then what?"

Omar kept his hand out, his gaze on hers.

Finally, Mia took it and allowed him to pull her into the van. The inside was dank and smelled like stale bread. All of the bench seats had been pulled out, leaving only the driver's and passenger seats up front.

Omar turned on the flashlight from his phone and pulled the back hatch closed.

Looking around, Mia thought it was even more dismal than she'd first thought. She moved a box to the side and sat in the corner of the van near the driver's side. It wasn't too comfortable in her fitted dress.

Omar rummaged around for a few moments. He found a couple of flour sacks and slid them over so they could lean against them.

"How are we supposed to stay hidden when the delivery man comes?" Mia asked.

"If he notices, I'll have to convince him with my gun to stay quiet."

Mia exhaled. This plan wasn't solid. It was liable to change at every moment. She drew her knees up to her chest and tugged her skirt, wishing she'd brought a jacket, or even a thick, warm blanket. It wasn't freezing, but the autumn night wasn't warm, either.

"You can use my shoulder if you want, or even my lap, if you need a pillow," Omar said, sitting about a meter away.

"Funny," Mia said, pulling her legs in tighter. "I don't plan on falling asleep."

Omar just smiled, leaned his head back, and closed his eyes.

4

Mia opened her eyes, realizing two things at once. First, she was leaning against Omar's shoulder with his arm around her, and second, she'd heard a door bang shut.

Omar straightened, awake too.

"Is that the delivery man?" Mia said, lifting her head. Her heart pounded, and not just because of the imminent discovery.

"Lie down," Omar said, pulling out a gun. "I can block his view of you."

Mia complied, even though she wasn't happy about it. Omar maneuvered in front of her so he was between Mia and the door.

But the back door never opened. When the driver's door opened, Mia's skin broke out in goose bumps. Omar shifted slightly so his gun was aimed at the driver's seat.

The man climbed in, whistling, and the smell of fresh pastries reached Mia. After some settling, and the sound of what seemed to be a box of pastries set on the passenger seat, the engine started.

Mia turned her head and caught Omar's gaze. He gave her a small nod then trained his eyes on the driver. If she hadn't been in such a precarious situation, she'd have given almost anything for one of those pastries. Omar had to be hungry too.

The van jolted onto a dirt road, and Mia wished she could change her position. With each bump, the van's floor dug into her right hip. The sky was definitely lighter outside, and Mia caught glimpses of a violet sky beginning to melt into blue.

When the van started to slow, Omar lay down next to her, moving very carefully. "Checkpoint," he whispered in her ear.

This close to him, she could see the pupils of his dark eyes and smell his spicy scent. And his body was touching hers. That didn't make her nervous. If anything, it made her feel warm . . . a thought she pushed away immediately.

Omar's eyes stayed trained on her as if he didn't dare move.

The van came to a stop, and the driver rolled down the window. He spoke to someone in Arabic.

Omar's gaze didn't falter, but Mia was surprised as she listened to the conversation. They were exchanging pleasantries, and by the expression on Omar's face, she knew he understood the language too.

The van lurched forward again, and Mia braced herself against Omar. His hand moved to her waist to steady her. The van turned once, then again, heading deeper into the compound. Mia's heart pounded, and she hoped Omar knew what he was doing.

FIRST HEIST

Every time she caught his gaze, it was steady, unwavering. How could he not be worried? If there was one thing about this man she'd learned in the past seven or eight hours, it was that he was pretty much fearless.

Like I've tried but failed to be.

There was a time she feared little. Well-trained and well-disciplined, she'd been in control—until her mother was blown up on the neighborhood street corner. Mia had moved, of course, unable to stand seeing the site of destruction each day. But the new place hadn't worked out much better. Within a few weeks, she'd left Jerusalem altogether and had taken a reassignment in Ankara.

Her eyes started to sting as she thought about all she'd left behind and about how she'd even lost touch with her stepfather. The memories were simply too painful. Now, as she met Omar's gaze, a bit of hope seeped into the hole of her grief. Here was a man who believed her theory, and he'd promised to help her.

Granted, they'd have to get out of this situation alive. Yes, Omar had a gun, but was that enough to allow them to complete the job and get out safely?

Omar's body heat warmed her through, and she was grateful the chill had lessened.

The van slowed, and Omar's grip on her waist tightened.

"We'll have a couple of minutes to get out of the van, but first we need to empty the flour sacks," Omar whispered. "Be ready."

Mia nodded, taking a deep breath. Omar moved slightly away from her, and the warmth dissipated, replaced by her racing pulse.

The driver got out and resumed whistling. As soon as

the door shut, Omar moved into a crouch and took a knife out of his pocket. He slit the flour sacks at the tops and dumped them out. Then he rolled them up and stuffed them into his waistband.

He held out his hand. "Come on."

She moved as fast as she could, but every part of her body was cramped and stiff. Once out of the van, Omar closed the rear hatch but not all the way. Then he grabbed her hand and tugged her toward a group of bushes. They crouched behind them until the delivery man came out and drove away, the tires of the van kicking up dust in its wake.

Now what? Mia wanted to ask, but she wasn't about to make any noise.

His fingers intertwined with hers, and she followed his lead as he stood.

They ran, and Mia kept up with him as they moved around the building. In the growing dawn, it reminded her of an embassy—nice stonework, heavily fortressed.

When they stopped in an alcove, Mia caught her breath and asked, "This was a military compound?"

"Former," Omar said. "They've done some renovation. You should see the inside."

Mia was about to question him when he put a finger to her lips. Her heart thudded. They stood together in silence as a low hum began overhead, growing louder by the second. Mia hadn't noticed a landing pad for a helicopter, but there had to be one very close.

Omar pointed upward, and Mia nodded, understanding that the copter pad was on the roof. Did that change Omar's plans? He seemed as determined as ever.

Mia's breath was calm now, and she met Omar's gaze. One of his eyebrows lifted slightly. "One more minute," he said in a hushed voice.

She waited, her mind involuntarily counting the seconds. Omar motioned for her to follow as he stepped out of the alcove. They took about three steps then Omar crouched to the ground. He pried up some sort of heavy plastic covering that stretched over a window well.

Mia didn't need to be told what to do. She slipped into the dark hole, Omar following and pulling the covering into place.

Omar reached for her arm, gained his bearings, and whispered, "The commotion of the helicopter leaving will give us time to grab the artifacts."

"We're just going to carry them out? With our bare hands?"

"Not exactly," Omar said with amusement in his voice.

What did he expect? He was only telling her things play-by-play.

"How then?" Mia asked.

His hand dropped from her arm, and he turned on his phone light. "Hold this," he said, handing her the phone.

She took it, and he pulled some metal object out of his pocket and popped the window open.

"No alarms?" she said in disbelief.

"Oh, alarms are going off all right, but I'm counting on Jamil's people being slow to react." Omar disappeared inside. A second later, his hand came back out. Mia grasped it and joined him inside.

They'd entered a large, cavernous room. Soft lights from the ceiling illuminated glass displays of what seemed to be artifacts. It was like a museum.

"Are these all stolen?" she whispered.

Omar nodded, his eyes scoping out the room. "The Olympic items aren't in here. Come on. There's another display room."

It was then Mia noticed a small red light flashing in the corner by the door. She couldn't hear an alarm, but a flashing red light was never a good thing. They moved around the display cases, and Omar paused at the door to withdraw his pistol. But before he could the door, it flew open.

A man barreled into Omar, and they struggled until Omar got the upper hand and knocked him out. The gun had fallen to the floor, and Mia retrieved it.

"This way," Omar said, panting. They moved into the next room. It was similar to the first. Inside were display cases containing artifacts. Omar zigzagged through them, seeming to know exactly what he was looking for. He stopped in front of a case and knelt beside it. Mia crouched next to him.

Omar used some sort of a pick to trigger the lock at the base. The glass lid lifted, and he withdrew the flour sacks from his belt then handed one to Mia. "Get as many as you can. Hurry."

Mia grabbed artifacts as fast as she could, her stomach clenching as she thought about the ancient relics knocking together in the sack.

"Let's go," Omar said, and Mia twisted the top of her sack.

He led her out into the hall, looking left then right. The hall was empty, but Mia had a feeling it wouldn't stay that way. For now it was eerily quiet—no alarms, no flashing lights, just silence. When they reached the end of the corridor, Omar opened a door. Shining his light, Mia saw a stairwell.

"We're going to a lower level," Omar said. He took the light, then started down, motioning for Mia to follow.

The stairs were narrow, with only room for them to

walk single file, and they spiraled into dark nothingness.

"Wait," Omar said, his soft footsteps halting. Mia caught herself in time and stopped without bumping into him. He switched his light off, and they stood in absolute black. The only sound Mia could hear was their almost imperceptible breathing.

Then the staircase rattled, and the whole building seemed to vibrate. Mia grabbed Omar's arm to steady herself. When the shaking stopped, she said, "What was that?"

"They know we're here," he whispered, coming up one step to be closer to her.

"So what, they created an earthquake?"

"Not exactly. They caved in the tunnel I was planning to take."

Mia wished she could see Omar's face, but the darkness was too complete. "What tunnel?"

"The one that led out of the compound. It would have given us a quick exit," Omar said.

Another vibration rattled the stairwell, and Mia's grip tightened on his arm. "Now what?"

Omar seemed to hesitate; Mia wasn't sure if that was a bad thing. "We go up, unless you have a get-away truck parked outside."

"No, not this time." She turned her body so she faced the ascending stairs. "What's up there?"

"Hopefully a helicopter."

"The one we heard taking off?"

"There should be two," Omar said. "But we need to go as quickly as possible."

Omar moved past her, leading the way again with the light. Mia started up after him. Within minutes, her thighs burned. She was in plenty good shape, but a sleepless night and no food, plus carrying at least fifty pounds in her sack, took its toll.

She was breathing hard but trying to control it. She didn't want Omar to think she couldn't keep up. When they reached the original landing, he didn't say anything as he took her pack, hoisted it with his own over his shoulder then started up the next flight of stairs.

"Omar," Mia protested, but he was already several steps ahead.

She climbed after him then came to a stop when it appeared they'd reached the next landing. They were still in the dark, but some light permeated the area, making everything gray.

"Maybe we should call for backup," Mia said.

"You are my backup," Omar said, and if there had been more light, she knew she'd see him smiling.

In truth, Mia was scared. Omar had already been attacked by one man, and they'd blown up a tunnel.

Omar's hand found hers. "Hey, I told you to trust me. We'll be out of here soon."

5

Mia didn't see how they could get out of this situation if the alarms were going off throughout the building, but she let Omar lead her across the landing. He set down both sacks and crouched. She stayed quiet, waiting for his next instructions. She heard him move, and then a sliver of light popped up, showing through a door Omar had cracked open.

He had one hand on the door handle, the other on his gun. He looked back at her, and when their gazes met, he tilted his head. Mia got his message—bring the bags—and gave a nod.

Omar watched as she got a good grip on each sack and hefted them over her shoulders.

His attention shifted, and a few seconds later, he was through the door, running across the roof of the building. Mia followed, staggering to keep up and ignoring the burning in her thighs and calves. She wouldn't let herself fall behind.

The roof was multi-leveled with what looked like a set of storage units in the middle. Omar stopped behind one unit, keeping his gaze on the sky. Mia stopped next to him and set down the sacks. In the distance, she could see the copter they'd heard on its way to the landing pad—which was about a dozen meters away.

Omar motioned with his finger to follow him into a crouch.

The air seemed to tremble with the copter's approaching blades. Omar grabbed a sack and motioned for Mia to do the same, but instead of holding his position to wait for the approaching helicopter, he moved around to the other side of the building, Mia following.

A second landing pad was there, along with a second helicopter. "Do you know how to fly?" Omar asked her above the sound of the approaching copter.

"No," she said.

His gaze moved from her to the dormant copter. "Hope you said your prayers then. Let's go."

Before Mia could question him—not that it was even possible right now—Omar motioned for her to follow. They ran toward the copter, and Omar yanked the door open, ushering her inside then handing up his sack.

"You know how to fly this thing?" Mia asked as she watched him flip switches, reconsider, then flip them the other way.

"I've had some training," he said.

The other helicopter landed, and the two men inside started pointing at them, obviously recognizing that Mia and Omar weren't authorized.

"They see us," she said, but Omar seemed absorbed in trying to figure out how to run the helicopter. The engine started up, and the blades slowly rotated.

Mia's heart pounded. Although it looked like Omar might have finally figured it out, more than one person was advancing on them, weapons drawn. She grabbed Omar's arm and slid down in her seat, expecting a bullet to come flying through the windshield any second.

"Omar, put your hands up," she said. "They're right outside."

He lifted a hand, and at first Mia thought he would comply. Instead he flipped one of the overhead switches. "Hang on," he said, and the helicopter jerked upward.

Mia screamed and ducked as bullets hit the windshield. The helicopter careened to the right, and bullets peppered the windshield, but they didn't penetrate. Mia's stomach churned as the helicopter rose several meters then dropped suddenly.

Omar had flown past the building, so they didn't hit anything when they dropped. He cursed and flipped some more switches. Mia gripped whatever she could hold on to, hoping she wouldn't throw up. She felt like she was on a rollercoaster that had derailed.

"Are you crazy? I thought you said you could fly," Mia said.

"That's not exactly what I said," Omar answered through gritted teeth as he maneuvered the copter above a group of trees. They were flying at a tilt. Mia didn't see how this could end well.

Omar's face was perspiring . . . not a comforting sight. She twisted and looked behind her. To her horror, the first helicopter had left the landing pad.

"They're coming after us!" Mia shouted. "Do you see them back there?"

"We're almost to the tanks."

"Tanks?" Mia exhaled. "You called for backup?"

Omar flashed a half smile. "Of course. I'm not that much of an idiot." He nodded his head. "See up there? Past the ridge."

Mia strained to see any semblance of a tank. As the helicopter rose, dark forms came into view. Three SUVs, with police lights flashing, came tearing over a ridge a couple of kilometers away. "Those aren't tanks."

Omar cursed. "They never follow my orders . . . I told them to send tanks."

Mia snapped her head around to see how close the other helicopter was. "They're almost on top of us!" she shouted. "We're not going to make it."

Omar kept his focus straight ahead, neither speeding up nor trying to maneuver away. It was like he refused to see anything but the flashing lights ahead.

"Hurry!" Mia ducked as the other helicopter bore down on them, as if she could avoid a collision by being lower.

Suddenly their copter stalled, and Omar frantically adjusted switches.

"What's going on?" Mia stared at blinking red lights on the panel. The helicopter started to spin, slowly then faster. She grabbed Omar's arm, too petrified to scream as they dropped.

"Relax your body," Omar commanded. "The impact will break fewer bones if you're relaxed."

Mia wanted to scream, but instead she tried to let her every part of her body soften. Seconds later, they hit the ground hard. The helicopter tilted and slid to a stop on its side. Mia thudded against her seat, nearly passing out, but she took careful, even breaths until the haze and confusion started to lift.

"Are you all right?" Omar asked, undoing her seatbelt. She nodded, not sure she could speak yet. He scanned her. "Can you move everything okay? Nothing broken?"

Mia lifted her arms and then her legs. She'd probably have a few bruises, but she had no shooting pain anywhere. The helicopter had tipped to the right, and her door was on the ground . . . no way she could get out through it. She looked up to find Omar still watching her.

"We're alive, right?" she said, her thoughts spinning with all that had happened.

"Yeah," he said, his eyes amused. But then he sobered. "Uh . . . sorry about the landing. It's been awhile since I've flown, and at my last training . . . well, things didn't go well."

She realized she was staring into those deep brown eyes, noticing how they were nearly black. "You're the worst pilot ever," she said, finding it hard to breathe normally with him so close. "I don't know whether to slap you or . . ." She flushed, realizing she was going to say "kiss you." It wasn't what she meant, but it had almost slipped out.

Omar's brows rose. "Or . . . thank me?" he practically whispered.

She wanted him to move back to give her some space, but then again, she didn't want him to move at all. What was wrong with her? Maybe she'd hit her head and hadn't realized it. "Yes, I need to thank you . . . for not killing me."

He nodded slightly but looked a bit confused at the turn in the conversation. He looked adorable—this confident, daring man at a loss. Without letting herself think about it too much, she wrapped a hand around his neck and pulled his face toward hers. She pressed her mouth against his, and for a second he didn't move. Then one of his hands brushed her cheek and slid behind her head, pulling her close.

And he kissed her back. Plainly, he was no longer confused. Fire spread through Mia as his kiss deepened. She supposed she'd thought about this when she'd first spied on him at the bar, but it wasn't until this moment that she wondered if he'd considered it as well.

His other hand cradled her face as his kiss slowed, and Mia was able to catch her breath. Then reality slammed through her.

She pulled away. "Sorry. I didn't mean—it wasn't . . ." She decided to stop talking.

Omar's eyes searched hers as if he was about to ask her something, but instead he said, "We have to get out of here in case a fire starts." He straightened above her and shoved the pilot's door open.

"Where's—" she started, then took another much needed breath. "The other helicopter?"

Everything was silent, or maybe it was Mia's hearing.

"Turned around," Omar said.

She stared at his hand, which was extended to help her out of the wreckage. "How?"

Omar grasped her hand, tugging her upward. "Climb out, and I'll show you."

Mia climbed out of the helicopter, feeling aches where she didn't know she had muscles. Once she was out, Omar joined her, standing close, but not touching. The butterflies in her stomach about *the incident* changed into something else as she watched the approaching SUVs, about a hundred meters away now, coming fast and hard. A fourth truck with a missile launcher in the bed had a gunman at the helm.

"Is that legal?" Mia asked, staring at the launcher.

Omar wore a grin. "I don't think so, but it makes a pretty good tank. And a nice deterrent."

Mia turned to see the retreating helicopter. Her heart still pounded from kissing Omar, or maybe it was from nearly dying; she was sure it would be awhile before she comprehended everything that had happened. It had all gone so fast, and she didn't know exactly how much had been planned by Omar, but the fact was . . .

"We'd better get the artifacts," she said.

Omar nodded. "Done. You were a bit dazed when we landed."

She stole a glance at him, and he winked at her. That woke the butterflies again. She looked away, hoping she wasn't blushing. The two sacks were on the other side of the helicopter. "You rescued the artifacts before me?"

"I knew you'd be fine," Omar said in a soft voice.

Mia shook her head, holding back her own smile. He was crazy, but his methods had somehow worked. They'd recovered the artifacts, and they were both still alive.

"Yeah, nothing's broken," Mia said, taking a step back. Somehow they'd ended up standing too close.

The first SUV arrived, and the next several moments were a flurry of questions and activity. Omar took a call from Abram, and Mia was whisked into one of the SUVs with a medic asking her a million questions.

She tried to see what Omar was doing, but after he got off the phone, he climbed into the truck with the launcher and was driven off. Mia stared after him for a few minutes, wondering what she'd just done.

6

Mia could have slept for two days straight, but her phone only let her sleep for seven hours. By the time the sun was up, she was on her second cup of coffee as she scrolled through the intelligence reports sent over by her boss.

It looked like Omar had written up the reports already, and now all Mia had to do was approve them. She wondered when he'd slept, if at all. After their rescue, Mia had been taken to headquarters for a couple of hours for debriefing, separately from Omar. She hadn't seen him since he was driven away.

She smiled as she imagined Omar checking out the missile launcher. As she read through the report, she continued to smile. Although she'd been scared to death half the time, reading back on the experience made her remember Omar's little quirks. Like how he seemed to always have a backup plan. How things like the escape tunnel being blown up didn't bother him. How he'd carried her sack when she was struggling to keep up. How he did what he said he'd do—recover the artifacts and get the two of them out of there.

She'd trusted him with her life, and he had protected her.

Her eyes widened as she read Omar's description of hijacking the helicopter. He made it sound like they'd taken off smoothly, hadn't been shot, and hadn't nearly careened to their deaths. There was no mention of Mia's panicked screaming. Thankfully, there was no mention of *the incident.*

Reading the report made the recovery sound perfectly executed. Abram could read between the lines well enough, which was why she'd been sent home to bed.

Her phone buzzed, and Mia checked the incoming text.

Awake yet? Want to meet at the CoffeeShop on Azza? I promise not to take you on a disastrous helicopter ride.

Butterflies went crazy in Mia's stomach. Omar hadn't signed his name, but it could only be him. How did he have her cell number? Then she realized she shouldn't question that—this was Omar.

Already had my coffee, she typed back. Her pulse fluttered as she waited for his reply.

A few seconds later, it came: *Me too. Maybe we can order tea. Twenty minutes?*

Mia smiled and typed: *Ok.*

It took almost that long for Mia to shower and dress. She lived about a ten-minute walk from CoffeeShop and was sure Omar had planned a place close by her apartment. She was in no hurry; Omar could wait for her. When she arrived at the café, she didn't see him immediately. Finally she found him sitting behind an arbor of grape vines that had turned yellow and orange with the autumn weather, mostly obscuring him from the street view. His back was to her, and he wore a dark fitted shirt and Levi's. He was scanning a newspaper, but when Mia approached, he set it down and checked something on his phone.

Her heart pinged at the sight of him, and her mind went back to *the incident*. What did he think about it? What did he think about *her*? And why did she care?

"Working already?" she said, stopping a couple of meters behind him, out of view.

He turned and stood. Their eyes met, and he held her gaze for a few seconds. "You look great," he said, and she felt her face warm.

"I'm alive."

One side of his mouth lifted into a smile. "You are definitely alive," he said, stepping toward her and kissing her cheek.

Mia hadn't expected that and was about to say something, maybe apologize for being so forward in the helicopter, but he'd already moved away and pulled out a chair for her.

"Is Abram going to give you a break?" he asked.

Mia sat in the chair he'd offered, passing close enough to know he wore some sort of cologne. Not strong, but evident. "I have the weekend off."

Omar's brow furrowed as he sat down. "That's not much, considering you just closed a major operation."

"What about you? How much time do you have off?" Mia asked, curious.

He lifted one shoulder in a shrug then leaned forward, his elbows on the table. "I found a cool feature that disables all GPS tracking on my phone."

Mia stared at him. "And your point is . . . ?"

"Abram can't track me, so I can take off as much time as I want."

"And how is that effective for job productivity?"

Omar smiled. "It's not in the least. But you must admit, I get the job done—just not on a normal timeline."

"I can agree to that," Mia said, finding that she was smiling back, and that the butterflies had returned in full force.

A waitress came up, and Omar looked up at her. "Tea, please. What do you recommend?"

Her bright red lipsticked mouth widened into a smile. "What do you like?"

"I'll try anything . . . as long as it's fresh."

"Everything here is fresh," she said, her smile growing wider, if possible.

"Then I'll take your freshest tea," Omar said with a wink.

The waitress laughed. "I'll make sure it's extra fresh. Anything else?"

Omar glanced at Mia, and she shook her head. She was having way too much fun watching the waitress flirt with Omar.

When the woman walked away, Mia leaned forward. "You have horrible pickup lines."

Omar blew out a breath. "I wasn't trying to pick her up."

"Oh really?"

His gaze narrowed. "I was just being nice."

"You're such a liar."

"Why would I flirt with that woman when I've got you sitting across from me?"

Mia straightened, her face flushing. "You're saving it for me?"

He held her gaze for a few seconds, not saying anything. "I wasn't going to take that blonde woman home, you know."

The woman at the bar. "Why were you there anyway?"

"Couldn't sleep. Of course, that's really no excuse. I'm a bit of an insomniac."

Mia found herself smiling despite her thudding heart. "Really? That's odd."

Omar's hand seemed to inch closer, or maybe it was her imagination. But she found she didn't mind at all. Reading him was a bit like reading the back of a cereal box in another language—familiar, because the cereal was the same, just like Omar was a man like any other, yet completely foreign because, well . . . Omar wasn't like any man she knew.

"Why is it odd?" he asked. "Fifteen percent of adults suffer from insomnia."

"Because it means we have something in common."

Omar laughed, and soon Mia was laughing too.

"That's all we've got in common, huh?" he said, lowering his voice. "I think we have a lot more than that."

Mia's face felt like it was on fire. Was he talking about the kiss?

His hand had definitely moved now. In fact, his fingers brushed hers. Mia met his gaze. Why bother fighting it? She wanted him to kiss her again. A soft chuckle sounded from Omar before he leaned across the table and did just that.

Mia's stomach flipped. They were sitting at a café, half concealed, but still in public. This must be breaking all kinds of rules. Still, she kissed him back, warmth pulsing through her as his hands moved from her face to her neck.

She sighed, and he pulled away slightly.

"Do we have something else in common?" he asked.

"Apparently," Mia whispered, feeling like her heart was going to pound out of her chest.

He moved back, but one of his hands captured hers, threading their fingers together. Tingles ran through her at his touch, but she deliberately ignored anything that common sense might be telling her. She was probably violating a coworker code of no dating, or at least no kissing, but it was really hard to think straight right now.

The waitress showed up with their tea; she was a bit less smiley now. She bustled around the table, much more business-like than before. Mia caught Omar gazing at her.

She felt herself starting to blush so she focused on stirring the steaming tea. When the waitress left, Mia said, "So why are we meeting again?"

Omar shifted his gaze and fished a thumb drive out of his pocket. He slid it over to her. "I copied some files on here that you might find interesting. They're highly classified and . . . relate to the bombing incident that involved your mother."

The butterflies that had been in Mia's stomach turned to stone. She picked up the thumb drive, feeling her throat tighten. "What's on it?"

"The complete profile of the bombing suspect. You'll find a lot of coincidences . . . things that shouldn't line up with a random attack."

Mia nodded, her breath coming short. She turned over the thumb drive, her hand shaking. "Will you read it with me?"

Omar didn't even hesitate. "Sure."

Mia put the thumb drive in her pocket then sipped her tea, letting the hot liquid calm her. They sat in silence for several moments, which was fine with Mia. Omar ignored the texts that kept chiming on his phone.

Finally, Mia said, "How did you get this information if it's classified?"

Omar hesitated at that, and Mia wished she could read what was going on in his mind this once. "It's probably better if I don't say. But I can tell you that it cost me a few hours of sleep."

"Did you have to break into any place or steal another helicopter?"

Omar smiled. "Nothing that drastic. But I did get a nasty bruise."

"Oh really? Where?"

"I can't exactly show you where, at least not in public."

Mia's heart rate sped up. She didn't know how he made that happen, and even though she laughed, she chastised herself inside. This guy was a little too flirty for her taste, and it seemed that every woman who met him thought so too. And he had no fear. Not the best combination to get involved with.

But he'd given her something priceless—something she'd almost given up hope of finding. Was kissing him a little so terrible? It wasn't like she'd let her heart get involved.

Mia only finished half her tea because she couldn't stop thinking about what could be on the thumb drive, and after Omar insisting on paying for their tea, they left the café.

"My place or yours?" he asked, guiding her around the tables, hand at her lower back.

Mia tried not to think about his touch. "Where do you live?"

"It would involve a taxi ride then possibly a motorcycle ride."

"Motorcycle, huh? Yours?"

"I'm not sure whose," Omar said as they exited the café. He slipped his hand in hers.

Mia let him hold her hand as they walked along the sidewalk in the direction of her place, although. "Do you ever use your own transportation?"

"Like what, a car?"

"Or anything. A bike . . . or maybe a truck?"

"I have a car, but it's in the repair shop."

Mia stopped under a tree and faced him. "Let me guess. You used it in a job, were chased through the streets of Jerusalem, then ended up wrecking it."

Omar's amused gaze soaked her in. "No, more like the transmission went out . . . no reason, just getting old, I guess."

"No reason?" Mia said, a bit disappointed.

Omar leaned toward her, his mouth next to her ear. "It was right after I drove it through the streets of Jerusalem at 3:00 a.m.," he whispered, "being chased by Mr. Jamil himself, though I can't confirm it."

Mia pulled away from him, laughing. "I knew it."

"Lucky guess."

"Maybe," she said, turning to walk again, her hand still in Omar's.

"I guess we're going to your place then?"

"Much safer than yours, I think," Mia said.

7

Mia re-read the files on her laptop from the thumb drive Omar had given her. She took a few more notes, then sat back, rubbing her eyes. She'd been at it for two hours. Omar was in the living room, asleep on the couch. After the first hour and answering a million of her questions, he couldn't stop yawning. It turned out he hadn't slept at all the night before, and hardly any the night they'd spent in the bakery van.

Mia reviewed her notes, her stomach churning at coincidences that were way too convenient to be anything but connected to her mother's death. First, the bomb was detonated by a live trigger, meaning that the bomber had been watching for Mia.

A quick glance at the framed picture on the kitchen wall reaffirmed to Mia, and had made clear to Omar, that Mia and her mom looked a lot alike. When "Mia" reached the corner, the car bomb was detonated.

Tears stung her eyes . . . All that she'd suspected had

now been made clear. The fear and regret that had been in her heart since her mother's death had now intensified. The truth was staring her in the face.

Her gaze went back to the name she'd written down. The bombing suspect was in jail, but the A'zam organization, which he worked for, hadn't been implicated. In a country like Israel, there were so many branches of larger terrorist organizations that the government focused on larger pods, often ignoring the smaller groups.

Mia rested her head in her hands, tears dripping onto the kitchen table. She didn't care if this had been only a two-man operation; it had to be stopped. The bomber had been hired, and now he was incarcerated, but the mastermind had to be caught as well.

She thought back to the case she'd been involved with at the time. It had been a high-security case, but nothing that had made her particularly concerned about death threats. A couple of million dollars in paintings had been stolen from a private collector in Jordan, and when Mia headed the recovery operation, everything went smoothly.

The paintings had been recovered near the Sinai border, just before the transport vehicle crossed into Egypt. Mia had worn her best disguise, yet she knew that with digital imaging, an advanced tech program could have matched her profile. She should have known better, relocated, and sent her mother to a secure location.

Mia blew out a breath of frustration and closed her laptop with a bang. She scrubbed her hands through her hair. How could she have been so stupid? Her confidence had cost her mother her life.

She stood abruptly; she had to do something. Shoving a chair out of the way, she decided to shower then pack up her place. She wouldn't risk staying here another night. Who knew what kind of fallout there'd be after the Jamil heist? She'd have to ask her boss to set her up in a safe house somewhere.

Maybe she'd made a mistake returning to Jerusalem.

She'd do whatever it took to find the A'zam operatives. She walked into the hallway only to be met by Omar, who looked like he'd just woken up.

"Hey," he said, taking one look at her and pulling her into his arms. "Are you okay?"

She let herself melt against him, feeling tears coming fast. She was a mess, she knew, and didn't want to blubber to anyone. But Omar was here, and his arms around her were comforting—or at least, they were holding her up for now.

"I'm just tired," she mumbled against his chest.

He slowly rubbed her back, holding her close. "Sorry I fell asleep on you."

She pulled away from him, giving him a watery smile. "You are human, you know, so I do expect you to sleep sometimes."

He smiled and moved a hand to her face. His thumb brushed her tears. "You're human too, so quit fighting it."

Mia brought her hands up and wiped her tears away. "Sometimes I forget."

Omar pulled her to him again and kissed the top of her head. She let him hold her for a few minutes, then she drew away. "I'm going to shower then pack. If the A'zam group was able to find me so quickly, what about Jamil's?"

Omar's mouth pulled into a frown. "Is this not a safe house?"

"No," Mia said, her heart thumping. "I insisted on living like a normal person, but that was before I knew . . ." Her voice cracked.

"You can stay with me then, until Abram gets something set up." Apprehension was plain in his voice. "I can help you pack . . . or shower."

Mia patted his chest. "There are boxes in the front closet."

He slid his arms around her waist and leaned in to kiss her.

"No you don't," she said. "Go pack."

He groaned and let her slip away.

Mia locked the bathroom door, telling herself that she was letting herself fall too fast for this guy. She hardly knew him. Well, that wasn't true. She'd learned almost everything about him when she was assigned to do the handoff. He wasn't in any relationship with a woman, he had never been married, and he didn't sleep around. So the way he was acting around her was surprising. Could he really like her that much?

It was clear he liked her, but was this just a game to him? Something told her it wasn't. He'd risked a lot, even though he hadn't admitted it, to get her the confidential files. He seemed to truly care about what happened to her mom, and when she told him she wasn't in a safe house, she'd seen genuine concern in his eyes.

Could she trust him? Could she trust that he wasn't playing games with her, trying to sleep with her for whatever reason, that he wasn't the wildcard Abram had painted him to be?

By the time she'd showered and changed, Omar had packed up the living room and was well into the kitchen. He looked up as she entered. Seeing him in her kitchen, doing something completely pedestrian, even though she knew he had a gun and probably a thousand plans in his head, made him look sweet and vulnerable.

Especially with the way he was looking at her. Maybe she shouldn't stay at his place tonight after all.

"Feel better?" he asked, and she wanted to kiss him for it.

"Much," she said. "I packed a few changes of clothing. Maybe Abram can arrange for the rest of my stuff to be moved when he finds me a place."

Omar raised his brows. "I said you can stay with me."

She folded her arms and smiled. "I know. I heard you. But—"

He raised a hand. "I've got it. Let's get you safe, and then we can plan out our strategy."

"Our strategy?"

"You didn't think I'd let you do this alone, did you?"

Mia flushed. She hadn't known what to think, but his words sent a jolt of relief through her. "I don't expect you to. I mean, you have your own assignments. You've had a bunch of texts come in today."

"They can wait. You're more important."

Mia didn't say anything, just held her breath for a couple of seconds. Then she finally let it out. "Look, Omar . . . I mean . . . you're a great guy, but I'm not—"

He was at her side in three steps. "Look, I'm not asking for anything. I like you, that's all. It's been a long time since I cared about any woman—or anyone, for that matter. I won't touch you if you don't want me to." But he was touching her now, his hands holding her arms, and his breath was soft on her face, making heat pulse through her body.

"You'll be safe with me, I promise," he said. "You can have my room, and if I sleep, I'll stay on the couch." His gaze bored into hers, and Mia's breath caught. "I just want to help. So you set the rules." He let go and stepped away.

"Okay," she said, her breath shaky.

"Are we good then?" he asked.

She nodded. "Yeah."

Something like relief filled his eyes. "Great. Let's get out of here and find whoever is running A'zam."

8

Mia wanted to cover her ears and drown out the sound of Omar's shouting. For the past twenty minutes, he'd been in the back bedroom of his apartment arguing with Abram. They went around in circles, coming back to the same point, only to start the argument all over again.

Mia's head was pounding, so she searched for ibuprofen or aspirin in his cupboards, but came up empty. She walked down the hall, cringing when she heard the expletives Omar was calling their boss. She found the bathroom and opened the mirrored cupboard.

A small bottle of ibuprofen looked about five years old. Didn't Omar ever have a headache or bruises? She blushed, remembering that he had one he couldn't show her in public.

"This is more important," Omar was saying, his voice loud through the bathroom wall. "Find someone else to clean up the Jamil case. I got the artifacts out, and that should make Greece happy."

A pause, then Omar's voice again. "How are you going to explain your lousy employee retention? You can't treat people like this . . . Mia can answer for herself . . . No, she's not here."

Mia came out of the bathroom and stood in the bedroom doorway, crossing her arms. She was nervous about talking to Abram after all of this but knew she couldn't concentrate on any other assignments until the A'zam organization was exposed. Yet it sounded like Abram wouldn't give them any resources. They were on their own, which meant they were extremely restricted in what they could do. Pretty much every strategy Omar had thrown out was illegal without clearance from the government.

Mia walked toward Omar, hand outstretched, and Omar reluctantly handed over the phone. She lifted the phone to her ear, but it was dead. "You hung up on him?"

"He'll get over it."

"What are we going to do without Abram's backup?"

Omar took the phone from her hand and slid it in his pocket. His expression was strained, but it softened when he looked at her. "You can be my backup, or if you want, I'll be yours." He turned to leave the room.

"Wait," she said, grasping his arm. "I'm serious. I don't want you to do this—Abram made his position clear. And he's right, it's too risky. I can't let something happen to another person because of another one of my mistakes. I wouldn't be able to live with myself."

Omar didn't say anything for a couple of seconds while he gazed down at her. "I can't live with myself if I let you do this alone."

"Omar—"

"Don't worry. Nothing will happen to me, or to you. I have a favor I can call in."

Mia let out a breath. That's what she was afraid of, some topsy-turvy plan barely held together by a thread. Despite her erratic pulse at what she was about to agree to, she said, "What are you planning?"

"Let's get on the road, and I'll fill you in."

She nodded, and he leaned down and kissed her cheek.

"Sorry. I didn't mean to do that," he said, taking a step back. "I'll be better."

Mia let a smile escape. "I don't mind the kissing."

His smile matched hers, but before he could say or do anything else, his phone rang. Omar looked at the number then answered. "Matan here."

He listened for a couple of seconds then hung up, a look of triumph on his face.

"*Matan?*" she said.

He placed a finger on her lips to shush her. "That name stays between us. Part of the favor."

For a charged moment, she wanted to kiss him again, but she didn't. Instead she stepped back and let him lead the way out of the room. She didn't know what to expect transportation-wise but was pleased when Omar unlocked the doors to a small truck parked outside, one that he had an actual key for.

"Yours?" she asked, climbing into the passenger seat.

"Government vehicle," he said with a wink, setting a backpack between them. "But let's keep that between us."

He pulled onto the street then made a U-turn.

"Okay, what's the plan?" Mia asked, her stomach forming into knots of anticipation.

"First stop is Bethlehem to meet our contact. Then we'll have to get creative with the transportation situation."

"Is there a situation?" she asked.

"Most definitely."

Mia shook her head. "I don't know if I should laugh or jump out of the truck."

Omar moved his hand on top of hers, intertwining their fingers. "Don't jump."

She leaned back and smiled at him. As they drove, he told her about Isham, the man they were going to meet. "He works grounds at the Church of the Nativity. He's my eyes and ears, and a few weeks ago when I was researching you, I asked if he knew anything."

Mia was paying attention now. "How would he know anything about me?"

"He didn't, but he was able to fill me in on A'zam, which didn't connect to you until I got those files last night."

"Okay, so we find A'zam. Then what?" Mia asked. "Without Abram, what are we going to do, haul the guy to a police station?"

"We won't have to. That's where Isham comes in." Omar paused as he slowed the truck, entering a long line of cars waiting to be admitted across the Bethlehem border. Thirty-foot high barricades rose above them, dividing the town. This famous tourist attraction was marred by high security, keeping in the resident Arabs, allowing only ones with a work visa to go back and forth.

Omar flashed his ID when they reached security. Once inside the town, he drove along a series of narrow streets. He nudged the backpack toward her. "There's a gun in there for you."

She took out the 9mm and tucked it into the inner pocket of her jacket. Minutes later, Omar parked beneath a drooping tree. Some of its leaves were falling off in the breeze and littering the ground. He and Mia climbed out of the truck, and he led her between two apartment buildings then down a flight of concrete stairs. He knocked on a heavy metal door, and when it screeched open, Mia was already second-guessing herself.

This would be so much easier with authorities backing them up.

The man who greeted them was tiny, with a few missing teeth, but that didn't stop his enthusiastic smile as he pumped Omar's hand in greeting.

"Isham, this is my partner," Omar said.

Isham's gaze showed disapproval, but he motioned for them to come inside.

They entered the dim interior, which turned out to be a small living room complete with a battered couch and fuzzy television. Mia perched on the couch as Omar spoke rapid Arabic with Isham, gesturing wildly. Mia followed most of it, catching on that Isham wasn't happy with Mia coming along.

When Omar turned to her, she braced herself. "We're going out to the fields to a Bedu camp. You'll have to wear a burka."

Mia stood. "I don't want to."

"Just to protect your identity. It'll be rather convenient, actually," Omar said.

Next to him, Isham nodded briskly then left the room.

"We're looking for a Bedouin?" Mia asked Omar.

"And apparently we're in luck. The Bethlehem police want him for something else."

"Are they our backup?"

Omar smiled. Isham rushed back into the room, carrying a burka and a UN ID. Mia grimaced as she pulled on the heavy fabric.

Isham smiled at her with approval then led them

through the apartment to another door, which opened to a spiral stairwell. He pointed upward and said something about a Jeep.

Omar nodded and thanked him. Then Omar was on his way up the stairs, Mia following. When she spotted the rusted-out Jeep in the dirt courtyard, she had her doubts. But if anyone could start it, Omar probably could.

Even with the keys, Omar had to try several times to get the vehicle running. He steered through the narrow gate then back through the main Bethlehem entrance. This time, Mia produced her fake ID, and they were waved through. The sun was just setting as they pulled off the main road onto a dirt lane that wound through the hills. Omar kept only his parking lights on, relying on the rising moon for most of the light.

They drove for about an hour before Omar finally stopped and killed the engine. "We're being followed," he said in a quiet voice.

"By who?"

"I'm hoping it's Isham's people."

A chill went through Mia at other possibilities.

"Come on, we're getting out. It's less than a kilometer anyway," Omar said.

Mia struggled with the burka a bit before climbing out. The extra material provided warmth on the chilly night, so she didn't mind it so much right now. Omar grasped her hand and led her up an incline, where they crouched behind some brush and waited. Omar kept hold of her hand, and for that Mia was grateful. It kept her nerves more steady.

Twenty minutes passed, and still no sign of anyone. "They must know we stopped," Omar whispered. "Let's start walking."

Mia rose to her feet, stretching her cramped legs, then they walked over a couple of hills until they could see the Bedu camp. A fire blazed as a woman cooked over it, and a few little kids ran around. Men sat in the background, crouching on rugs and talking.

Mia's grip tightened in Omar's hand, and he squeezed back. "We'll move around back then surprise them from the side."

He let go, and then they made a wide circle about the camp. Mia stayed about six meters from Omar, walking slowly and listening for every little sound. When they reached the back of the main tent, they both paused. Omar motioned with his finger for her to follow, but before Mia could take a step, someone grabbed her from behind.

Mia tried to twist free of her captor, but he had twice her strength. He shoved her to the ground face first and wrenched her arms behind her. She cried out in pain.

Omar spun, gun in hand, but a second person dove against his legs, buckling them and sending Omar forward into the sand.

"Who are you?" the second man asked, the one who'd pinned Omar.

Omar twisted furiously and managed to deliver a punch at the guy holding him down. They wrestled for a few seconds, ending with Omar getting control of his gun again. "Both of you, against the tent!" Omar shouted.

"We'll shoot the woman first," the man holding Mia said.

"You're surrounded . . . this whole desert is crawling with police," Omar said. "Give up now, and you can enter a plea deal. Maybe get out of prison before you lose all of your teeth."

The man holding Mia tightened his grip; she grunted.

"Let go of her now, and stand against the tent," Omar commanded.

Mia tried to catch her breath. The burka was suffocating, along with the pressure of the man pinning her down. Her ears started humming, and she wondered if she was about to pass out. The buzzing grew louder, and then Mia recognized the sound—trucks were approaching.

The distraction was exactly what Mia needed. She got one arm free and threw her elbow back, making contact with her captor's nose. As he cried out in pain, Mia twisted to her side and pulled out her gun.

"Get off me!" she said.

The man held his nose and shifted his weight.

"You can move the easy way or the hard way," she said. "At least you have a choice. My mother never did."

The man's eyes widened, and Mia wondered how many deaths this man was responsible for. He moved off of her and stood next to the other man.

Mia sat up. Omar crouched beside her and put his hand on her shoulder. "Are you all right?"

"Yes," she said, her voice hoarse.

"Move behind me, then."

She scrambled to her feet and stood next to him, pointing her gun at the men. They were tall for Bedu men, with thick beards and flashing dark eyes. One was nearly two meters, the other about Omar's size.

A child started crying, and a woman called out, telling her children to get inside the tent. The women must have seen the approaching vehicles.

"Which one of you operates A'zam?" Omar asked.

"I don't know what you're talking about," the taller man said, but his gaze slid to his companion's.

"All right, then I'll shoot you first, because I came here for information." Omar's finger moved to the trigger.

"Wait," the shorter man said, looking from Omar to Mia. "We may know a little. Tell us why you're here, and maybe we can help you."

"They're stalling," Mia said.

"You're right," Omar answered. "Who should I shoot first?"

Mia's gaze went to the shorter man, the one who'd pinned her. "Him."

"No!" the man shouted as everything flashed around them.

Mia dove for the ground, and someone landed on top of her. A grenade had gone off, but she wasn't sure where. Hot pain shot through her ears, and she gasped for breath. "Omar!"

"I'm here," he said, his voice just above her.

He rolled off and tugged up her face covering.

"You're alive," she said, her eyes burning, her body trembling.

Omar stood and helped her up. "Are you hurt?"

"I don't know." She grasped his arm to steady herself. "Get this damn thing off of me."

Omar helped her out of the burka then grabbed her around the waist with one hand, keeping his gun in the other. The tent had caved in, and the shorter man they'd been interrogating wasn't moving. The taller man was crawling away from them, crying out for his family.

Mia almost felt sorry for him.

The place swarmed with officials shouting to each other and running in all directions. A couple of men ran toward the Bedu man, dragged him to his feet, and handcuffed him.

FIRST HEIST

"Omar!" someone shouted. Mia recognized the voice—their boss was here. She stared in disbelief as the trim man jogged toward them. "Looks like you missed my message."

Omar stiffened, his hold tightening around Mia. "I thought you'd bailed."

Abram rubbed his neck and grinned, his thin mustache turning up. "You thought wrong." His eyes turned to Mia. "Let's get you out of here."

"Wait," Omar said, putting himself between Mia and Abram. "What are you doing here, and why did you change your mind?"

Abram folded his arms. "Turns out the A'zam are not as obscure as we thought. They've called in a couple of bomb threats over the past two weeks, one as far away as Tel Aviv." He spread his hands out. "Thought I'd kill two birds with one stone."

"Fabulous that you showed up just in time," Omar said, the sarcasm oozing from his voice. "How'd you find us?"

"Mia didn't turn off her tracker like some employees did." Abram stepped toward Mia and wrapped an arm around her shoulders. "Didn't I tell you to stay away from him? You could have been killed."

Mia glanced from Abram to Omar. When Mia had tried to get Abram to look into her mother's death more closely, she had been ignored. It took Omar to make him consider it seriously. She shrugged off Abram's arm. "I'm fine. My mother was killed by these men. I wasn't worried about myself."

"We'll talk more about that," Abram said. "But first let's get you into a truck and checked out at the hospital."

"She doesn't need a hospital," Omar said.

Abram shook his head and steered Mia around the tent

toward one of the SUVs. He peppered her with questions, none of which Mia wanted to answer yet, but she followed his lead and settled into the passenger seat of an SUV. Through the window, she watched Omar talk to a few people; it appeared he was chewing everyone out. She almost laughed at the sight.

The shorter Arab was alive after all, and two men were carrying him to one of the trucks. The women and children all appeared to be safe, and they stood in a huddled group, crying and refusing to talk to any of the officials.

Mia leaned her head against the cool glass, watching as Omar stalked to one of the trucks and climbed into the driver's seat. Apparently he was driving himself out. A weight had been lifted off of her shoulders. Her mother was still gone, but the men behind her death would finally be brought to justice. Omar might do things a bit outside of the box, but he'd given her a priceless gift: closure.

Before she could think about what she was doing, she popped open her door and hurried over to the truck Omar had climbed into. He'd started the engine and was pulling forward when he saw her. He braked, and she ran around the front and climbed in the passenger side.

Slamming the door after her, she looked over at him. "Hi."

"Hi, yourself." He smiled and threw the gear into drive. The tires spun out on the sand, then made purchase, and Omar gunned the engine, barreling into the dark night. About a hundred meters out, he started to laugh.

"What's so funny?" Mia asked.

He slowed the truck, then stopped. Mia looked behind them; no one was following. When she turned to ask why he'd stopped, he took her face in his hands and kissed her.

Electricity shot all the way to her toes. Omar's mouth moved against hers, possessing her as he hadn't before, and Mia let herself melt. She slid her hands around his neck, and her fingers tugged at his hair to get him closer. He didn't seem to mind, and his kissing slowed, yet intensified at the same time. Mia realized that from the moment she first saw him, this man had intrigued her. She wanted to know everything about him—why he had no fear, and why he was drawn to her.

His mouth moved to her jawline, then to her neck, and warm shivers traveled throughout her body. "You still haven't told me why you're laughing," she whispered.

"Hmm," he mumbled, his lips moving back to hers, taking his time kissing her.

She didn't mind; she could wait for his answer.

When he pulled away, they were both breathless. Omar smiled and rested his forehead against hers. "I was imagining the look on Abram's face when he saw you climb into my truck. It looks like I got the girl after all."

More Omar Zagouri Thrillers:

Finding Sheba, a novel

Beneath, a digital short story

ABOUT HEATHER B. MOORE

Heather B. Moore is the *USA Today* bestselling author of more than a dozen historical novels and thrillers, written under pen name H.B. Moore. She writes women's fiction, romance and inspirational nonfiction under Heather B. Moore. This can all be confusing, so her kids just call her Mom. Heather attended Cairo American College in Egypt, the Anglican School of Jerusalem in Israel, and earned a Bachelor of Science degree from Brigham Young University in Utah.

Blog: MyWritersLair.blogspot.com
Website: www.hbmoore.com
Twitter: @HeatherBMoore
Facebook: Fans of H.B. Moore

Literary awards include: 3-time Best of State Recipient for Best in Literary Arts, 3-time Whitney Award Winner, and 2-time Golden Quill Award Winner

LETTER FOR TWO

Sarah M. Eden

Other Works by Sarah M. Eden

Seeking Persephone

Courting Miss Lancaster

The Kiss of a Stranger

Friends and Foes

An Unlikely Match

Drops of Gold

Glimmer of Hope

As You Are

Longing for Home

Hope Springs

For Elise

1

Sophia Davis lived in one half of a historic home in downtown Phoenix. The bungalow had been divided into two quaint apartments with two very distinct, well-labeled mailboxes. Yet, every day, she and the tenant in the other half of the house received a haphazard mixture of their own mail and each other's. They met each evening at five-thirty on the wraparound porch to sort out the pile.

Her neighbor, Ethan Williams, was well worth the hassle of a mixed-up mail delivery. Sophia was half tempted to ask the mail carrier to mix things up on purpose. Those few minutes of laughing and talking with her handsome and witty neighbor were the highlight of her day.

She set her messenger bag on the hall table and glanced up at the clock. She'd managed the walk from her office building in record time. Mail sorting wasn't for another ten minutes. Time enough to smooth out her hair and freshen her makeup. October had finally turned cooler, so she no longer arrived home drenched in sweat.

Ten minutes proved just the right amount of time. By the time the clock read five thirty exactly, she looked less ragged and more refreshed. Maybe today would be the day Ethan finally noticed.

She stepped out onto the porch. He was there already, sitting in one of the patio chairs. What was it about a man in scrubs that made her heart tie itself up in knots?

"Hey, there." He pulled himself up as she stepped outside.

Sophia had moved into the house six months earlier. They had the mail sorting ritual down to a science now. They pulled the mail from their mailboxes and sat in chairs on either side of the small glass-top table.

"I think it's your day to take the junk mail," Ethan said, holding up a stack of flyers and envelopes of coupons as if offering her a real treat.

She shook her head, as she always did. "My recycle can says otherwise. It's still full from yesterday, when you pawned the ads off on me."

He dropped the stack on the table next to him, acting like it was a big burden. "I guess I'll be the recycle guy today."

Sophia covertly watched Ethan over the tops of the envelopes she was supposed to be looking through. She'd always had a thing for guys with dark hair and the ability to hold up their end of a conversation. Ethan had both.

He waved around a brochure. "A programmers' conference in Denver. Sounds exciting."

She smiled as he handed it over. His eyes dropped right back to the mail.

"How were things at the hospital today?" Sophia asked, setting a letter addressed to him on his side of the table.

"When people asked my mom how her day was, she always used to say, 'No one died.' I don't think that's the best answer for a post-op nurse, though." He flashed a quick, mischievous look.

"I'll start using that," she said. "'How was my day? No computers died.' That sounds like a disclaimer at the end of a movie, doesn't it?"

He chuckled and slid a magazine toward her. "Exactly. 'No computers were harmed in the making of this film.'"

They laughed together a minute. She watched him, but his gaze didn't linger. Why was it she never could catch his attention? The five minutes a day they spent switching letters and flyers and junk mail wasn't doing the trick.

"What's this?" Ethan held up a yellowed envelope, turning it around a few times. "Do you know anyone named Eleanor?"

Sophia shook her head. Ethan set the letter on the table right between them.

"It has the house address," he said. "But no Apartment A or B."

"For a former tenant?" Sophia suggested. She looked more closely. "Wait. Look at the postmark—1953." She couldn't make out the entire date.

She took the envelope and turned it around a few times. It looked old, the corners bent and worn. There appeared to have once been a return address written on the back flap, but it had long since been smudged beyond recognition. This mysterious Eleanor had once had a last name, though it had faded. The house number and street were still visible, along with the word Phoenix, but nothing else.

"This was mailed sixty years ago." Sophia set it back down. "And I don't think it's ever been opened."

Ethan looked at the envelope for a drawn-out moment before looking up at her. Those brown eyes melted her every time.

"What should we do with it?" he asked.

"I don't know. It doesn't belong to either of us, but who knows where this Eleanor is now." She leaned back in her chair, letting her eyes wander back to the letter. "After sixty years, she may not even be alive."

Ethan flipped the envelope over again, then slouched in his chair. He fiddled with his hospital badge. Sophia tapped her foot, thinking.

A look of determination crossed Ethan's face. "I know this makes me sound like a sap, but if this letter managed to stay around for sixty years, we can't just throw it away."

A sap? Not at all. She liked him even more knowing he had a sense of fairness and a touch of sentimentality.

"So we should try to find Eleanor?" Sophia asked, casually throwing in the *we* to see if he'd object.

"We absolutely should."

A bubble of excitement started in her stomach. "How do we do that? She probably hasn't lived here in decades. We don't even have a last name." Between the two of them, they'd used the word *we* four times in four sentences.

He shrugged. "It'll take some time. Wouldn't it be worth it to get this letter to Eleanor?"

Time. Time with Ethan Williams. "Let's do it."

He smiled, and Sophia swore she saw a sparkle of light shimmering off his pearly white teeth. The man was perfect and, at the moment, romantically oblivious to her. He was friendly, but not interested. Perhaps while they searched for the mysterious Eleanor, she'd find a way to get him to notice her as more than merely the neighbor he exchanged mail with.

"When do you have an evening free for researching?" Ethan asked.

For researching. That was a disappointing phrase to hear tacked on to the end of that particular sentence. Still, she'd take it. "Tomorrow?" she suggested.

"Sounds good." He grabbed his stack of mail and stood. "If you provide the computer expertise, I'll provide dinner."

She tried to act casual. "Oh, do you cook?"

He nodded. "I think you'll be impressed."

"Tomorrow night then." She stood as well, taking her mail and the sixty-year-old envelope. "It's a—deal." She barely stopped herself from saying "date."

Maybe, just maybe, while they searched for Eleanor, she'd figure a way to snap up Ethan's attention as well.

2

Ethan could cook a couple of dozen dishes that would impress even the pickiest foodie. He'd finally found a way to ask Sophia over for dinner without seeming like a creepy housemate stalker, and he had nothing remotely impressive to serve. It hadn't even occurred to him that being on his second twelve-hour shift in two days, with a third looming on the horizon, would mean dinner would have to be something out of the freezer.

He pulled the two-serving-sized lasagna from the oven. The pan was hot enough to nearly burn his hand through the hot pad. He dropped it on the stove top, shaking the heat off his fingers. "This is ridiculous."

He glanced at the clock. She'd be here in a few minutes. The table was set, and he'd cleaned up the place. Ethan slipped down the hall to take a quick look at himself in the bathroom mirror. He'd looked better. But three twelves took a toll on a person. He mussed his hair a little with his fingers. Better. At least he wasn't in scrubs.

The bell rang in the very next moment. Sophia.

He looked his reflection dead in the eye. "Don't blow this. It may be your only chance."

Ethan kept his posture casual. He was already afraid he reeked of desperation; there was no point looking pathetic as well.

He pulled open the front door. There stood Sophia in a black skirt and blue top. She looked amazing in blue.

"Hey." *That was lame.* He jumped right to, "Come on in."

"Smells good." Sophia smiled as she stepped inside. She had a great smile. A really great smile. "Lasagna?"

He nodded, walking beside her on the way to the kitchen. "And steamed broccoli." He hoped she liked broccoli.

Ethan moved the lasagna from the stovetop to the table.

"Is this the fancy meal you bragged you were going to cook?" Sophia asked, eying the pan.

"I ran out of time," he confessed. "I had a five-to-five shift today."

"I'm not complaining. Frozen Italian food happens to be one of my specialties as well. Though microwavable enchiladas is my signature dish."

He set the glass bowl of broccoli on the table. "I did steam these from fresh. That's impressive, right?"

"Sure."

Sophia Davis was in his house. At his table. Smiling at him. *Don't mess this up.*

"How was work?" he asked. "Did the computers behave themselves?"

"They always do." She dished herself some lasagna. "Computers only do what we tell them to."

He spooned broccoli on his plate. "And if my computer runs slow and freezes up all the time?"

Sophia laughed a little. "You're sending it mixed messages. Or you seriously need an upgrade."

He pointed at her with his empty fork. "Computers really hit their stride in the late 90s. Why would I replace a classic?"

"Please tell me you don't actually have a twenty-year-old computer."

He kept his expression naïve. "Why, would you recommend something newer?"

"As a general rule, the age of your computer should be single digits."

Ethan shook his head, pretending to be frustrated. "If only I'd known this eleven years ago."

"Don't be too hard on yourself." Her serious expression was exaggerated to the point of being comical. "I am a professional, after all."

Ethan poured her a glass of water; he had nothing else to offer. He always made a desperate grocery run at the end of his three days.

"How was your day?" Sophia asked.

"Not too bad," Ethan said. "One patient was finally discharged after a long, tough few days. It should have been a simple recovery." He shrugged as he swallowed a bite of lasagna. "Sometimes you just don't know."

Sophia nodded, not pressing for more information. He'd explained once, during one of their first mail exchanges, that HIPAA laws and privacy rules prevented him from saying much about his patients—nothing specific, and no names. She'd accepted that without question or complaint. He appreciated that. His last girlfriend—not that

Sophia was his new girlfriend—had resented that, insisting he "didn't want to talk to her" and heavily hinting he was hiding something.

"A five-to-five shift?" Sophia asked. "That sounds brutal."

He nodded, swallowing another mouthful. "Three days on and three days off. The three on is killer."

"I'm surprised you had the energy to pull the lasagna out of the freezer."

Ethan shrugged. "I do what I can."

They laughed and talked through dinner without a single awkward pause. Sophia was easy to talk to. She didn't ever seem bored by talk of his work. And he enjoyed hearing her talk about what she was working on—he didn't understand all the technical aspects of it, but she got so excited explaining it all that he listened, mesmerized.

When they were done, she helped clear dinner and rinse the dishes before he loaded them in the dishwasher. It sure beat doing it all on his own.

"Where's your ancient computer?" she asked when they'd finished. "We have a letter to research."

"Living room," he said.

"Does it even get on the Internet?" she asked as they walked out of the kitchen. "That was pretty new stuff back in the nineties."

"No, it sends telegrams."

A minute later she was sitting on his couch, his laptop—the one he'd bought only a couple years earlier—on her lap. Ethan tried to act nonchalant as he pushed a dirty sock under the couch with his foot. He sat next to her, telling himself to not be a complete loser.

"So how do we find out who was living here in 1953?"

Her eyes narrowed as she looked at Google open on the screen.

"Census records?" Ethan suggested.

"Good idea." She nodded. "How about the 1950 census? That would be the closest."

"Sounds good to me." He watched her as she typed. Did that make him a stalker?

Sophia's forehead scrunched up as she read the words on the screen. It made him smile. She was even cuter that way than usual, and that was saying something.

"Hmm."

"What?" he asked.

"Doesn't look like the 1950 census is available online." She looked over at him, disappointment heavy in her brown eyes. "Should we try 1940?"

"It's worth a try. If Eleanor was here in '53, she might have been there in '40."

Sophia leaned back. She typed a new search in. After a few more clicks, her face lit up. "Here we go."

She turned a little so the screen faced him more. Ethan hesitantly took that as an invitation. He moved ever so slightly closer but made sure she could tell he was doing so to get a better look at the computer. For all he knew, she thought of him as nothing more than a friend. Pushing that wouldn't do his cause any good.

Sophia filled in the state, county, city information then the street name and nearest crossroad.

Ethan let out a long whistle when the search completed. "Thirty-six pages of results."

She scrolled up and down on the census image. "This isn't exactly straightforward. We'll have to scroll through to find the right street."

"I've got time." Did that sound casual enough?

They scrolled through page after page searching for their street name and house number. He'd never looked through census records before but kind of enjoyed it. They got caught up reading about people's occupations, where they'd lived before coming to Phoenix, how many children they had. There found unique names they'd never heard before and tried to pronounce them.

"Here it is." Sophia sat up straight, her eyes darting from him to the computer screen and back again. "Our address. Right here."

He scooted a little closer. Man, she smelled good. *Focus, Ethan.*

"Is there an Eleanor?" he asked.

She moved her finger along the screen, not quite touching it. She went from one line to the other, shaking her head as she did.

"No Eleanor." She sounded as disappointed as he felt.

"Her family could have moved in after 1940." That seemed more and more like the case.

Sophia leaned back against the couch again, watching him. "Where should we look next? We can't get to the 1950 census or the one from 1960."

Ethan gave it as much thought as he could while sitting this close to her. "Tax records?" It was the first thing that came to mind.

She typed in a new search. Then another. Part of him was glad the task hadn't proven quick and easy. He'd spend the whole evening with her, looking for Eleanor. Once they found her, Sophia would leave.

"The county assessor's site is down," Sophia said.

"Sounds like they need an IT professional." Ethan gave her a pointed look.

"They can't afford me," she answered.

"I'll have to remember that next time I have a computer emergency."

"Nah." She pushed his shoulder with hers. "I won't charge you for consultations if you'll check out my next sore throat."

"Deal." A very welcome deal, in fact.

"And maybe we can check the assessor's site tomorrow."

"Over dinner?" he suggested, doing his best to keep the hopefulness out of his face and tone.

"My place this time," she said.

"Sounds good." But in his head, he was saying, *That counts as a date, right?*

3

If Ethan could thaw out a frozen lasagna the night before and call it cooking dinner, then Sophia felt confident she could order in Chinese and fulfill her obligation to feed him that night. She could cook okay, but even simple cooking required time, and she didn't have any. She'd spent the day trying to get a server running again and had left work almost a full hour late, ordering dinner on her cellphone as she walked home.

Ethan was on the front porch when she got there.

"Sorry I'm late," she said. "Work was nuts."

"Yeah, for me, too." His smile was quick and weak. He looked tired. Yesterday he'd said that today would be his third twelve-hour day.

"Dinner's on the way." She held up her cell. "Maybe we can do some searching while we wait."

"Sounds good."

She unlocked the door and stepped inside. Ethan came in behind her. She was very glad she'd cleaned up that morning.

"Make yourself at home." Somehow she managed to make the offer without sounding like a teenager with a desperate crush. She felt like it but hoped she at least sounded like an adult.

Sophia moved quickly to her bedroom and dropped her bag on the bed. She took a minute to smooth out her hair and check her makeup. Of course, Ethan had seen her in all her glory when she first got home. Fixing herself up wouldn't help much now.

She pulled off the walking shoes she always wore home. If only she'd had a chance to change them before running in to Ethan—walking shoes with a skirt suit was not the most fashion-forward ensemble. She slipped on a pair of ballet flats, a better pick than the walking shoes, though not as fabulous as a pair of heels. But heels would make her look like she was trying too hard. She wanted to look like she wasn't trying at all. Guys could smell desperation from three blocks away.

She pulled her laptop out of her bag and headed for the living room. Ethan was sitting on the sofa, his head tilted back, his eyes closed. Was he asleep already? That didn't bode well for a fun, borderline romantic evening.

Sophia approached quietly and cautiously. Just as she reached the sofa, he opened a single eye.

"Hey." It was all she could manage with him looking so mussed and casual and cute.

He sat up straighter, blinking a few times as if shaking off sleepiness. "Did I miss dinner?"

"It would have served you right if you had." She dropped onto the couch by him. "You snooze, you lose."

"'You snooze, you lose?' Man." He chuckled low in his throat. "I haven't heard that since elementary school."

Sophia laughed and set her laptop on the coffee table. "I spent elementary school desperately in love with all of the Backstreet Boys. So 'Quit Playing Games with my Heart' always takes me back."

"The Backstreet Boys?" Ethan shook his head. "I think I just lost all respect for you."

"You weren't into boy bands in your impressionable younger years?"

He made a noise that sounded very much like, "Puh-shaw."

"You were too cool for that?" she guessed.

"Actually, probably too lame. I was one of those weird kids into retro before being into retro was a thing, you know? I was in middle school before I listened to anything more recent than Etta James or Frank Sinatra, and I stopped wearing a bow tie and fedora to school only after the gym teacher warned me I was probably going to get beat up for it."

She could picture him walking around his elementary school playground in a zoot suit, snapping his fingers while singing "Come Fly with Me."

"My sister refused to be seen with me in public," Ethan said. "So I told her if she couldn't be hip to my beat, she could just ice it. She hated when I used old-school slang."

Sophia settled into the corner, warming to the topic. "I'm going to guess she was your older sister."

"How did you know?"

"Because *younger* brothers are the worst."

He grinned. "You have a younger brother, don't you?"

Sophia nodded dramatically. They talked about their families and childhoods. Dinner arrived, and they kept talking all the way through their meal. He got along with his family. He didn't badmouth people. Sophia liked that about him. He was the kind of person you felt comfortable with, safe. He didn't seem likely to rip into a person behind their back, and he was proving easy to get along with.

As they finished off the last of the moo goo gai pan, Ethan told her about the first time he administered an IV and how he thought he was going to pass out. She loved hearing his laugh and seeing him smile. Not only because he was ridiculously handsome, but also because she knew he was enjoying their time together as much as she was. Maybe she should quit pretending she saw him only as a friend. Maybe she should try actually flirting, being more obvious that she was interested.

Ethan pushed his plate away and nodded toward her laptop. "Guess we'd better get to work finding Eleanor."

And just like that, they were back to business. She hoped he was hanging around for more than the mystery they were solving. She almost asked him. Almost. But Sophia wasn't that brave.

She threw herself into the search, trying not to think about how lopsided their interest in each other might very well be. The county assessor's site was up, but no matter how they searched, they couldn't find any historical information. Maybe it simply wasn't available.

They ran at least a dozen Google searches, trying their address and the year, the street name and "Eleanor," anything that came to mind. Nothing panned out.

Sophia set her feet up on the coffee table, the computer on her lap, trying everything she could think of to find the names of the people who lived in their house sixty years earlier. "This is going to be harder than we thought."

Ethan didn't answer. She looked over at him, and her

heart fluttered just a bit. He was asleep, curled a little bit into the corner of the couch. He looked cute even sleeping. She pulled a light lap blanket out of the storage ottoman and spread it over him. She'd wake him up eventually, but after hearing of the long, difficult hours he'd put in the past three days, she couldn't bear to now.

Sophia sat in the armchair and continued searching for Eleanor, though her eyes wandered to Ethan more than once. She liked him more than she should, especially not knowing how he felt. Maybe it was a good thing that finding Eleanor was proving difficult. The longer it took, the more time they'd have together. Perhaps she'd convince Ethan she was what *he* was looking for.

4

The next afternoon, Ethan made himself a sandwich and sat at the table on the porch. Fall was the best time of year in Phoenix. The days were finally cool enough to sit outside in the shade. The nights were perfect.

Mrs. Garcia walked past with her daughter. Ethan waved to them.

"Lovely day, isn't it?" Mrs. Garcia called out to him.

"Perfect."

She was the neighborhood grandmother and treated everyone like her grandchildren. She had to be in her mid-eighties. Her daughter had moved back from Detroit a couple of years earlier to help take care of her. From what Ethan had learned over the years, the Garcia family had been in Phoenix before Phoenix even existed.

The ladies came slowly up the walk. Ethan got out of his chair and offered it and the other patio chair to them. He took a seat on the front steps.

"Any luck with that pretty friend of yours?" Mrs. Garcia

was well aware of his interest in Sophia—this wasn't the first visit they'd had on the front porch.

"I think so," he said. "We've had dinner together the last two nights."

Mrs. Garcia nodded her approval. "But have you kissed her yet?"

Mrs. Garcia's daughter gave her mother a scolding look, but Ethan couldn't take offense.

"I'm working up to that. I don't even know if she's into me yet."

"Kiss her good, and you'll find out soon enough." Mrs. Garcia looked absolutely convinced of her strategy.

Ethan, however, was certain it wasn't the best.

"Anything interesting happen lately?" Mrs. Garcia's daughter asked.

Ethan realized he didn't know her actual name. Everyone called her "Mrs. Garcia's daughter."

"Sophia and I got a letter," he said. "To this address, without apartment A or B, addressed to someone named Eleanor. We couldn't make out the last name or the return address. The postmark is from 1953. We've been trying to figure out who she was and if there's any way to get it to her."

"'53?" Mrs. Garcia's daughter repeated. "That's the year I was born, so I'm not much help."

But Mrs. Garcia seemed to be pondering it. "The Bartletts lived here in '53," she said. Mrs. Garcia's mind was sharp as ever.

Why hadn't he thought to ask her? She'd lived in the same house since the late 1940s. "Was there an Eleanor Bartlett?"

Mrs. Garcia thought for a moment. "Caroline, Norma, and . . . Delores. Those were all the girls in the family. No Eleanor."

Ethan leaned back against the railing. If Mrs. Garcia didn't know of an Eleanor living at their house in 1953, maybe they'd never find her.

"Were there any Eleanors on the street? Maybe the envelope was addressed wrong."

But Mrs. Garcia was quick to shake her head. "I can't think of any."

"I'm friends with Norma Bartlett on Facebook," Mrs. Garcia's daughter said.

Both Ethan and Mrs. Garcia stared at her for a minute.

"Don't look so shocked. I'm hip to social media."

Ethan had a momentary flashback to his childhood years of using terms like *hip to* and *square*.

"I'll ask Norma if she has any idea who this Eleanor might have been," Mrs. Garcia's daughter offered.

"Thanks," Ethan said. "We'd appreciate it. We've hit a bunch of dead ends."

"Why don't the two of you come over for dinner tonight?" Mrs. Garcia said. "We'll make enchiladas."

Ethan was game, but he didn't know what Sophia's plans were. "I'll ask her when she gets home."

"Do." Mrs. Garcia wiggled her white eyebrows.

Ethan couldn't help laughing.

"Enchiladas. Mmm."

Sophia walked at Ethan's side down the street toward Mrs. Garcia's house. She had agreed to their dinner appointment without hesitation. Ethan hoped the promise of his company was as much a part of her motivation as Mrs. Garcia's enchiladas were.

"Do you think she'll make tamales at Christmas again

this year?" Sophia asked. "I was the most popular person in the office last December when I brought them in."

"I convinced one of my colleagues to switch shifts with me so I could have a five-day weekend thanks to Mrs. Garcia's tamales," Ethan said. "They're worth their weight in gold."

"Just don't tell her that," Sophia said, a twinkle in her eyes. "She'll start charging us their weight in gold."

Ethan had the strongest urge to hold her hand. He had to tuck his hands into his jeans pockets to keep from acting on it. He'd made progress with their sort-of relationship, but he didn't think he'd reached that point yet.

Mrs. Garcia's daughter let them in. The house smelled amazing. Ethan's stomach growled loudly, earning him a shoulder push from Sophia.

"It's not my fault," Ethan said. "I missed breakfast."

"You probably slept through breakfast. You were pretty wiped last night." She didn't seem embarrassed or annoyed by it.

"Sorry about that. I feel like an idiot. You feed me dinner, and I crash on your couch."

She waved that off. "It's not like you're a total stranger."

Mrs. Garcia hugged them both and welcomed them. They took seats next to each other at the table. The dinner was every bit as mouthwatering as Ethan knew it would be. And Mrs. Garcia and her daughter were every bit as matchmaking minded as he feared they would be.

When he filled Sophia's cup with water, Mrs. Garcia commented on how sweet it was of him. When Sophia passed the salsa without him having to ask, Mrs. Garcia's daughter wondered out loud when the two of them had come to know each other so well. They helped clear the table, and Mrs. Garcia declared they were "such a great team."

Sophia's cheeks pinked up. Was she embarrassed? Or was she blushing because she was interested in him but hadn't admitted it yet?

Either way, he wasn't going to let her face the teasing alone. He set his arm around her shoulders. She didn't pull away. Not even a little. He might have been deluding himself, but Ethan thought she even leaned a little closer.

For just a moment, his breath caught too much to talk. But he found his voice. "The two of you'd better be nice to Sophia," he said. "She'll give your computers a virus."

Mrs. Garcia shrugged like it didn't matter at all.

"Speaking of computers," Mrs. Garcia's daughter said, "I went on Facebook today and left a message for my friend Norma."

Sophia turned to look at him. He still stood with his arm around her shoulders, which put them nearly nose to nose. He had to think hard to keep breathing.

"Norma is the friend who used to live in our house, right?" she asked.

He nodded. *Breathe.* He liked that she called it *their* house.

"Come on into the living room, you two," Mrs. Garcia's daughter said. "I'll read you what she said."

As they followed, Ethan let his hand drop from her shoulder to her back, leading her along beside him. She didn't object to the touch. She didn't pull away.

"Do you know what Mrs. Garcia's daughter's name is?" Ethan whispered directly into Sophia's ear. *Breathe,* he reminded himself again.

"Everyone's always called her 'Mrs. Garcia's daughter,'" Sophia whispered back. "I think that may be her legal name."

They settled onto the loveseat, which was conveniently smaller than a sofa. Ethan had the perfect excuse to sit very close to Sophia. He couldn't be certain, but he thought she sat a little closer than necessary.

Mrs. Garcia's daughter sat at the desktop in the corner and put on a pair of reading glasses. "Here it is. Norma thinks her aunt Ellie lived with them for about a year while her husband was fighting in Korea. She's going to check with a cousin of hers and find out."

"'Ellie'?" Sophia repeated. "Could that be short for Eleanor?"

Mrs. Garcia's daughter looked over her spectacles at them. "I'd say so. I asked about any Eleanors at their house, and she thought of her aunt right off."

Sophia looked up at Ethan, excitement twinkling in her beautiful brown eyes. "This could be it. We might have solved the mystery."

"Sounds like it." He tentatively set his arm around her again. She leaned against him.

Breathe. Breathe.

"Will you let us know what Norma hears from her cousin?" Sophia asked Mrs. Garcia's daughter.

"Of course."

They spent the rest of the evening comfortable on the love seat. She stayed there with his arm around her shoulder while they talked to the older women. Ethan's heart pounded so hard, he expected it to pop right out of his ribs. But Sophia was there with him. He wouldn't change a thing.

The walk back to their house was slow and leisurely. They didn't talk much, just walked.

They stopped on their porch, standing there in awkward silence. Ethan wasn't sure what to say. Should he talk about

Eleanor? That was what had finally brought them together. But if that was all they had to talk about, where could their relationship even go?

"I can't wait to hear if the Bartletts' aunt Ellie is the Eleanor from our letter," Sophia said.

"That'd be cool." *That'd be cool? What is this, high school? I'm being a complete idiot.*

Sophia leaned against her door. Did that mean she was anxious to go inside? Ethan never had been good at figuring those things out. "I wonder if Ellie is still alive," Sophia said. "She's probably Mrs. Garcia's age."

"Probably."

Sophia brushed a stray ebony hair out of her face. The gesture was mesmerizing. Either he was totally gone on her or . . . No. He was totally gone on her. That's what it was.

"So . . . uh . . ." What could he say? Sometimes they talked about work, but he'd had the day off. "Maybe you could come over tomorrow night. I'll cook."

"Frozen pot pies?" Sophia's smile got to him every time.

"Nah," he said. "I have the day off. I'll actually cook this time."

"You really do know how to cook?" Obviously she doubted it.

Ethan leaned his shoulder against the wall near her, close enough for a conversation but with enough distance that she wouldn't panic if he was interpreting this whole thing differently than she was.

"My brother and sister and I all had to learn to cook growing up," Ethan said. "It wasn't optional."

"That's smart. Your parents didn't have to cook every night." She turned so she was facing him more directly. "And now it makes you popular with your neighbors."

"With *all* my neighbors?" *Lamest pick-up line ever.*

Sophia shrugged. "Probably not with Mrs. Garcia or her daughter. They can outcook anyone."

"I'll give it my best shot," Ethan said.

She brushed at that same stray hair, which made Ethan wonder if doing so was some kind of signal he didn't know about.

"So, I guess I'll see you tomorrow night," Sophia said.

Disappointment settled like a weight in his chest. He wasn't the smoothest of guys, but he was making some progress. If she went inside this soon, he'd never get past the standing-near-her-on-the-porch stage to any of the other stages that came next. He'd had his arm around her at Mrs. Garcia's house, but she hadn't held his hand on the way home, hadn't lingered very close by when they got home.

"Yeah." He did his best to act like it was no big deal. "See you after work tomorrow."

"See ya."

She slipped inside, closing the door behind her. Ethan stayed on the porch, telling himself he was an idiot. Either she wasn't interested and he was chasing after her pointlessly, or she *was* interested, and he just blew it.

5

Sophia left work about an hour early so she'd have time to shower and change before walking across the porch to Ethan's side of the house. Something had gone wrong the night before, but she still had no idea what. He'd sat with his arm around her on Mrs. Garcia's couch. He'd walked home with her, and a couple of times, she'd thought he was going to hold her hand. But he never did. Then, on the porch, she'd leaned in a little close to him, fussed with her hair, given him her best *I'm interested* smile, and he still didn't take her hand or try to hug her. He certainly didn't look like he'd wanted to kiss her.

Though Sophia didn't think she could blame her personal hygiene, she wasn't taking any chances. She blow-dried her hair and added some curl with her flatiron. She pulled on her favorite pair of skinny jeans, coupling it with a great top she'd found at a boutique nearby and a pair of yellow ballet flats.

She gave herself a quick check. Casual but on trend. Nice, but not like she was trying too hard.

"Just don't blow it," she told her reflection.

Sophia knocked at Ethan's door. She was even more nervous than she had been three nights before when she'd first had dinner with him. Had it really only been three days? She'd known him for months, but the past week had seemed the longest part of it, in the best way. She'd started believing it was possible that he returned her feelings. The combination of hope and doubt was exhausting.

The door opened.

"Hey, Sophia." He always greeted her with *Hey*. Was she just imagining that he'd said it with more feeling than he used to?

"Hey."

"Are you up for a car trip?" Ethan asked.

She hadn't seen that coming. "Trying to get out of cooking dinner again?"

He chuckled. She loved the sound of his deep, rumbling laugh. "Nope. Mrs. Garcia's daughter talked to Norma's cousin."

"I hope I'm not expected to repeat that."

His smile was adorably lopsided. She couldn't help smiling back.

"This cousin," he said, "is the daughter of her aunt Ellie, whose full name, as it turns out is Eleanor Gibbons."

Sophia's heart leapt at the name. "Is she *our* Eleanor?"

Ethan stepped onto the porch next to her. "It looks like she is. She did, in fact, live in this house with the Bartletts in 1953 and part of 1954."

Excitement twisted her stomach around. Her mind raced. No words would fully form on her lips.

"Grab the letter," Ethan said. "We're headed to Paradise Valley."

"What's in Paradise Valley?"

He set a hand on each of her arms just below the shoulders and looked excitedly into her eyes. "Eleanor."

"She's still alive?"

He nodded. "She's living with her daughter, the one Mrs. Garcia's daughter found. They're expecting us tonight."

"I can't believe this. We found her in less than a week."

"Grab the letter," he repeated. His eyes danced with as much anticipation as she felt.

In a matter of minutes, she had the letter, her phone, and her purse and was sitting in the passenger seat of Ethan's car heading north on Central. Would Eleanor be glad to see the letter? What if her memory was gone, and the letter meant nothing to her? What if it brought bad memories or sadness?

Her misgivings must have shown in her face. Ethan reached over and briefly squeezed her hand with his. "Whatever happens with Eleanor," he said, "at least the letter will finally be delivered to the right person."

"I'm dying to know what it says," Sophia confessed. "I've been tempted to open it so many times. Do you think she'll let us read it?"

"I don't know." He turned into the drive-through lane at Lenny's Burger shop. "It's not a gourmet meal, but—"

"Are you kidding? Lenny's is the best. Besides, I could really go for a cheeseburger right now."

"Bacon cheeseburger for me," Ethan said. "And a chocolate milkshake."

"So basically you're going to die of heart disease right here in the car."

"What a way to go, huh?" he said.

Ethan didn't let her pay for her meal, insisting he was treating, since he didn't cook her the dinner he'd promised. Sophia decided to let that mean it was a date. A person could do that, right? Decide something was a date without actually asking the other person?

"My mom would kill me if she knew I was eating in the car," Ethan said as he turned off Central and on to Indian School Road.

"Because it's not healthy?" Sophia was digging into her own meal, so she certainly wasn't criticizing.

Ethan nodded. "And messy."

Sophia would have added *dangerous* to the list, except Ethan put his burger down whenever he was actually driving, only taking bites at red lights. Either Ethan was a very safe driver, or, as a hospital nurse, he'd seen too many people after car accidents.

"Would you do me a favor?" Ethan asked.

"Sure." She'd happily do just about anything for him.

"Grab my phone and turn on the GPS. I know basically where we're headed, but not exactly."

She picked up his phone from the between-seat console and turned on the screen.

"You seriously need a phone upgrade." She searched through his apps until she found the GPS.

"Tell me about it. My contract's up in a couple months, and I'm definitely getting rid of that dinosaur."

The GPS app already had a Paradise Valley address entered, so she tapped "Navigate." The phone voice told them to get on the Piestewa Freeway, something Ethan was already doing.

"So, you wanna come with me?" he asked.

Her immediate answer was yes, but she traded that out for the less desperate, "Go with you where?"

"To pick out a new phone," he said. "You probably know all the new stuff."

"Because I'm a computer geek?" She wiped ketchup from her mouth with a paper napkin.

"Exactly. And there's nothing better than a computer geek helping out a wannabe technology geek, especially if that wannabe doesn't want to end up stuck with a lame phone for another two years."

Going shopping together. She liked the idea. "Does this mean you only like me for my brain?" *Please don't let that sound weird.*

"Among other things." He made the comment off hand, but it struck Sophia with tremendous force.

"Among other things." What other things? But she didn't ask. Sophia, when it came down to it, was a chicken.

They followed the phone's directions all the way to a home that was modest by Paradise Valley standards. Sophia checked her teeth in the visor mirror. When she looked back toward Ethan, he was watching her with a completely unreadable look on his face. "What?"

He just shook his head and shrugged, the same half-smile, half *something* on his face. "Shall we go meet Eleanor?"

Sophia grabbed her purse—the letter was inside—and got out of the car. Ethan came around and met her there.

"I don't know why I'm nervous about delivering this letter," she said.

Then Ethan did something she wasn't expecting. He held his hand out to her. She tentatively put hers in it, half convinced he'd pull away. Instead, he wrapped his fingers around hers and walked with her up the concrete walkway toward the front door.

"Don't sweat it," he said. "The worst they can do is slam the door in our faces. Or let their mastiff attack us on the doorstep."

"Nice." But she appreciated the teasing and the hand to hold.

Ethan rang the bell, and they waited. He didn't let go of her hand but stood there as if it were the most natural thing in the world.

A woman answered the door, probably about the same age as Sophia's mom.

"Hello. I'm Ethan Williams."

"Yes." The woman's face lit up. "You've come with the letter. Come in. Come in."

They stepped inside. Ethan squeezed her fingers for a moment, not letting her go. Sophia didn't know which made her stomach flutter more: her nervousness over the letter or the feel of Ethan's hand around hers.

"I'm Georgia," the woman said.

"Sophia."

"My mother is in the living room, but, if you don't mind, I'd like to see the letter before we show it to her." Georgia's eyes moved from Ethan to Sophia and back again. "I haven't told Mother about it. Her health is fragile, and since my father died, she's so easily disappointed. If it's not a letter to her, or nothing more than an old bill or something like that, I'd rather not get her hopes up."

"Of course." Sophia pulled the letter out of her purse and handed it to Georgia. She watched the woman's face for some sign of recognition. Georgia turned the letter over in her hand a couple of times.

"I can see why you were stumped," Georgia said. "I can't make out a last name or a return address or anything. But my mother was living at that address for most of 1953, so I'd guess this letter was for her."

A bubble of excitement began expanding in Sophia's chest. They'd found Eleanor. She looked up at Ethan and saw the same eagerness in his face.

Georgia broke the seal on the envelope and carefully pulled out the paper. Sophia held more tightly to Ethan's hand. She'd wondered again and again what was in that letter. They would soon know.

"Oh, good heavens." Georgia gasped, pressing a hand to her lips. "This is a letter from my father." She glanced at the two of them before returning her gaze to the letter. "He wrote it just before he left for Korea."

This *was* the right Eleanor! Sophia grasped Ethan's arm with her free hand, hardly able to contain her excitement.

"I know," he whispered, not needing her to explain her enthusiasm.

"Mother will be beside herself." Georgia's grin spread ever wider. "Do you mind staying a few minutes? I'd love for her to meet the couple who found this letter."

Ethan agreed without even a word of correction on their couple status. Sophia wasn't about to make any objections.

"Mother," Georgia said as they came into the living room. "This is Ethan and Sophia. They live in the Bartletts' old house."

A woman seated in an easy chair near a tall window looked up at them as they approached. She had hair the brilliant shade of white that never failed to look sophisticated. Her face bore the tell-tale wrinkles of age, but her eyes looked as alive and alert as a twenty-year-old's. This was their Eleanor.

"How is the old house?" Eleanor asked. Her frail frame

trembled as she sat there, but she kept her gaze firmly on them.

"It's charming." Ethan sat on the sofa nearest her. "And the ash tree in the front yard, I'm told, was a sapling when you lived there."

Eleanor nodded. "I helped my nieces and nephew plant it while I lived with them."

Sophia leaned against Ethan as he talked to Eleanor about the house and neighborhood. He had a way with people. Had he developed that ability out of necessity in his profession, or had the talent led him to his chosen career? Either way, Sophia knew he was good with his patients. She hoped they appreciated him.

Ethan leaned back and shifted so his arm rested around Sophia. He'd done that the night before at Mrs. Garcia's. He tucked her into the crook of his arm. Sophia gladly settled there.

"They brought something for you, Mother," Georgia said when the conversation lulled a bit. She gave her mother the yellowed envelope with the letter folded alongside it. "This was delivered to their house, but it's addressed to you."

"For me?" Curiosity filled every line of Eleanor's face. She put on her reading glasses hanging from a chain around her neck. "1953? My, but this was late in coming."

Sophia and Ethan watched in silence as Eleanor read the letter. Her eyes slowly filled with tears.

"Mother?"

Eleanor pressed the open letter to her heart. "It's from my Jerry. My sweet, sweet Jerry."

Georgia watched her mother with an equally teary expression. A lump started to form in Sophia's throat as well.

"Oh, I can't tell you what this means." Eleanor's voice

broke a little. "He says he misses me. That he hopes I'll find something to pass the time while we're apart, that he'll see me again soon." Her lips and voice trembled. "I can hear him saying those words, those exact words to me now. Then he was off to Korea. Now he's..."

Sophia pressed her lips together to keep them steady. *Now he's passed on.* Eleanor missed her husband, likely more than she had when he'd gone to war. And this letter, lost for so many decades, was like a voice from the past, helping ease the loneliness.

Eleanor insisted on hugging them both several times and thanking them over and over. She and Georgia were in tears by the time Ethan and Sophia left. She got as far as the curb before she had to blink back a tear herself.

Ethan hadn't gone around to get in the car. He stood beside her, one hand on the door handle. "Sophia?" He looked a little concerned.

She shook her head and smiled at him. "I'm so glad we got that letter to her. It meant so much."

"So am I." Ethan glanced back at the house. "She obviously misses her husband. It's nice to give her back a piece of their life together."

"Makes me hope we'll get another sixty-year-old letter," Sophia said.

Ethan opened her door. "Maybe we will."

In another minute, they were on their way. Night had fallen and, with it, a calm peacefulness.

"We make a pretty good mystery-solving team," Ethan said.

"Yeah. Look out, Scooby-Doo," she said. "Although I was sad that no one blamed something on us 'meddling kids.'"

"That would have been awesome." There, again, was that deep chuckle she liked so much.

They talked about inconsequential things all the way back home. It was an easy conversation, comfortable, and blessedly not awkward. But it also wasn't deep or personal. Not promising.

She'd only fallen more in love with him over the hours they'd spent searching for Eleanor. She desperately wanted him to feel the same way.

6

Putting on a blue button-up business shirt and black dress slacks to meet Sophia for their daily mail sorting was probably overkill. But if he was going to ask her out, he wanted to make a good impression. That was also the reason for the red roses.

She's gonna know I'm crazy about her. He didn't really care anymore. Two evenings spent with his arm around her had driven home an inarguable fact: having her in his life was too important to leave it up to chance. Maybe she'd brush him off or laugh at him, but at least he'd know.

Ethan tapped the corner of the pile of mail on the patio table. Sorting mail didn't usually make him jittery. Maybe if he practiced what he planned to say his nerves would calm down?

"We should go out." *No. Too abrupt.*

"I'm pretty much in love with you." He dismissed that opening line as well.

"Are you busy tonight? Wanna have dinner with me?

No pressure. You can say no if you want." That just sounded stupid.

Before he could try out any other approaches, Sophia's door opened. Was it his imagination, or did her face light up a little when their eyes met?

"Hey, Sophia," he said.

"Hey. You're all dressed up." She was absolutely checking him out. That was promising. "Do you have a date or something?"

She was not only checking him out; she sounded disappointed at the possibility of him seeing someone else.

"I may have a date," Ethan said. "Depending on how the mail sorting goes today."

"She's sending her answer by mail?"

Ethan decided to play it cool and mysterious. He sat in his usual chair and started dividing the mail. "Computer-parts catalog." He held it up before sliding it across the table toward her. "This bill's mine, but you can have it if you want."

Sophia didn't sit across from him like she usually did. She just watched him silently.

Ethan kept sorting the mail. "Who gets the junk mail today?"

Sophia hadn't moved, hadn't looked away from him.

"You okay?" he asked.

Her eyebrows scrunched in, worry in her eyes. "*Do* you have a date . . . or something?"

He didn't need any more encouragement than that. "I'm not sure." Ethan snatched the dozen red roses from under the table. Sophia eyed them suspiciously.

"I was hoping these may help convince her," Ethan said. "What do you think?"

Sophia's shoulders drooped, and she looked away. "She'll love them."

He immediately changed tactics. He set the roses on the table and crossed to where Sophia stood, very near her door. She looked nervous, which actually helped him be less so.

He took both of her hands in his. "Sophia."

She didn't quite look at him.

"I've been sitting out here waiting for you, trying to think of a way to ask you what you're doing tonight."

That brought her eyes to his for just a moment.

"And I almost got thrown out of the flower shop because I kept changing my mind about red roses versus white roses." He slid one hand up her arm, pulling her a little closer. "I have reservations at three different places because I didn't know which you were more likely to say yes to."

With that, he had her full attention. "*Me*?"

Ethan nodded. "We're a good team, and not just with solving mail mysteries. We both know how to promise to cook someone dinner but end up serving fast food."

The corner of her mouth tugged upward.

"And we're both good at eating enchiladas with neighbors," he added.

Her smile grew. Ethan snaked one arm around her waist. Sophia set a hand on his chest. She could probably feel his heart pounding. They were close enough he could see flakes of gold in her brown eyes.

"So, you wanna go out . . . or something?" he asked.

"I've been hoping you would ask me that for months."

Her candid confession inspired one of his own. "I almost have, a dozen times since you moved in. But I always chickened out."

"I'm glad you didn't this time."

"So is that a yes?" He hoped so.

Sophia nodded. Her gaze wandered to his lips, and her cheeks reddened. That was all the invitation he needed.

He slipped his hand to the back of her neck and pulled her up to him. Slowly, so she could tell him if he'd made a mistake, he lowered his mouth to hers. She leaned in, meeting him in the middle. Neither of them initiated the kiss, it simply started between them. He held her as closely and as tightly as he could. She clung to him, and he held her in return.

Sophia whispered his name against his lips, and he was a goner. He kissed her long and good there on the porch. Ethan lost himself in that kiss, putting months of longing into every moment. He knew without a single doubt that she felt the same way. They'd wasted enough time. Two people, sharing a house, sharing a porch, but living separate lives, brought together by a single, long-lost letter.

ABOUT SARAH M. EDEN

Sarah M. Eden is the author of multiple historical romances, including *Longing for Home*, winner of *Foreword* magazine's IndieFab Gold Award and the AML's 2013 Novel of the Year, as well as Whitney Award finalists *Seeking Persephone* and *Courting Miss Lancaster*.

Combining her obsession with history and affinity for tender love stories, Sarah loves crafting witty characters and heartfelt romances. She has twice served as the Master of Ceremonies for the LDStorymakers Writers Conference and acted as the Writer in Residence at the Northwest Writers Retreat. Sarah is represented by Pam van Hylckama Vlieg at Foreword Literary Agency.

Visit her website at www.sarahmeden.com
Twitter: @SarahMEden
Facebook: Sarah M. Eden

SILVER CASCADE SECRETS

Rachelle J. Christensen

Other Works by Rachelle J. Christensen

Wrong Number

Caller ID

Diamond Rings are Deadly Things

1

"Again!" a little girl squealed as she brushed leaves off her pants.

I smiled and continued digging in the flower bed, planting tulip bulbs. Silver maple trees lined the sidewalks of Silver Cascade Park, where I worked five days a week as caretaker. My nails were bad because I didn't like gloves, and I had perpetual dirt stains on my knees, but it was my dream job.

I watched the girl sail into the pile of leaves and seconds later run to a man screaming, "Again! Again!"

As I wondered if they were father and daughter, a woman approached and hugged the girl. The man put his arm around her in a side hug, and they talked for a few minutes before the woman left with the little girl.

Hmm, didn't seem like a divorced couple, but then my people-watching skills had proven that there was always more than meets the eye. The man sauntered down the sidewalk. I thought I heard him humming something.

Carpenter jeans with a good fit were a weakness of mine, and his retreating form was straining my eyes, so I put some muscle back into the flower bed and grabbed another handful of tulip bulbs.

A few minutes later, a light wind picked up several leaves and sent them skittering across the sidewalk. The points of the maple leaves made a distinct sound, signaling that autumn had taken root in Boise, Idaho. I watched the leaves swirl and ignored thoughts of raking and leaf blowing.

The man had come back and was on his hands and knees, searching through the grass. His carpenter jeans had a dark wash, which complimented his olive-toned skin. He appeared to be in his late twenties, maybe a few years older than my twenty-five years. I approached him, kicking a few leaves up as I walked.

"Not to ask the obvious, but did you lose something?"

He looked up. "Yeah, my keys."

"I'm Jillian Warren, Silver Cascade Park caretaker and finder of many sets of lost keys. Would you like some help?"

He stood and brushed his hands on his pants then held out his hand. "Travis Banner. I'd love some help, because it helps to have keys if you want to drive home."

With a laugh, I shook his hand then knelt in the grass and began combing through the leaves. I stole a few glances in his direction. With dark hair and stubble along his jawline, he reminded me of Hook on my favorite TV show, *Once Upon a Time*, minus the sexy accent. "I saw you playing with that little girl. Is she your daughter?"

"My niece. I'm not married, but I like playing favorite uncle."

"It looked like you're were definitely in the running."

Hook, or Travis, looked even better with that info, and I

had to remind myself I was searching for keys, not a date.

"Four-year-olds are pretty easy to please." He nodded toward the flower bed I'd been digging in. "So do you like your job? The park is beautiful, by the way."

"Thanks. I do enjoy working here. I graduated in landscape architecture, and this seemed like a great stepping stone into the field. My grandma was a bit underwhelmed—not many bragging rights—but I really do like it more than I thought I would." I ducked my head, embarrassed at all the information I'd just given a stranger. Well, I knew his name, so he wasn't a complete stranger.

Travis met my gaze, picking up on my admission. "It's okay to love your job, even if it's different from what everyone else expects. I'm a diesel-engine mechanic. My white-collar dad definitely didn't approve of me donning the blue collar, but I love what I do and hope to have my own shop one day."

My hands stilled in the leaves, and I looked at Travis. He had dark brown eyes, unlike Hook, so surely he couldn't be an evil villain. "It's so nice to talk to someone who understands."

He paused, brushing a hand across the stubble on his chin. "I was thinking the same thing."

My heart felt jittery, and a rush of heat came to my cheeks. "Um, don't laugh, but I'm going to use my favorite trick to try to find your keys."

He raised his eyebrows. "I can't make any promises. I might laugh."

I shrugged. "Fair enough." Glancing behind me, I saw the remains of the leaf pile Travis had been tossing his niece into. The leaves crunched under my feet as I walked to the pile; I kicked some of the leaves then backed up a few paces.

Travis was hot, so it was worth embarrassing myself to find his keys. I lay flat on my belly and squinted at the millions of blades of grass and crumbled leaves scattered in the distance. A few strands had come loose from the knot of hair I'd fixed earlier, so I tucked them behind my ear. I heard Travis chuckle but ignored him and continued using the Warren Secret Spy Method, angling my head so my view skimmed along the ground.

Leaves crunched beside me, and I looked over to see Travis mimicking my pose. He winked at me. "I know this trick. My brother and I used to do it to find stray marbles in the gravel."

"Most kids know it, but most adults have forgotten."

"Or maybe they have more pride than we do."

I giggled and rolled over in the leaves, moving to a different vantage point. The sun chose that moment to break through the mass of cumulus clouds scattered across the sky. The leaves turned from red to golden, and I caught a glint of metal about ten feet in front of me.

"Aha!" I shouted and jumped up, keeping my eyes trained on the sparkle I'd seen. When I picked them up, the keys jingled together. "Found 'em." I dangled the keys triumphantly as Travis approached.

"Thanks, Jillian." Travis held out his palm, and I dropped the keys into it. "You're amazing." His tone was light, but I chose to find a deeper meaning in his words.

"Glad to help."

"I really appreciate you helping me out." Travis pocketed his keys. "There's this great café a couple of blocks down. They serve the best Mexican hot chocolate. Could I treat you to some?"

"I love The Sugar Cube. Let me just finish up with these bulbs."

"Ah, so you know the place. Let me help. I owe you big time." Travis followed me to the flower bed and plopped a tulip bulb into one of the holes I'd dug.

"Thanks." I examined his work with a nod. "I'm impressed you knew which way to plant the bulb. My brother doesn't know anything about flowers."

"I may be a bachelor, but my mother had a prized flower garden, and she taught me a few things." Travis pointed at my fingernails. "Her hands always looked like that in the fall—mine, too. She's been gone for almost ten years, but for a while, I had my own bulb garden in her honor."

I had started to curl my fingers inward at his attention, but the affection in his voice made me proud to show my work-worn hands. I patted the earth down around the new plantings. "Really? What was her favorite flower?"

"Daffodils. She must have had a dozen varieties. I always liked these little miniature ones she used to plant around the tulips." He got a faraway look in his eyes as he grabbed a handful of bulbs. "How about you?"

"Hyacinths. I'll be planting a pink variety tomorrow that I think smells a little like heaven."

As he reached for the last tulip bulb, his hand brushed mine. He liked the dirt under my fingernails. I almost laughed at the thought. Too many dates with businessmen, lawyers, and would-be doctors had me feeling ashamed of my chipped nails. Travis was different. We'd just had a conversation about varieties of flower bulbs. He was handsome and looking better by the minute.

We stood and brushed the dirt from our clothes. "Thanks for the help. I usually don't work this late, but I got a little carried away with this flowerbed."

"I'm sure it'll be beautiful. I'm glad you were still here."

His smile widened. "I have to say, I'm kind of glad I lost my keys."

The blush tinting my cheeks had me feeling like a school girl, so I hurriedly gathered my tools and tossed them in the back of the Gator—my golf cart on steroids. I loved driving it around the park.

"Can I give you a ride to The Sugar Cube?" he asked.

I looked at my dirt-smudged jeans and wrinkled my nose at the dark smear of mud on my t-shirt. "I'm kind of a mess."

"I think you look cute." He motioned to his right knee. "And look; I have a matching stain."

"Okay, let's go." I stowed my tools and followed Travis to his car.

2

The sunset tinged the sky with purple as we drove to the city center. Travis opened my door and grabbed a booth in the back corner of the café where it was quiet and the lights were dim. A few minutes later, we were warming our hands on mugs of hot cocoa topped with whipped cream. The jitters in my stomach were pleasant, but I wasn't ready to give in to them yet. This was a thank you, not a date—it had been too long since I'd had a good date.

"Have you lived in Boise long?" Travis asked.

"I'm pretty much a full-blooded Idahoan. How about you?"

"I've spent some time in Montana, but I'm back to my roots. It's nice to be close to family, especially since, well, Heidi is growing up fast."

I could tell he meant to say something else, and judging by the shadow that crossed his face, it was something painful. My curiosity reared its persistent head, but I sipped my cocoa and steered the conversation elsewhere.

"Guess how many bulbs I'll be planting in the park this fall."

Travis looked up and pretended to calculate. "Three-hundred."

I laughed. "I wish."

"More than that?" he asked, his eyes bright with interest.

"Only about five times more."

Travis whistled. "That'll mean a beautiful park come springtime, but that's a ton of work."

"I don't mind. We've never had this many to plant before, but someone donated money for a special memorial garden. I'm thrilled with the plans I've drawn up. It really is going to be beautiful."

"That's nice." Travis sat up straight and clenched his fingers into a fist.

"What's wrong?" I blurted before remembering that I barely knew him.

He swallowed, and when he looked at me, I could see a sparkle of moisture in his eyes. "I wasn't going to say anything, because it kind of kills light conversation, but I know about that memorial garden. The reason I moved back here has to do with my sister and my niece. It's a part of my reality that I can't get away from no matter how hard I try."

Again, I swallowed back my questions. "I'm sorry. We can talk about something else." I was ruining things by dominating the conversation with talk of bulbs and gardens. Did I really think this gorgeous guy would be interested in my fall planting plans?

"No, it's okay. That memorial garden is for Craig Simmons."

"Did you know him?" Something pinged in my brain at the name. The guy had been some kind of business consultant, and his firm had made the donation for the garden. I couldn't remember all of the details, but judging by the look on Travis's face, he was going to tell me.

"He was my brother-in-law. He was murdered six months ago."

I gasped. "That's terrible. I'm so sorry. I didn't mean to dredge up sad memories."

"Not at all. It's kind of a neat coincidence to meet the person in charge of Craig's memorial. His firm, True Assets, wanted to do something for the family. Kami suggested the park, because Heidi loved to go there with her dad."

I thought of the sloping ground covered with gravel on the north edge of the park, which had been cleared of crabgrass, dandelions, and June grass. It had been a sore spot in my park for the past two years, and I was happy to make something beautiful out of the offensive weeds.

"I'm sorry for your loss." I licked my lips before continuing. "I'll work extra hard on that garden."

"I'm sure you will. More than one person in this town has bragged about that beautiful park, and that's thanks to your care of it."

"Thank you." The boost to my ego was almost enough to drown out my curiosity. Almost. "Did they catch the person who killed Craig?"

Travis shook his head. "And they don't have any leads." He pushed his mug forward and rested his forearms on the table. "Before Craig died, he told Kami that she'd always be taken care of. The last time she saw him, he said that when the time was right, she'd understand everything. He died that afternoon. Kami said it was like he knew he was facing death, but there was nothing he could do about it."

"That's terrible. I remember hearing about the murder. I'm so sorry."

"I feel bad for Heidi. That's why I bring her to the park a couple of times a week."

"She's lucky to have such a wonderful uncle."

"Thanks. I wish I could help her more." He turned his mug slowly in his hands and took another sip. "Kami thinks Craig knew his killer—and that it wasn't random."

"Have the police included her in their investigation—you know, to see if he left a clue she'd recognize?"

He tightened his fingers around his mug, the tension of the conversation flowing out of his fingertips. "As much as they can," Travis answered. "It's been tough on her. She said that every time she searched through his stuff, it felt like he'd died all over again."

"That's awful. Is she doing any better now that you're here?"

He nodded. "She seems to be coping. She says it's helpful to see Heidi smiling more."

"I hope the police can solve the case, so you all can have closure."

He pressed his lips together then exhaled slowly. "We may have to find closure another way. I wish the police had more evidence to go on."

"How frustrating." I wanted to ask more questions, but I could see that the conversation was taking a toll on him. I sipped my cocoa and waited for him to take the lead.

He stared off into space for a moment, and I took the opportunity to study the flecks of gold in his brown eyes. His hair looked light brown from the front, but it darkened as it approached his collar. It was a bit on the shaggy side, and I surprised myself with the sudden impulse to run my fingers through the thick strands. He looked up and gave his head a gentle shake. "See? I told you it was a conversation killer."

"Not at all. I'm glad you shared it with me. It'll put more meaning into my work."

"So what do you do for fun?" he asked.

I jumped at the chance to lighten the mood. "Anything outdoors. Hiking, mountain biking, a little white-water rafting."

He smiled and nodded. "Sounds like my kind of fun."

My stomach flipped. "What's your favorite?"

"Hard to choose, but my bike hasn't seen any action since I moved back. Would you like to go for a ride with me?"

I nodded. "Sure. There's a path that runs along the river. It's beautiful this time of year." I tried to tone down the grin spreading across my face, because Travis had just asked me on a date to go mountain biking, *and* he liked the dirt under my fingernails.

"When do you get off tomorrow?" he asked.

"I was hoping to get an early start so I could finish up by three."

"Oh, do you already have other plans?" The disappointment on his face made my cocoa taste even sweeter.

"Just some errands. Nothing that can't be rearranged." I watched a smile return to his face. "But I'll need time to change. I could meet you at the park at four." It was mid-September, but already the nights were chilly. Afternoon was the perfect time to enjoy the outdoors. Biking was much more fun when I wasn't freezing.

"Sounds great. I'm only working a half day tomorrow,

because I've pulled too much overtime lately." He stifled a yawn. "This cocoa is making me sleepy."

"Me, too." I glanced at my watch and was surprised to see that an hour had already passed. It was almost eight o'clock. "Thanks for the treat."

"Thank you," Travis replied. "I'll give you a ride to the park."

On the way back we shared mountain-biking stories. He told me about being chased by a "bear" that ended up being a large and friendly dog. I laughed until my sides hurt and found myself wishing the park was farther away so I could enjoy his company longer.

Travis offered me his arm as he walked me to where I'd left the Gator. I could feel his bicep underneath my fingertips, and for a minute I forgot where we were headed.

"You're so easy to talk to, Jillian. I'm looking forward to seeing you tomorrow." He covered my hand with his and gave it a gentle squeeze.

"Me, too." I liked the feel of his hand on mine. He released my fingers and took a few steps back as he fished his keys out of his pocket.

"I'll hold on to these." He jangled the keys and chuckled.

I pulled my keys out and held them up before sliding into my seat. Travis waved goodbye as I started the engine and turned the lights on his retreating form. Those carpenter jeans looked even better in the headlights.

3

Travis looked different when he rode up on his mountain bike in a pair of biker shorts that accentuated his muscular legs. I couldn't decide which I liked better, jeans or shorts?

"You look nice," he said. "I like that shade of blue on you." He pointed to my aqua t-shirt, which I'd selected because it accented my blue eyes.

"Thanks. It's my favorite color."

He slipped his sunglasses onto his head and swung off his bike. "I hope you don't mind the smell of diesel oil. I got caught finishing up a truck and didn't have time to shower."

I noticed dark spots of grease embedded in the lines of his hands and caught a whiff of motor oil. For some reason, the mechanic's cologne was a total turn-on. "Not at all. Besides, if you can keep up with me, you'll need a shower when we're done."

He lifted an eyebrow. "Competitive, huh?"

With a smile, I began pedaling. "Who, me?"

We biked the trails and did a little off-roading in a few spots. During a sprint, I ran Travis off the path. When we returned to the park, I was sweating and laughing.

"That was awesome." Travis stood and then groaned. "It's been way too long, though. I won't be able to walk tomorrow."

"Me, neither, but I'll be on hands and knees planting, so that's okay."

Travis chuckled and looked about to say more when his phone rang. "It's Kami. Mind if I take this?"

"No prob." I finished off my water bottle while he talked to Kami.

His tone turned urgent. "Are you sure?" He glanced at me and grimaced. "I'll be right there." He ended the call and pocketed his phone with a sigh.

"Is everything okay?"

"Kami was going through some more of Craig's stuff and thinks she found something important. She's a wreck. I'm sorry to do this, Jillian, but I'm going to have to run."

"Don't worry about it. Maybe it's something that will help you find his killer." I stowed the empty water bottle and wiped my hands on my shorts.

He scrubbed his foot along the grass. "I think that's partly why Kami's so upset." He stepped forward and took my hand. "I was hoping to extend our date—grab some dinner or something. Can I call you later?"

I was nodding before he finished. "Sure." Then I wrinkled my nose. "You need a shower anyway, remember?"

Travis laughed and squeezed my hand. "Thanks for understanding." He brushed his fingers across my cheek and tucked a strand of hair behind my ear. "I'll call you."

"I'll answer."

With a grin, he rode off in the direction of the parking lot, leaving me wondering what it would feel like to be kissed by him. That, and my ever-present connection to Nancy Drew had my mind occupied as I walked across the park. What did Kami find that had her so upset?

I rode home and showered, determined to look my best if there was a chance of seeing Travis later. My tan capris accentuated my long legs—I'd seen Travis checking me out a few times. I took a few minutes to swipe some dark-pink polish on my toes before slipping on my sandals. I straightened the lace on my fitted tee in a shade of fuchsia that matched my toes. I liked the contrast of the pink with my dark hair. I might have checked my phone a bit obsessively while I applied eyeliner and mascara.

The mystery of what Kami discovered had my mind whirring with possibilities, and if I'd had a bit less pride, I would've texted Travis to see if everything was okay. My heart felt hopeful about the possibility of dating him. We'd had so much fun earlier, and he seemed to really get me. Plus, he wore carpenter jeans.

While checking my phone for the umpteenth time, it started playing Taylor Swift's latest hit, and I almost dropped it when I saw Travis's number.

"Hello?" I tried to sound demure but failed terribly.

"Jillian, I'm so glad you answered."

"Me, too." I wondered if he could hear the smile in my voice.

"Look, this is going to sound forward, but could I bring some dinner to your place? And, well, I need to talk to you about something concerning Craig's death."

"You can come over now. How's that for forward?" I answered.

He chuckled. "Chinese or pizza?"

"Sesame chicken, please, and an egg roll."

"I'll be there in half an hour. Just tell me how to get there."

I rattled off directions and held in my squeal until after I ended the call. I had just enough time to tidy up. As I got the table set for Chinese takeout, I thought about how Travis sounded nervous. Threads of anxiety competed with the butterflies in my stomach. I was excited to see him but apprehensive about having anything to do with his brother-in-law's tragic death.

My last relationship started off similar to this one. I pushed thoughts of Caleb from my mind, but not fast enough. I still felt the twinge of the broken pieces of my heart, which I'd thought would be mended by now. Was I strong enough to take another chance at dating? Maybe I shouldn't have appeared so eager with Travis, but there was something different about him.

My doorbell rang exactly forty minutes after his call, and my heart pinged happily in my chest as I walked to answer it. My mouth started watering as soon as I opened the door. It might have been the steamy aroma coming from the takeout boxes in Travis's hands, but he also looked delicious. He wore a brown bomber jacket, and when he smiled, his brown eyes crinkled around the edges.

"Hope you're hungry." He lifted the boxes and waggled his eyebrows.

"I'm starving," I replied. He had a nice mouth, and I mentally slapped myself when I thought about how it would feel to kiss him. *Don't rush it, Jillian.* "Come on back to the kitchen."

He followed me and set the food in the center of the

table. "You have a nice place. Thanks for letting me come over on such short notice."

"I'll admit that I was more than a little curious as to what you found out from Kami."

"Good. Let's eat, 'cause I'm hoping you can help me figure something out." He draped his leather jacket over a chair and took a seat.

"I should warn you that my dad likes to call me Nancy Drew."

With a chuckle, Travis popped open a box of egg rolls. "That may come in handy right about now." He bit into one of the spring rolls and fanned his mouth. "Mmm, these are good."

"Yes, they are. Now chew faster so you can tell me what's up."

He dumped some sesame chicken on his plate and smiled. "Kami was sorting through Craig's things again and found a card that seemed out of place. She didn't remember seeing it before, but it was from Craig and addressed to her." He finished chewing a bite of chicken and pulled a card out of the pocket of his jacket.

"She let you have it?"

"I told her I'd make a copy and then see if I could figure out what it means. The note's cryptic. We think he was trying to say more than what is here." He handed me the yellow card, which was decorated with tulips.

With a quick breath, I flipped open the card and glanced over the flowing script printed in pink.

"Thank you for being the love of my life"

Below that was a handwritten note in black ink.

Kami,

I love you. I'm so glad that you brought your mother's love of flowers into our home. I especially loved our late-night walks to the park. I always want you to be safe. I'm glad Travis is such a great brother to you. We're lucky to have his support. I hope you understand that I'll always do my best to protect our family.

Love,
Craig

"Is there a date anywhere?" I flipped the card over, looking for more writing.

"No, but Kami's sure she never saw it before."

"It does seem like he's hinting at something, but what?"

Travis shook his head. "By the time I got there, she'd already ripped apart the tool shed, looking for bags of tulip bulbs and hidden messages. I helped her go through every box of mementos, cards, and anything else before I told her to wait and see if something else turns up."

"I think that's wise. Maybe she'll think of a connection later. He obviously wanted you to see the note." I tried not to let my disappointment show. I was hoping for something that would shed light on Craig's murder. A love note didn't help at all. If anything, I was more curious now.

Travis and I chewed in silence for a moment. He reached across the table and covered my hand with his. "Thanks for letting me come over. It's really nice to talk to someone about this." He squeezed my hand before pulling away and taking a drink of water.

"I'm glad you could come. I just wish I were more help." The feeling of his hand over mine lingered, and I didn't want him to leave yet. Unfortunately, my phone buzzed from the kitchen about the time I was going to ask him to stay and watch a movie.

Travis glanced at the clock, and I think we were both surprised to see that it was almost ten. "Look, I'd better go. I have a full day tomorrow, but can I see you again?"

My insides were fluttering with butterflies, and I felt like I had a perma-grin. "I'd like that. I'm heading to the park super early tomorrow to finish up planting. Maybe we can do something early evening?"

"I'd like that." My phone rang, probably because I'd ignored the text. "I'm guessing that's my sister. She'd better have something good to say."

"No worries. I'll call." Travis gave me a hug, and for a moment I thought he was going to kiss me. He hesitated near my face, then pulled back. "Thanks again for letting me come by."

4

The front-room window shades were slanted, so I could see Travis get in his car and drive away. I touched my lips, surprised at how much I longed for a kiss from him while, at the same time, I was grateful he'd held back. We'd only known each other for a day, but already I missed his presence.

As I headed to grab my cell phone, which was ringing for probably the fifth time, I thought of the losers I'd dated in the past. I snatched it and pushed accept at the same time I noticed that it wasn't my sister calling.

"Damn," I said as I put the phone up to my ear and contemplated just ending the call.

"I'm guessing that 'damn' was meant for me, but I hope you'll listen for ten seconds."

"Caleb, I thought I blocked your number."

"Don't hang up! Just give me one minute," my ex-boyfriend pleaded.

"It's late, and we agreed not to call each other anymore, remember?" At one time, I'd fallen for Caleb and his rugged good looks. He'd seemed so put together—an anesthesiologist with a nice home and no baggage—or so I thought. We'd been dating for two months when he told me that his divorce wasn't final yet, and that his wife wanted them to give it one more shot.

I wanted to shoot him.

"Please, Jillian. I promised to always be honest with you, and I really need to tell you something." The urgency in his voice chipped away at my resolve.

"One minute. And I'm timing you." I glanced at the clock—it was fifteen after ten.

"My divorce is final. Turns out Sandra was just hoping to squeeze more money out of me. For the past six months, I've lived with regret because I messed everything up with us. I love you, and I'm begging for you to give us one more chance."

My mouth opened and closed. Had Caleb just said he loved me? My mind warred with anger and memories traced with the happiness I'd felt while we dated. I'd really cared for him, but he broke my heart when the truth came out and he went back to his wife.

"I know it's a lot to take in," he said. "But I can't live like this. Please. Can I come see you?"

"It's getting late, and I have an early morning tomorrow."

"Could I see you tomorrow to talk for a few minutes?" His voice was soft.

"You really hurt me—"

"And I promise never to do that again. I just want to see you," Caleb cut in. "I made a mistake, and I've been paying for it ever since. I know it's a lot to ask you to forgive me, but I love you so much. I need you."

The emotion in his voice had me cracking; I couldn't allow that. "I'll think about it, but I probably can't see you tomorrow or maybe ever. Good night." I ended the call, even though he'd started to say something else.

I went to the kitchen and got a drink of water. My emotions were boiling, and suddenly I felt like crying. That made me angry; Caleb had ruined my chance to bask in the warmth of Travis's closeness as we'd sat at my kitchen table and talked. I shook my head. I didn't want to mess things up with Travis when we were barely connecting, but I also couldn't ignore the feelings of longing rising from memories laced with heartache, all featuring a man with eyes the color of a stormy day.

My breath caught around a sob working its way up my throat, and my eyes filled with tears. But I wouldn't cry over Caleb anymore. Every minute with him had been perfect until I found out it was all a lie. With a hard swallow, I swiped a hand across my eyes.

My phone pinged with a text, and I grumbled as I opened it, but the grumbling stopped when I saw it was from Travis.

Hey, Miss Curious, thanks again for giving up your night to help me puzzle things out.

The tingles that had evaporated with Caleb's call returned full force as I relived the tender way Travis had held me. But the moment couldn't compete with the memories crowding at the edge of my consciousness, all revolving around Caleb.

I'd loved Caleb for a few weeks and thought that maybe he was the one. It took me nearly six months to get over him and the hurt. It was so unfair that one day after meeting Travis, Caleb was confessing his love to me, dredging up all of the feelings I'd swept from my broken heart.

Rolling my shoulders back, I replied to the text.

My pleasure. I'm glad you shared the note and your Chinese food with me!

A minute after I hit send, my phone pinged again. I shook off my errant thoughts, smiling at what I expected would be a reply from Travis. My screen flickered, and I saw Caleb's name. I couldn't resist reading the text.

You're the only one for me. I'm sorry I messed things up the first time. Please give me another chance.

I groaned, grappling with mixed emotions of anger, hurt, and betrayal tinged with an unsettling fondness for the man responsible for the cracks in my heart. The sob inched its way farther up my throat. I was just about to turn my phone off when it pinged again.

The message was from Travis.

Sweet dreams, flower girl.

The sob turned into a hiccup, and I felt an echo of my earlier smile tug at the corners of my lips. No way would I mess things up with Travis because Caleb thought he had VIP status in my heart. For a moment, I considered texting Caleb my thoughts, but I knew he'd only argue back. Better to turn my cell phone off and have a good night's sleep.

5

The smell of damp earth and tulip bulbs topped my list of aromatic memories. I could almost see my mother's hands guiding my own small fingers to place the flower bulbs in the soft mulch of our flowerbed.

I thought about Travis Banner and his sister Kami, her grief over the loss of her husband, and the mystery of the cryptic notecard Craig Simmons had left his wife.

What was he involved in that got him killed? My best ideas always came when my hands were working the soil. Now I willed my mind to think of something, anything, to explain the note and Craig's premonition of his own death.

Something about flowers. Travis had mentioned his mother's love of flowers and how Kami shared that love and did her best to mimic their mother's talent. The mention of late-night walks in the park was also significant. Travis was sure Craig meant Silver Cascade Park. My mind turned over the possibilities as I planted dozens of tulip, hyacinth, and daffodil bulbs in a pattern I'd drawn on a piece of paper sitting in the dirt next to me.

"Jillian! I'm so glad I found you."

I jumped in surprise as I turned to see Travis jogging toward me. My heart did a triple flip, and I stood as he approached. "Good morning."

He cleared his throat, and I noticed his breath coming in short puffs. "Could you take a short break now? It's important."

"Uh, sure." I glanced at the bulbs arranged in neat piles, and Travis followed my gaze.

"I know you're really busy, but I need your help." His eyes were bright with excitement.

"Let me just cover the bulbs." I knelt in the dirt again and began packing the soil back into the holes, the dark earth cushioning the last fifty bulbs I'd planted. "Grab those burlap sacks, and cover the bulbs in that pile. I don't want them to dry out."

"Can I help you finish up? I don't want to mess up your hard work."

"If you'll cover those bulbs, I can finish planting this last row." I could see he was anxious, and for a moment I wondered if I should just leave the work; but a light wind had picked up, and it wouldn't take five minutes to plop the bulbs into the ready-dug holes. "Thanks for the help."

"I'm sorry to interrupt, but it's urgent." Travis covered the bulbs and dusted his hands off on his pants.

"No worries." I packed the last of the bulbs. "I needed to stretch for a minute anyway." I stood, and he grabbed my hand, tugging me in the direction of the parking lot.

"You won't believe what I got in the mail today."

I quirked an eyebrow. "Must be good for nine o'clock in the morning."

"Nine-fifteen. I was at the post office when it opened. I got a letter from Craig."

I sucked in a breath. "Another clue?"

Travis nodded and gave my hand a squeeze. "C'mon. I'll show you." He opened the door to his Subaru, and I climbed inside. The interior smelled like vanilla, and I noticed a few granola-bar wrappers on the floor. My stomach grumbled.

"Where are we going?" I asked after he sat in the driver's seat.

"Nowhere. I wanted to show you this where no one else would see." He pulled out a manila envelope from under his seat and waved it in front of me.

"Gee, that doesn't make me curious at all."

Travis chuckled. "I'm counting on your curiosity to help me figure this out."

"What is it?"

He lifted the flap and looked at me. "This was rerouted from Billings, Montana, and the original postmark was two months ago. Apparently, it was misdirected."

"Two months ago? Then how can it be from Craig? He died over six months ago, didn't he?"

With a nod, Travis pulled out a sheet of computer paper and handed it to me. "My guess is that he set it up with an automated service. If he lived, he could cancel the delivery. If he died . . ."

"Then it would go out in the morning post, but then you moved," I finished for him.

Travis scrubbed at his eyes then handed me the page. "See what you think."

The note was typewritten on plain, white paper with no header.

To: Travis Banner
From: Craig Simmons, True Assets Financial Support

Hey, bro. I'm worried about my family. I'm not sure what to do, but if you got this letter, it means something bad has happened to me. My first priority will always be my family, so I want you to know that if the police can't answer your questions, you're safe, and there's no need to worry. If you do need answers, try to console yourself by reliving the memories I made with Heidi in the park. She loved the flower gardens, especially the one with orange and white daffodils.

I'm sorry I can't say more. Please let Kami know that I did my best to stick around for her and Heidi.

I love you all.

Craig

"He's trying to tell you something." I handed Travis the page. "Do you know what it is?"

He took a deep breath. "I have a hunch, but it may sound wild, so don't laugh."

"Probably not any wilder than my imagination is right now."

Travis leaned closer to me, his relief evident as some of the tension from his face relaxed. "I think Craig hid something in your park—something that will identify his murderer." His voice was low and urgent.

"Why not in a safe-deposit box? Isn't that where people hide stuff before they get killed?"

"He must have been too afraid of giving his murderer any hints. Remember, his first priority was protecting his family."

I twisted my watch around my wrist. "And if Kami found a clue to his murder, she might be in danger. If so, it doesn't bode well for you."

"I'll be careful. But I don't see how anyone could know about this letter or Craig's hiding place."

"This sounds like a Grisham novel." I turned in my seat to survey the parking lot. "Do you think someone's watching your family?"

Travis followed my line of sight. "I'll admit I've been kind of jumpy since I got the mail, but I think we're safe. Enough time has passed that even if someone used to be watching Kami, they probably have become bored."

"Craig was an investment planner, right? That isn't supposed to be a hazardous occupation. So what happened?" My heart pumped faster as I thought about the danger we could be in. I watched Travis stow the manila envelope under his seat again.

"Craig was a smart guy. His clients loved him for his sharp eye and ability to put their money to work for them." Travis drummed his fingers on the steering wheel. "I've seen him investigate financials with a fine-toothed comb and find something that could completely change a person's life for the better. But maybe he found something dangerous—some information that could change a person's life by putting them behind bars."

I shivered. "That's scary. Are you going to take that letter to the police?"

Travis pressed his lips together and blew out a breath. "I probably should, but the way they've acted recently has my confidence waning. Besides, this wouldn't mean anything to them. Craig wrote to me for a reason."

"He knew you wouldn't be afraid to figure it out." I flicked a piece of dirt from the cuff of my jacket. "How can I help?"

Travis reached for my hand with a smile. "This is your

park. You know those flowerbeds like the dirt under your fingernails." He squeezed my hand, and I looked at my stained fingertips. "What are the chances that I'd meet the very person who could help me days before I received this letter?" His eyes were hopeful, and I couldn't argue with the providence of our meeting, but Craig had died because of what he'd discovered.

"I'm scared, but I'll help you."

Travis leaned closer and whispered, "I won't let anything happen to you."

His words sent a tingling of goose bumps down my arms. My face heated as I realized how much I wanted him to kiss me. I cleared my throat. "So, you want to know where the daffodils with the orange centers are?"

"It's a safe place to start, since you're already digging in the flower beds. Do you have some sort of map of the landscaping?"

I pulled the sketch out of my pocket that I'd been consulting earlier. The paper crinkled as I unfolded it. "This is the design for the memorial garden. I've made one of these for each of the flowerbeds I've worked on in the park. There are nine."

"Perfect. Can we take a look at the maps?"

"Sure. I keep a binder in the tool shed." I reached for the door handle, but Craig stopped me.

"I didn't mean to hijack your work. Are you sure you have time right now?"

"If I didn't, I'd make time, because I want to figure this out almost as much as you do."

The shed was on the other side of the park. I noticed Travis scanning the area more than once as we headed that direction. How nervous was he about the threat Craig had implied? I unlocked the shed and turned on the light. My insides felt jittery as I grabbed the binder and began leafing through the sheet protectors holding my designs. I'd made some of them in my college classes, and I remembered how proud I'd been to implement them into beautiful creations everyone in the city could enjoy.

"Do you change the flowers every year?" Travis asked as he leaned over my shoulder and studied the layouts.

"No, I planned these gardens as perennials, so the upkeep is substantially lower. Each year I do a little rearranging, but the main design stays the same." I flipped through a few more pages. "There are daffodils in about half of the flower beds, but different varieties in each, because I like to experiment to see which grows the best in our climate."

"Wow, you've done a ton of work here." He motioned to the binder. "This is really great."

"Thanks." I tapped the page. "The daffodils with the orange centers are only in two flower beds, if I remember right."

"But we can't just dig up the whole flowerbed," Travis said.

"We won't have to. The daffodils were blooming when he buried whatever he might have hid, so he would have to work around the flowers. Come on." I tucked the binder in between a few gardening catalogs on the shelf, then closed up the shed and headed straight across the park.

Travis walked briskly to keep up with me. "Thanks again for helping me. I hope it's not a wild goose chase."

I slowed and studied his expression. The sincerity in his eyes was touching, making me want to help him even more. "I just thought of something. I'm not sure he would have actually buried something. That seems too risky. What if he hid something by a tree, or a rock, or even by one of the garden statues? That's what I'd do."

Travis nodded. "Good point."

"Here's the first one." I motioned to the flowerbed devoid of daffodil blooms but still beautiful in its autumn wardrobe of decorative purple cabbages and bushy remnants of a dark-orange mum.

We knelt at the edge of the rich, brown soil. Travis scanned the area, scrunching up his eyes in thought. He turned to me and shrugged. "I guess we start digging?"

I handed him one of the two trowels I'd brought along. "You dig here. I'll check around the bushes and paver stones on the north edge."

We hunted around for the next twenty minutes, with me instructing Travis where to dig. He dug up a few bulbs, but we found nothing significant. We walked across the park and dug around in the other flower bed, with no luck.

Travis sat on the grass with a sigh. "I guess it was too much to hope that it would be easy."

I sat next to him on the grass. "I think we'll figure it out. Maybe we're missing something. You know, we may need to look at the letter from a different angle. Maybe there's a different code word we missed, and he mentioned the park to throw off any criminals intercepting it."

Travis frowned. "I doubt it, but I do think you're right that we're missing something."

He stood and pulled me up. My breath caught at his nearness. He stared at me for a moment, and the depths of his brown eyes were full of kindness and something else that made my heart do the cha-cha.

"Craig would be happy that you're helping his family," I said.

"'My family,'" Travis murmured. "Not much of our family left. I don't want to let him down."

"You won't. I'm going to help you."

Travis smiled. "I have a good feeling about you. You're smart. Maybe you'll be the one to figure it out."

I started to shake my head.

"Could I take you out to dinner tonight? I have a busy day ahead finishing a couple of trucks, but I'd like to repay your kindness." He touched my arm, resting his hand near my elbow.

"I can't think of anything better. Especially if it involves Mexican food."

"And I know just the place," he said. "Can I pick you up at five thirty?"

"Si, Señor."

Travis chuckled. "Hasta la vista, baby." He gave me a quick peck on the cheek, then lifted two fingers in a wave, his keys dangling.

My smile stayed in place the rest of the day. I kept thinking about the cryptic message Craig had sent Travis, vowing that I'd crack the code and help his family heal.

6

Dinner was fabulous. Travis took me to a local dive for some of the best nachos and enchiladas I'd had in quite a while. We laughed and talked as we worked on our monstrous plates, each moment lingering with the sparks flying between us.

"Man, that hit the spot." Travis rubbed his flat stomach and stretched as we walked to his car.

"I have a love affair with guacamole and good salsa."

"Good to know you have some weaknesses," Travis teased.

"Whatever. I'm a work in progress," I replied.

He opened my door and leaned toward me, his voice husky. "I think you're pretty wonderful."

I felt as if a rocket had launched in my chest. He closed my door and walked around the car, giving me time to cool the jet flames before he slid into the driver's seat. As he drove toward my house, I caught myself looking at his mouth. He gave my hand a gentle squeeze and didn't let go. The warmth of his fingers pressing against mine was comforting, and I found my mind wandering toward the gated area in my heart—the one I hoped to open again someday to a man worthy of my love. It was too soon to ponder any future with Travis, but that didn't keep me from longing for the companionship of someone who understood and loved me.

A few minutes later, we stood on my doorstep, holding hands. He smiled at me, and our eyes locked until I felt the warmth of my cheeks giving away my inner thoughts. I cleared my throat. "Um, maybe you could stay awhile, and we could watch a movie or play a board game?" As soon as I said it, I realized how needy and geeky I sounded. Dang. I should have just asked him to make-out on the couch. My face burned even hotter.

"Sounds fun. Do you have Yahtzee?"

My head jerked up, and my mouth opened, but before I could say something sappy, my witty side kicked in to save me. "Technically that's not a board game, but it'll work in a pinch."

"I wouldn't want to get hung up on technicalities, but if you're scared you'll lose, we can play something else."

I lifted my chin and rolled my shoulders back. "You're on, but I hope you know what you're in for." I shook my hand vigorously as if rolling dice.

With a nod, he followed me inside. "This day just keeps getting better."

I was certain he saw the flaming heat on my cheeks, but I hoped he thought my blush was cute instead of juvenile.

A few minutes later, the dice clacked in the little red cup, and Travis had me laughing with his whoops and hollers, but in the end, he won with a bonus Yahtzee. He jumped out of his seat and cheered, pulling me up with him.

"And the grand prize goes to Travis Banner, Yahtzee Champion."

"And what is the grand prize?"

He stopped cheering and stepped closer. "Isn't there usually something about a kiss from the fair maiden?"

My cheeks lifted in a grin. "I thought that was only in jousting or some other medieval game."

"Nah, I don't think so." His glanced at my lips, then met my eyes.

His aftershave smelled woodsy, and I leaned forward, breathing it in. He lowered his head, and I tipped mine instinctively to meet his mouth. The kiss was soft and tentative at first, but then I felt the space between us disappear as he put his arms around me. The sparks I'd felt earlier turned into full flames when his lips touched mine. His kiss was tender, and I let myself relax into his arms, my mouth moving against his as he held me close.

When he finally pulled back, his grin had brought out a small dimple under his eye I hadn't noticed earlier. "Can we play again?" he whispered.

I laughed and lifted up on my toes to place a kiss on either side of his mouth. "If I win, what's my grand prize?"

He pulled me closer and nuzzled my ear. "Maybe I'll just give you the consolation prize right now."

"Oh?" I tilted my head, my eyes focusing too much on his strong jaw and the bit of stubble on his chin, which made me want to kiss him again.

His hands ran up and down my sides, and suddenly he was tickling me, and I was screaming like a ten-year-old. I got away and ran into my living room. "That's not a prize." The couch stood between us, and I darted from side to side, laughing.

"It is." Travis jumped over the couch and grabbed me, pulling me down on the cushions.

I squealed, and he started laughing. "Let me explain how it works." His voice was husky. "I tickle you until you beg for mercy, and then I give you the consolation prize."

He kissed me again, and when I parted my lips, I could taste the desire he'd been holding back. My arms encircled his neck, and I returned the kiss, loving the way he held me gently against him, when moments before, he'd elicited squeals by tickling me. The moment felt perfect, like I never wanted to let go of Travis.

Then my phone buzzed from the kitchen.

Travis pulled back slightly, his face inches from mine. "Do you need to get that?"

"Definitely not."

He chuckled, kissing my top lip and then sucking on my bottom lip before sitting up on the couch. "Wow. I definitely want to beat you at Yahtzee again."

"You know this means war." I tried to sound serious.

He raised his eyebrows. "This soldier is tired, but I'm seeing you again tomorrow, right?"

"I wasn't quite finished with my consolation prize."

Travis tickled me, and I squealed again. "Not that!"

"Oh, okay. Just one more." He gave me a quick peck. "Would you like to get together for lunch tomorrow?"

"Yes, but how about if it's my treat? I make a mean picnic with the best macaroni salad you've ever tasted."

"A man never turns down home-cooked lovin'."

I blushed and scolded myself for wanting to kiss him again. The tips of Travis's ears were pink, and I stifled a giggle as he opened the door. "Good night, Jillian. Can't wait until tomorrow."

As soon as the door closed, I sighed, because Travis was the best kisser ever, and he'd pretty much ruined me for any other guy. Ten minutes later, my phone buzzed again. I checked my texts. The first was a banking reminder, but the second had my lips tingling.

Hey Yahtzee queen. I think we need a rematch. Thanks again for tonight.

7

I mixed up the macaroni salad and set it to chill in a large cooler before leaving for work. Travis said he could meet me just before noon. We wouldn't be staying in the park. I planned to take him up to some magnificent rose gardens I admired on the other end of town.

It took me about an hour, but I cleaned up the shed in preparation for winter. Most of my work for the fall was done, which meant I needed to start thinking about the lean times of winter and where I might make a little extra money. Last year I did some substitute teaching during the snow-covered months to offset the few hours I worked at Silver Cascade, but this year I had some ideas brewing about landscape design consulting for larger companies on their grounds. It was a big dream but one I felt was possible. I wanted to talk to Travis about it to see what he thought. My mouth twitched with a smile, because I knew he'd think the idea was great and encourage me to pursue it. He was that type of person.

After the shed was organized, I walked around the park, mentally drawing up a list of what else needed to be done before November. I stood in front of the fountain for a few minutes, watching the light dance across the water. Behind me, someone cleared their throat, and I startled, dropping a bag of tulip bulbs at my feet.

"Hi, Jillian."

I turned to face my ex-boyfriend. "Caleb?"

He took a step forward; I took a step back. "What are you doing here?"

"I've been trying to find you all morning. I really need to talk to you." He held out a paper bag with a large green ribbon tied at the top. "I brought you something."

I tentatively took the sack and pulled the ribbon off. Inside was a set of new gardening tools—nice ones. Sharp silver blades met the dark red ergonomic grip of the trowel. I pulled out the shears and the trowel, examining them. "Thank you. These look like they're high quality."

"I'm glad you like them. I hoped I'd picked out the right kind." He stepped forward again, and this time I didn't back up, although my body tensed at his proximity.

"You didn't have to bring me anything, but I appreciate it."

He put his hands on my arms. He was thirty-three, but he looked younger and more vulnerable when he was freshly shaven. I could smell his expensive cologne—he must have shaved before coming to see me.

"I love you, Jillian. I made a huge mistake—actually, a lot of mistakes, but if you'll just give me a chance, I can show you how much I've changed. You cared for me once, and I hurt you deeply. I understand why you don't want to see me, but please, reconsider."

His words flowed out and tumbled around in my mind, mixing with old emotions I'd tried desperately to banish. I shook my head. "I'm not ready to have my heart broken again. I don't want—"

Caleb pulled me close and kissed away the end of my sentence. For half a second, I relaxed into his embrace and savored the familiar softness of his lips. Then my mind snapped back to attention, and I pushed Caleb away.

"What are you doing? You can't kiss me like nothing has happened."

"I want another chance," he said. "Please?"

I turned and folded my arms, directing my gaze away from the helpless expression in Caleb's eyes. As I turned, I caught sight of a figure retreating down the sidewalk.

"Oh no!" I brushed past Caleb and ran after Travis. I started gaining on him near the parking lot, but by the time I reached the asphalt, he was already getting into his car.

"Travis, wait!" I yelled as he peeled out of the lot, zooming toward the road.

Just before he turned, I thought he caught sight of me in the rearview mirror, but I couldn't be sure. My shoulders slumped in dejection. Could anyone have worse luck?

"Jillian, what's going on?" Caleb ran up beside me and moved to put his arm around me.

I clenched my fists and swallowed a scream as I pulled away.

"I'm dating that guy. He must have seen you kissing me."

"Hey, you were kissing me back."

"Seriously?" I wanted to slap him, but I refrained. I rested my forehead on my hand, feeling a tightness behind my eyes. Blinking rapidly, I looked up and glared at Caleb.

"I'm dating someone else—or at least, I'm trying to. Please give me some respect and leave me alone."

"I'm sorry," Caleb said.

I turned and walked back to the flowerbed. He started to follow me. "If you'd just give me another chance."

"No!" I spun around, putting my hand out to stop him. "My answer is no. Go home." I turned and ran in the opposite direction.

When I reached the flowerbed, I saw the gardening tools Caleb brought me, and I growled. Stupid, stupid men messing up everything. I hated the way my heart was pumping with anguish, fear, and the tiny, niggling voice that said maybe I should give Caleb another chance. I shook my head. If Travis would listen, I could explain everything. But my hopes deflated, knowing how I'd feel if I caught him kissing another woman.

Lunchtime arrived and passed by. I didn't bother to look for Travis. I'd called and left him a message explaining my persistent ex. It was a safe bet that he'd heard my message, so I kept praying that he'd believe my words instead of what he saw with his own eyes. At two o'clock, my stomach rumbled so loudly I couldn't ignore it anymore. I broke down and ate some of the macaroni salad, but it didn't taste right without Travis there to share it with me.

I left the park at three forty-five, dirty and dejected, with a hot shower in mind to melt away my problems. When I got home, the shower helped, but the peanut-butter brownies I'd made for our picnic were just what I needed. A large dollop of vanilla-bean ice cream and hot fudge were practically anti-depressants in my book. I swirled the brownie around the melting ice cream and sucked the concoction off my spoon, closing my eyes and wishing I'd punched Caleb instead of letting him kiss me.

Ladling another sugar-coated bite chased the thought away, and I sighed as I munched the creamy goodness that only came from the perfect proportions of chocolate and peanut butter. My doorbell rang, and I sat up straight, glancing at my bowl full of illegal goods and swiping my hand across my mouth. When I checked the peephole, my stomach flipped, and I licked my lips, checking for any stray bits of hot fudge. Travis stood on my doorstep with a worried expression. I swung the door open.

"I'm so sorry about today," I said. "I've been having a pity party all by myself, wishing you'd seen me punch Caleb instead."

"You punched him?" Travis's eyebrows rose.

"No, but I wish I had." I stood to the side. "Come in."

Travis hesitated. "I'll be honest; I would be home licking my wounds, but something important has happened, and I needed to make sure you were okay." He stepped inside, and I closed the door.

"What is it?"

"Someone broke into my apartment and searched through everything."

"What?" My knees felt weak with fear. "Let's sit down." I motioned toward the loveseat.

"They broke out a back window and climbed through." Travis followed, sitting close to me and resting a hand on my arm. "They didn't trash the place, but it's a mess. At first, I panicked, thinking they'd go for you next, but the police wouldn't let me come until they took a statement and searched everything."

His worry was evident, and my mind was already racing through scenarios. What if someone was waiting outside right now?

"My house looked fine when I came home, but now I'm scared." I didn't like how tense Travis looked.

"The police will patrol the area around my home, Kami's, and yours. I told them everything and gave them the letters—all the info I had. They're taking it seriously. Nothing was stolen, so it has to be connected to Craig's murder."

My mouth felt dry, and I swallowed away the taste of terror building in my throat. "But how could they know that you found anything?"

Travis shrugged. "Maybe they don't. I'm hoping that they were just being thorough, but my gut tells me that isn't near the truth. Someone must have been tailing me."

"You mean tailing *us*? Because we've spent a lot of time together the past few days." I shuddered.

He pulled me into his arms. "I know it's scary. I don't want you to be worried, but then I can't stop worrying either."

Not gonna lie, I loved the feeling of his arms around me. I nestled my head against his shoulder. We sat there for a moment, the clock on my living room wall ticking against the otherwise silent room.

"What did the police think of Craig's letters?" I asked.

"They were interested, but there wasn't much time to discuss them. Maybe they'll come up with something. In the meantime, we're supposed to be extra cautious."

I swallowed. "I don't like the idea of some crazy person out there watching us."

"Me neither."

The way he looked, I knew Travis wasn't trying to be macho by pretending this wasn't the real-deal-freak-out we both knew it potentially was. I sniffed and caught the tiniest whiff of fudge brownies. My mouth watered, remembering the decadent dessert I'd been devouring moments before. I reluctantly moved out of his embrace and stood. "Come in the kitchen. I'll make you the most sinful treat you've ever tasted." I tugged on his hand, and he smiled.

"That sounds dangerously good." He stood and stretched.

I went ahead so I could grab my bowl before he saw just how big my sweet tooth was. The fudge needed to be reheated, but the brownies were still perfectly moist. I topped off my bowl and fixed a larger helping for Travis. "Here you go."

Travis took a seat at the table and loaded his spoon with a giant bite. "Mmm, this is amazing," he said around a mouthful of brownie. He chewed for another moment. "Is there peanut butter in here?"

"Gluten-free chocolate and peanut-butter brownies—my secret recipe. The best remedy when you're stressing over crazed murderers invading your house."

Travis laughed. "I'd have to agree with you there."

My spoon clanked against the bowl as I scraped more hot fudge from the side. "I want to apologize again for what happened at the park today. I know it sounds lame, but Caleb took me completely off guard, and it didn't help that I was pretty messed up emotionally after we broke up."

"I was mad, but I've been thinking about it all day, and I realized two things—first, I don't own you. You can date whomever you please."

I sat up straight, shaking my head. "But—"

He held up a hand. "Second, you're not the type of girl to lead guys on or play hurtful games."

I relaxed. "Thank you. That means a lot."

"But that doesn't mean I don't have some make-up kisses coming my way." Travis took another bite of brownie and winked when I blushed.

We finished our brownies over light banter and more veiled teasing about kissing. Travis helped me clean up the dishes, then waltzed me around the kitchen and into the living room. We were both laughing; this was the best I'd felt all day. He pulled me close, and our eyes met.

"Jillian, you're a smart woman, and I know your mind is working hard on solving the mystery I dragged you into, but I want you to stop now."

"Stop what?" I tilted my head, drawing my focus away from his lips.

"Let's not do any more investigating. The police will figure it out."

"But we're so close," I replied. "I can feel it. The missing piece is hovering right there." I motioned to the air around us.

Travis chuckled. "All the same, I'd feel better if you gave it a rest. Please be careful at work. I'm sure someone's been watching us."

I shivered, and Travis held me tighter. "I don't like that feeling."

"I know. Would you consider going to work a little later tomorrow? You know, so more people will be at the park? I don't want you to be alone." Travis rested his chin on top of my head. "I thought about taking off work and spending the day with you, but the Freightliner I've been overhauling is almost finished, and the owner is breathing down my neck."

I touched his cheek. "Don't worry about me. I'm a big girl, and the bad guys are after you, not me, right?"

"I hope so." He stared at me, and I could see the gears of

his mind working and worrying. I leaned forward and kissed him, felt his mouth smile against mine with his arms encircling me.

He kissed me tenderly, then with an urgency that I sensed conveyed his feelings for me. My heart double-timed a staccato beat, and my mind whirred with possibilities. Caleb hadn't ruined everything. Travis was giving me another chance. Did I dare hope that my heart could finally be healed with someone I could trust? My fingers threaded through his hair, and I leaned into the kiss. Hope felt good on my lips.

008

The next day, I immersed myself in my work, continually pushing the questions and worries about Craig's murder from my mind. It worked for a while, and the way my lips tingled when I thought of kissing Travis helped distract me further. He called to check on me a couple of times during the day and apologized that he wouldn't be off work until seven. We arranged to meet at his place.

After work, I showered and dressed in denim shorts with my new favorite blouse, a sheer red top over a snug white tank top. While brushing through my hair, my mind wandered again to the clues we'd found. A new idea came to me. I set the brush on the counter and stared at the gray circle around the blue of my iris.

"It has to be," I whispered.

Glancing at the clock, I hurried out the door and headed to Travis's house. It was barely ten after seven. I hoped he'd be home from work so I could share my idea. When I pulled next to his driveway, he was just getting out of his car.

He smiled at me then, frowned at the grease and dirt stains on his shirt. "It's great to see you. Sorry I'm so dirty."

I placed one finger on his chest and leaned forward. "This spot doesn't look too bad." I carefully placed a kiss on his cheek.

"You look beautiful. Give me fifteen minutes, and I'll be ready. I'm starving."

"I came early because I thought of something—I think I know what Craig was trying to tell you."

Travis shook his head slowly and frowned. "I talked to the detective today. They have some leads, and he seemed optimistic about the possibilities."

"Good, but I think Craig did hide something in the park, and I know where to look." I felt buoyant with the idea of solving the murder. "We can go there as soon as you're ready."

Travis shook his head slowly. "I can't risk your safety. Let's go down to the station so you can tell them your hunch."

"I need to check out my design binder first to see if I'm right. It won't take long. We could figure this out."

"It's too dangerous," Travis said flatly. "I don't want you to get killed."

I felt my hackles rise. "You don't need to worry about me. I can take care of myself."

Travis grabbed me by the shoulders. The desperation in his eyes took me by surprise. "Jillian, I care about you. Please listen to me. Craig wouldn't want anyone else to get hurt."

The excitement I'd felt about discovering the missing piece evaporated. "But we can't give up. How do you know that Kami and Heidi will ever be safe?"

"I have to trust the police to do their job."

"Don't you want to know who killed Craig?" I felt anger rising in my stomach. "How can you give up so easily?"

Travis sighed. "Because I care about you, and I want to see your beautiful face and have a chance to kiss those freckles on your cheeks again."

"But I think I know what Craig meant."

"I don't want to hear anymore." Travis let his hands drop to his sides. "I have to honor his wish to keep his family—and you—safe."

"Craig didn't know me, so I'm not part of the deal. I'm sorry, but I feel strongly that I can help." I studied his face for any softening, but his eyes remained hard.

"No. That's not an option anymore. If you want to talk to the police, they'll be happy to meet with you." Travis's stance was determined, and I felt my neck flush with my own stubborn streak.

"Fine!" I whirled around and headed back to my car.

"Jillian! Wait. Please don't be angry," Travis called after me. "Nothing is worth you getting hurt."

Although the sentiment was touching, I'd never liked being bossed around. Besides, I knew I was on to something. "I'll talk to you later." My car door banged shut a little louder than I intended. But by tomorrow, I'd have answers that would finally allow Kami and Heidi to have the peace they deserved.

9

I knew my hunch was right. Craig had mentioned a daffodil with an orange center, so I'd immediately thought of the Narcissus variety—pearl-white petals with a dark-orange center. I'd completely forgotten about the other variety of orange-centered daffodils—the Scarlet Gem was a butter-yellow with orange centers.

Two years ago, when I'd first started at the park, I'd removed those yellow and orange bulbs from the flowerbeds encircling the fountain on the north side and moved them to a smaller bed near some pine trees on the south end. Some large rocks were in the flower bed, and one of them had several cavities in it perfect for growing a bright-green moss with dainty white flowers. My pace quickened as I approached the flowerbed and the rocks came into view. The moss-covered rocks would be the perfect hiding spot.

Stepping carefully through the dark earth, I leaned over the rock, now half-covered with a carpet of English moss. On the back side, the moss trailed through a crack that ended in a small divot. I lifted up the edge of the moss, feeling the fibers stretch as I uncovered a jagged opening in the rock.

Kneeling in the dirt, I twisted my body around the rock to see the hole. My fingers brushed against an object that clanked softly on the side of the rock—something metallic with a green tint. I pulled the object out of the rock—a four-leaf-clover-shaped USB drive. I sucked in a breath. The evidence to Craig's murder had to be on the tiny USB drive in my hand.

"Working late?"

I bit down hard on my lip to keep from screaming while quickly tucking the USB drive into the sleeve of my jacket. "Michael, you scared me." I turned to address my boss, the head of park development for the city. The light was fading, but I could still see the gray in his dark sideburns. Michael Nester wasn't tall, about the same as my five-foot-nine-inches, but his trim figure made him appear taller than he was. "I haven't seen you in a while," I said. "You been busy on that new park?" I stood slowly and put my hands in the pockets of my jacket, dropping the USB drive deep into the corner of the right pocket.

Michael nodded. "It's going to be beautiful. That park's actually why I came down here to find you. I want you to plant a few of the flower beds using your designs."

My face broke into a smile, and the pulsing anxiety coming from my pocket lessened. Michael wasn't here to kill me; he was here to offer me more work. "I'd love to help. It would be an honor."

"I have permission to pay you some overtime, because we want to get it done by next weekend."

"Wow. I'm pretty sure I can make time in my schedule." I tiptoed through the flowerbed and stood at the edge of the grass.

"Good. Walk with me, and let's talk about what I'm picturing." He adjusted the silver frames of his glasses. "You still have that binder with your designs, right?"

"Sure. I keep it in the shed."

"I'm a fan of the design where it looks like the daffodils are multiplying from the center."

"Thank you." It was always nice to receive a compliment from someone who really understood my work. We walked briskly to the shed, where Michael unlocked the door with his keys. He flipped on the light, and as the door swung open, I noticed my binder lying open on the top of a five-gallon bucket. Not where I'd left it. I noted the keys in Michael's hand. He must have pulled out my binder to look at a few of the designs he wanted to talk to me about. But he'd never done that before.

Michael went in and motioned for me to follow him inside. "Don't be shy. You have a lot of talent, Jillian. The city's lucky to have you."

I gave him a tight smile and took one step over the threshold. The binder was open to the very flower bed where I had just retrieved the USB drive. The hair on the back of my neck stood, and my nerves sizzled with fear.

As Michael bent to pick up my binder, I grabbed the shiny new hand trowel sitting on a box of tulip bulbs and held it nonchalantly by my side.

He turned to face me. "I didn't want to bring it up, but I noticed you've been spending some time on the clock with your boyfriend. When I found out it was Travis Banner, I thought I should warn you that he's dangerous."

My fingers clenched the spade. "I can assure you that it wasn't time on the clock. I always come in early to beat the heat, and I'm always honest with my hours."

Michael pressed his lips together. "But you weren't on the clock tonight, were you? What are you up to Jillian?"

His dark eyes hardened, which was all the urging I needed. I raised the thick metal spade and whacked him across the side of the head. Michael cried out and stumbled. I kicked him to speed up his fall. Jumping back over the threshold, I slammed the door and jammed my key into the lock then clicked it in place. I heard a groan and a thump against the door. In a panic, I sprinted toward the parking lot. There was no telling how long the shed would hold Michael.

10

As I ran, my breath came in short puffs, one hand clasped tightly around the four-leaf-clover. I knew I hadn't overreacted. Michael wanted me in that shed to take what I'd found. That was the only explanation for him finding me at the specific flower bed he'd just been studying in my binder.

But how could Michael be involved in Craig's death?

Michael had been my boss for only the past year. He'd moved over to city planning after the stressful job of being director of Parks and Recreation. Why did Craig hide the USB drive in a park if the bad guy worked for the parks? There had to be something I was missing. I felt in my pockets for my cell phone, then remembered I had left it tucked neatly in my purse on the passenger seat of my car.

In the distance, I saw Travis jump from his car and head in my direction.

I skidded to a halt. "Travis! Call 911!"

He stopped and pulled out his phone. "Are you okay? What happened?"

"It's my boss, Michael Nester. I locked him in the tool shed. We've got to get out of here before he breaks out."

"C'mon. We'll take my car. Maybe he'll think you're still in the park."

I climbed in, and a new wave of panic overtook me. What had Michael meant about Travis being dangerous? Travis slid into the car and handed me his cell phone.

"Here, I just pushed call."

Before I had a chance to think about whether I knew Travis well enough, if he was someone dangerous or not, he was pulling out of the parking lot and the 911 operator had answered. I rattled off the address to the park and the location of the shed, struggling to remember to breathe.

"My boss, Michael Nester, is locked in the tool shed."

"Are you injured?"

This was the tough part, because she would think I was totally psycho. "No, he was trying to trap me in the shed, but I hit him in the head with a hand trowel."

"Please stay in the area until emergency personnel arrive."

"I can't do that. He's dangerous. When you have him locked up, I'll talk to the police."

"Please stay on the line, ma'am."

I waited for what seemed like an eternity, glancing at Travis and trying to figure out where he was taking us. What if he was more than a great kisser? Had he planned all of this so I would uncover the clues he needed to keep secret?

"Ma'am, the officers would like you to stay in the parking lot so they can take your statement."

I shook my head. "I'll meet them at the police station. I don't feel safe in the park."

The operator started arguing again, but I interrupted,

"I'm sorry. You're cutting out. I'm safe now, and I'll get to the police station as soon as I can." I ended the call and handed Travis his phone.

"You hit the guy in the head with a shovel, huh?" Travis quirked an eyebrow.

"With a little one." I frowned. "I probably should have hit him again, but I ran as fast as I could."

"And what makes you think this Michael guy is evil?"

"He knew I'd been spending time with you. He knew your name. He had to have been watching you." I clenched my hands into fists, struggling with the tightness in my chest. "He'd already been to the shed to search my design binder. Somehow he figured out the same thing that I did: Craig hid evidence in a flower bed at Silver Cascade Park."

"Take deep breaths. You've had a good scare, but you'll be fine now." Travis squeezed my knee. "Did you find it?"

"Find what?" My panic increased, and Michael's words rang in my ears. What was on the USB drive in my pocket? I cast a sideways glance at Travis. He turned his head sharply, flicking his gaze toward me. Could I trust him?

"You're scaring me. Should I take you to the hospital? You look like you're going into shock."

I leaned back and closed my eyes and analyzed everything I knew about Travis. He was kind and loving and had been completely honest with me. I didn't have a reason not to trust him. "I found a USB drive in the cavity of a rock in one of the flower gardens. It had a metal four-leaf-clover covering it, so it was protected from the weather."

Travis slowed and looked at me, his eyes wide. "Do you think it will solve Craig's murder?"

"Probably." I briefly told him about how I'd figured out which flowerbed to look in based on the flowers I'd transplanted.

"You are one smart cookie. Are you comfortable handing that over to the police?"

"I think we should check it out first." The hammering of my heart had eased into a steady rhythm now that I knew Travis wasn't really dangerous.

He reached out his hand. "I'm sorry that Michael scared you."

I interlaced my fingers with his. "I'm so glad you came looking for me."

Travis's lips twitched. "I was in the shower and kept feeling rotten about everything, so I wanted to try to convince you that I really do care about you."

"I know." With a deep breath, I pulled the clover-leaf USB drive out of my pocket. "Let's stop at The Sugar Cube. The police station is about two blocks from there. We can check the contents at the café and then hand it over."

"Great idea."

Travis held me close to his side as we hurried into the café and sat in front of a computer. I pushed the drive in and opened it to find two documents and a video message. My hands shook as I clicked play. Craig's face appeared on the screen, and Travis sucked in a breath.

"If you're watching this video, something bad happened to me. I wasn't sure how far Michael Nester would go, but apparently he's not above murder." Craig's face pulled into a deep frown, and his chin trembled. "This USB device contains tax and legal documents recording the payoff and kickback I found that were paid to Michael Nester utilizing Boise City funds. It was well hidden, but after digging through layers, I found the evidence I was looking for. Michael Nester is guilty of embezzling funds and racketeering. He used his position to secure ground for a new park that an elderly couple owned. He offered them a payoff to relocate, but the price was doubled when the actual check was cut. The couple received only half of the money. The rest was deposited in Nester's account."

Craig paused and looked behind him as a loud bang sounded from the video. I flinched as he turned back to the camera and spoke rapidly. "I'm so sorry. Please tell Kami and Heidi that I love them so much. Travis, if you found this, you are rock solid, and I'm so glad I could be your bro. Love you, man. Do right by me and set the record straight. Gotta go."

The last image was of his face filled with fear as he reached toward the screen. I toggled the mouse to open up the other documents but stopped when a heavy hand landed on mine.

"That's all you really need to see, right?" Michael's face had blood streaming down the side of his head. I screamed.

"You didn't really think you'd got away, did you?" he said.

Michael reached for the USB port to grab the drive, but Travis punched him in the side of the head. Michael went down hard on the tile floor. Other people in the café shrieked, and I heard the manager say he'd call 911.

Travis pressed his foot into Michael's back. "Don't move."

I clicked the documents open and scanned them to see exactly what Craig had described and found plenty of evidence to convict Michael.

Travis looked over my shoulder then leaned in to kiss my cheek. "You did it, Jillian."

With a smile, I turned and kissed him full on the mouth. "No, we did."

11

When faced with the evidence, Michael confessed to killing Craig, then rolled over on another city employee who'd helped cover Michael's tracks. That partner had followed Travis, searched his house, and kept tabs on me as well. Both were convicted, and Michael was sentenced to life in prison.

That spring, with daffodils blooming, a special memorial service was held at the new garden in honor of Craig Simmons. Travis and I both received applause for helping to solve Craig's murder. The mayor placed a large, decorative compass in the garden because he said it signified that Craig had chosen the right path even though he knew it would endanger his life.

"That's how I feel about you," Travis murmured in my ear. "Thanks for never giving up." His whispers sent tingles down my spine, and I leaned into him.

"Thanks for losing your keys," I replied.

He laughed and pulled me into a hug. "I love you, Jillian."

My heart thrummed in a happy rhythm, and I breathed deeply. The hurt had mended, and I knew Travis would keep my heart safe. "I love you too."

I closed my eyes as his lips met mine, and I kissed him like nobody was watching while we stood next to the flower garden I had designed for Silver Cascade Park.

Recipes from *Silver Cascade Secrets*

Macaroni Salad
1 pkg of small sea shell or elbow macaroni
½ cup mayonnaise
3 Tbsp mustard
1 cup of diced pickles
3 Tbsp of pickle juice (or more according to taste)
½ cup of medium cheddar or pepper jack cheese, cubed in 1/8-inch pieces
Salt and pepper to taste

Cook pasta according to directions. Rinse with cool water and set aside to drain. In large bowl, mix drained pasta with other ingredients. The mixture should be slightly wet. Chill in refrigerator for at least two hours or overnight. Once chilled, stir the mixture to test consistency. Add more pickle juice, mayonnaise, or mustard to desired taste and consistency.

*If chilling overnight, I set aside the cheese and don't add it until morning.

Gluten-free Peanut-butter Brownies
Makes one 9" X 13" pan

2 cups oat flour
1 cup sugar
½ cup cocoa
1 tsp. salt
¾ cup melted butter

4 eggs
2 tsp. vanilla
½ cup of peanut butter, chunky or creamy

    Grease pan. Melt butter, sugar, and cocoa together. Beat all ingredients until smooth. Fold in peanut butter. Bake at 350 degrees for thirty minutes. Let cool for twenty minutes, then score brownies. Serve with ice cream, hot fudge, and/or a small dollop of peanut butter dusted with cocoa powder.

ABOUT RACHELLE J. CHRISTENSEN

Rachelle J. Christensen is a mom of four cute kids. She has an amazing husband, three cats, and five chickens. Her first novel, *Wrong Number*, was awarded Outstanding Book of the Year from the League of Utah Writers and was also a 2010 Whitney Finalist. Her second suspense novel, *Caller ID*, was released March 2012. She is also the author of a nonfiction book, *Lost Children: Coping with Miscarriage for Latter Day Saints*.

Rachelle enjoys singing and songwriting, playing the piano, running, motivational speaking, and of course reading. Visit www.rachellewrites.blogspot.com to learn more about upcoming books.

Rachelle's FB Author Page: Rachelle Christensen Author

CHOCOLATE OBSESSED

Annette Lyon

Other Works by Annette Lyon

Band of Sisters

Coming Home

The Newport Ladies Book Club series

A Portrait for Toni

At the Water's Edge

Lost Without You

Done & Done

There, Their, They're: A No-Tears Guide to Grammar from the Word Nerd

1

Manhattan—November 2010

Whitney's morning shift on the last day of the New York Chocolate Show could not end soon enough. She glanced at her watch as she finished ringing up a customer who'd bought two pounds of her handmade, cocoa-dusted truffles. Five more minutes, and her shift would be over. Thank heavens she didn't have to work the afternoon shift; she was starving for something not sweet, and her feet were killing her.

In the four years she'd been Canyon Valley Resort's executive pastry chef, this was the first time she'd worked the booth—and it would be her last. She much preferred her job of creating chocolate masterpieces for the event's competition and fashion show. But Ellie, the resort's exhibit manager, was short staffed, with two workers coming down ill—one with chicken pox, of all things, and the other with bronchitis. They were both holed up in their hotel rooms, so Whitney had ended up manning the booth, selling the very chocolates she'd spent weeks preparing for other people to sell.

She wasn't used to even seeing the show floor, let alone working it. A nearby booth sold kitschy posters and postcards with chocolate images and phrases. Another had children's cooking supplies—which had nothing to do with chocolate but were plenty popular nevertheless. Farther down was a booth with three chocolate fountains, followed by a display of actual cacao pods cut in half, a bowl of cacao beans and roasted nibs, with explanations showing how chocolate was made and placards defining terms like *ferment* and *conch*, along with a sign assuring parents that chocolate liquor had no alcohol in it.

She tried to assure Ellie that she could handle the shift alone, but for some unknowable reason, Stephen, from Snow View Lodge, had offered to fill the second slot. Ellie had welcomed the extra help, so Stephen ended up working the same hours as Whitney.

His offer was puzzling, as he was not only from a different—competing—Park City resort, but he was Whitney's greatest chocolate-sculpting rival. He'd beat her every year she'd competed in the New York show, and he almost always got better reviews. He had an ego the size of Hershey, Pennsylvania. He always tried to catch her eye after a win, as if he deserved her praise or something. To make matters worse, he was drop-dead hot. It would have been easier to ignore him if he'd been beanpole-thin, fat, or gay. Most of the other chefs in the field tended to fit into one of those three categories.

Stephen probably even likes Hershey's, Whitney thought with a smirk as she finished with the cash register and handed the bag of truffles to the middle-aged woman. "Here you go," she said. "Enjoy."

I know you will.

Whitney used only the best Vahlrona and Amano products, which made them expensive, but oh, so worth every mind-numbingly amazing bite. Her creations were practically bits of heaven on the tongue. She turned around, planning to grab her purse and coat in preparation for a speedy exit when the clock finally hit twelve. She did so fully ignoring Stephen, who stood by a set of wooden shelves filled with product. He was showing product to a young, flirting co-ed.

The bottle blonde flipped her hair and giggled at something he said then touched Stephen's bicep. "Thanks for your help. I don't know the first thing about chocolate, except that I like it." She giggled again, making Whitney roll her eyes. "Maybe you can teach me about it sometime?"

The girl left without buying anything, but she walked with a definite sway to her hips, which she obviously hoped Stephen would notice and appreciate. As Whitney crossed to the table under which they stowed personal belongings, she tried to watch Stephen out of the corner of her eye to see if he was indeed watching the girl's hips retreat. The angle wasn't quite right, though; to see him clearly, she'd have to turn her head, and she wouldn't give him the satisfaction.

I'd bet my Chocovision tempering machine that he got her phone number. Whitney reached the table and lifted its skirt to find her purse—and found her eyes making their way over to Stephen anyway.

He must have felt her gaze, because he looked over right then and smiled. Whitney's eyes flew the other direction. She focused her attention under the table as if the very fate of the world's cacao crop depended on it.

What was I looking for? Purse and jacket—right.

Had she imagined it, or had Stephen's smile turned into

a smirk when he'd caught her looking at him? With disdain, she tossed his jacket to the side as she hunted for hers. *Always winning the sculpting contests, even when my stuff is better*—higher percent cacao, better execution, innovative design. *I bet half of his stuff blooms, and he hides it under all that glitter.* He really did use an awful lot of edible glitter, so maybe it wasn't just his trademark; maybe it was to camouflage the white discoloration of improperly stored and handled chocolate.

That, or he had an in with the judges. Nothing else could explain why he always took first place while she took second.

She'd just grabbed her purse when a deep voice sounded near the register.

"Whitney. Fancy seeing you here."

She lifted an eyebrow, not quite recognizing the voice, but knowing she should. Furrowing her brow, she straightened and slipped her purse over her shoulder then turned to see Jeremy Stoddard. He'd recently graduated from a questionable culinary school and had competed in a dessert contest that she'd judged. He'd placed dead last. He hadn't taken the results well.

"Hi," she managed with a forced pleasant tone, reminding herself that he deserved her low ranking. His pastry had been soggy and chewy, his custard had curdled, and the plating and presentation were amateurish. At the time, she'd wanted to pull him aside and encourage him to pursue a different career, but she hadn't gotten the opportunity.

But why was he here? She'd assumed he'd eventually find a position somewhere in Park City, as that was where he'd interviewed, even if that meant being a waiter instead of an assistant executive pastry chef. Yet here he was on the East Coast.

She cleared her throat and chased away the uneasy feeling settling in her stomach. "Have you enjoyed the chocolate show?" she asked, making an extra effort to sound casual. She stepped away slightly, making sure to keep the table with the register between them.

Jeremy shook his greasy hair out of his eyes and leveled a gaze at her, one she couldn't read. "I didn't come to New York for the chocolate show."

Getting into the show wasn't cheap, and while a ticket probably wouldn't break the bank, the New York Chocolate Show wasn't exactly something you wandered into when you had nothing better to do and just happened to be in the neighborhood. Unless he'd recently gotten a job, Jeremy had no regular income. He could be with one of the exhibitors. Except that he wore only a dirty t-shirt and jeans with holes, while most attendees wore business casual. Maybe he was just in the neighborhood.

But who visited Manhattan in November for sightseeing? That was only slightly better than frigid January. The Rockefeller tree wasn't even up yet.

She gripped the handle of her purse. "So. What does bring you here?"

Jeremy's reply wasn't an answer. "You never answered my last email."

"Oh. Right. Sorry about that." She'd purposely deleted the email unanswered, thinking he'd sent it in the middle of an emotional storm; she understood all too well how hard it was to lose. So she hadn't responded; chances were good that the next day, he would realize what an idiot he'd been to send the message and felt embarrassed about it. Besides, what was she supposed to say to a string of profanity?

As Jeremy stood in front of her now, an eerie smile spread across his unshaven face. Her eyes darted to the side of the hall. She'd have to navigate through the maze of exhibitors to get out. But she couldn't leave now; Jeremy would follow. She could stick around for the next shift, but she was starving, and her feet were killing her.

He glanced in the same direction she had. "Going somewhere? But I came all the way from the other side of the country."

"Why are you here?" she asked, narrowing her eyes, unwilling to let him scare her. She wished he was at the show in some professional capacity, but his clothes and lack of a lanyard with the right ID said otherwise.

"To see you."

At those words, Whitney could have sworn spiders were crawling up her back. "How did you know I'd be here?" Of course she'd be at the show—she flew out with other resort staff for the competition and chocolate fashion show—but how had he known she'd be at the booth, right now, when she'd never worked it?

Jeremy laughed. "You practically begged me to come after tweeting about a hundred times that you'd be here, and that you had to work the booth this afternoon." He tilted his head one way and then the other. "I considered popping in at the Met yesterday morning when you checked in on Foursquare, but then I thought that seeing you here in you element would be more . . . apropos." He looked around, arms outstretched.

This booth was hardly her element, and he knew it. Her element would be the professional kitchen back in Park City, where she made sculptures for competitions and desserts for celebrities who were on ski vacations in the Rockies.

He stepped to the side, coming around the register's table, making Whitney hold her breath and take a matching step back. "Last night's contest results were more your style, am I right? You look radiant in royal blue, by the way."

A different deep voice spoke behind her. "Okay, that's enough."

Whitney's eyes widened as she turned to see Stephen coming up behind her. He didn't so much as look at Whitney. He had his eyes on Jeremy.

"It's time you left."

Whitney nodded in agreement. "Please go, Jeremy." He'd been there last night, watching her. And he admitted to practically stalking her Twitter feed and Foursquare check-ins. He knew exactly when she'd been at the Met. *Get the heck away from me.*

Jeremy chuckled. "Or what?"

Stephen took a step closer to Jeremy. "Go, or I'll call security."

"You don't need to do that," Jeremy sneered. "Whitney's leaving. I'm leaving. She can come with me." He looked at her. "Right?"

Whitney took a step closer to Stephen; rival or not, he was on her side. "I'm not going anywhere with you."

Jeremy raised one hand in surrender. "I get it. Just one more thing." He took two quick steps to her, so fast she didn't realize it until she smelled his body odor and alcohol breath.

Stephen pushed past them and hurried into the corridor. "Security!" he called, trying to get someone's attention.

But while Stephen was looking the other way, Jeremy

drew even closer, patted Whitney's cheek and said, "We both know I'll be anywhere you go."

A hand grabbed Jeremy by the shoulder and whipped him around. Stephen took Jeremy by the front of his jacket and shoved him away from Whitney, pinning him against the register. "You stay away from her."

Jeremy struggled to get away, but Stephen held on and swung a punch that landed squarely on the nose. The only response Jeremy gave was a smile, but it wasn't sheepish or defeated. If anything, he looked amused and victorious. "Enjoying yourself?" he said as blood dripped from both nostrils.

Finally two big security guards arrived. Stephen still held Jeremy down.

The black guard, the bigger of the two, folded his arms and eyed Jeremy. "What's going on here?"

"Take this guy," Stephen said, panting. "He's threatening Whitney here."

Jeremy shrugged—as much as he could with Stephen holding him down. "Sir, who does it look like is causing the scene? I'm the one bleeding."

The guard took Jeremy away, his arm pinned painfully behind his back.

"It's not like you're a cop," Jeremy protested as he was led away. "You can't hold me."

The security guard muttered something, but they'd turned a corner, so Whitney could no longer hear their voices. She let out a breath. "Didn't expect that today." She held her right hand out, palm down. It was trembling. "What's my problem? He's just a creeper."

"Look. Our replacements are here," Stephen said, pointing at the two staffers who'd just arrived.

"What happened?" Stacie asked.

"Yeah," Jenny said as she took her jacket off. "We saw security taking away this guy who had blood all over his shirt. He was swearing up a storm."

Whitney shook her head, exhausted. "I'll tell you later. For now, I'm getting out of here and finding something to eat. See you guys."

She headed along the path between booths, where Jeremy had walked only moments before. Stephen caught up and walked beside her. Whitney's normal response of not wanting him around was tempered by the fact that he'd basically saved her from a jerk. "Thanks," she told him. "For what you did back there."

"He deserved a lot worse," Stephen said, shaking out his hand, which looked bright red from the punch.

"Punching a nose that hard must hurt," Whitney said, eying his hand. "Oh, I hope he doesn't try pressing charges of assault or anything."

"Nah," Stephen said, waving the idea off. "I'm pretty sure we have enough witnesses to back me up. You would, anyway, right?"

"Right," Whitney said with a smile. She still didn't have to like Stephen, but she could at least admire his convictions. And his right hook.

Stephen stayed close as they walked through the hall until they'd meandered through the path of booths and out to the lobby, where a five-foot-wide globe of chocolate rotated on its axis. She pointed at the globe. "When I first saw that, I wanted to study it for hours. But right now, I just want to get out of here, get something to eat, and take a long bath."

"Long day?"

"You could say that. The whole show's been rough. Today a guy I judged in a contest followed me. Oh, and last night I lost the sculpture competition. Again. But you'd know that, because you took the grand prize."

They headed out the front doors and onto the bustling streets of Manhattan. The frosty November air bit at her skin, making Whitney realize she'd never picked up her jacket. It had to be under the table. Stephen didn't have his either; they'd both left them behind after the craziness that was Jeremy.

"You didn't lose," he said. "You took first place."

"But you still beat me; you took grand prize," she countered.

"First place is still fantastic. Yeah. We're pretty much the best."

Whitney couldn't help but wonder if he'd be okay with forever placing behind her in contests. They walked to the end of the block and turned a corner, where Stephen hailed a cab. When one pulled over, he opened the door and gestured for her to get in first.

"You really don't have to come with me. I'm a big girl."

"Hey, you said you're hungry," Stephen said with a shrug. "So am I. Besides, in your shoes, I'd like to get far from Jeremy, and I know a place he definitely won't wander into." He opened the cab door open and waited for Whitney to get inside.

She hesitated for a moment before getting inside. After he climbed in and shut the door, she said, "So where's this restaurant away from Jeremy?"

"I didn't say it was a restaurant." Then Stephen leaned forward to speak to the driver. "259 West 55th Street, please."

Whitney had no idea where—or what—that was, but remembering Jeremy's bloody nose, she opted to trust Stephen to get her a decent meal.

The drive lasted ten minutes or so. Stephen checked the digital counter and paid the fare. They got out, and he led Whitney along a road that seemed to have a lot of apartments along one side, and most of the buildings had reddish brick. He stopped by a big white awning—a white circle with the words The Original Soup Man on it. Below that, a service counter. No door, no tables or chairs.

"What's this?" Whitney asked.

Stephen leaned in to whisper. "Ever watch Seinfeld?" When she nodded, he grinned. "This is the home of the original Soup Nazi."

"No way!"

"Shh!" Stephen laughed. "He hates the attention from the show, so don't mention it. But his soup really is amazing, and you get a whole meal with it—bread and fruit."

As they approached the counter and the day's menu, Whitney blew on her hands, which were getting cold in the nippy air.

"Here," Stephen said, taking her left hand and sandwiching it between his warm ones. "Better?"

"Yeah," she said. His hands had to be so warm that they'd melt the chocolate he sculpted with. Was that his secret?

"What do you want?" he asked.

"The lobster bisque sounds good."

Stephen spoke to the man behind the counter, who looked strikingly like the guy from the Seinfeld episode. "Two large lobster bisques, please." Then, just like in the show, he stepped to the left, paid, and waited for their food.

After the soup man's assistant handed over their order, Stephen and Whitney walked down the block in silence. She was waiting for the chance to laugh and exclaim over meeting the Soup Nazi. Right before the corner, she noticed a big vertical sign that read Soup Man at Work, with an orange arrow pointing toward the awning.

"How did I miss that before?" Whitney said with a laugh.

Stephen got out the cups of soup and the spoons. "We can warm up with the soup as we walk. Central Park's not too far from here. We can eat the rest on a bench there."

From the first bite, the lobster bisque tasted heavenly, and it was the perfect temperature—enough to warm her from the inside without burning her mouth. Whitney breathed in the cold air that smelled so different from autumn in Park City—New York asphalt and hot dogs and a special something that belonged to Manhattan alone.

As they headed for the park, they talked about all kinds of things. Stephen told her about a chocolate-sculpting class where a student—a sixty-year-old woman—had used a length of chocolate and gold-dusted chocolate spheres in a way that inadvertently looked like a piece of anatomy. "The class had several younger people in it, and they weren't at all shy about calling it out by name. That poor lady, though. She looked ready to crawl into a hole—or have a stroke. I wasn't sure which."

Whitney laughed so hard at the image that she nearly spurted lobster bisque from her nose, something Stephen seemed to beam at.

She told him about a time a big-name actor had come to her resort and sent back every dessert he got, declaring that they were all too "French."

"I had no idea what he meant; he'd ordered a mousse, an éclair, and tiramisu—"

"Which isn't even French," Stephen interjected with a laugh.

"Exactly! I had a mind to go out to the floor and dump the mousse on his head."

"What did you do?"

"I figured he had to have a bland palate, so I made the most boring thing ever: chocolate-chip cookies . . . with store-bought dough."

"You didn't." Stephen said it as if she'd suggested using dirt.

"Seriously. I had one of the staffers run to the grocery store and get the cheapest stuff possible. He had to wait for his dessert, but he loved it." She shook her head. "Some people aren't worth wasting the good stuff on, am I right?"

Stephen looked into her eyes then, and her laugh caught in her throat. "I bet we'd work well together . . ." His voice trailed off, but then he finished the thought with, "In the kitchen," as if the statement needed clarifying. But she was pretty sure that's not what he'd been thinking at first.

"Yeah. I bet we would," she said. In the kitchen . . . and out.

2

By the time their soup was gone, they'd made it to Central Park, but they hadn't eaten the bread and grapes. They crossed the street at Columbus Circle, navigating three of the traffic circle's crosswalks before reaching the park itself. Stephen led the way a couple of hundred yards into the park.

As he walked, he couldn't help but remember the first time they'd met. He'd noticed her brilliant smile and flawless skin; he hadn't known what her hair was like, because at the time, it was pulled back in a bun and tucked under a chef's hat. He glanced over now as they walked, shoes crunching dead autumn leaves under foot. Her hair was dark, but not quite brown—more auburn.

He'd admired her as a professional for years, and he'd hoped to impress her with his skills the way she'd impressed him. But besting her in competitions only turned her away. Why he'd ever thought winning would help him get the girl, he'd never know; always beating her out was the equivalent of pulling her pigtails at recess, made worse by the fact that he knew the judges were often sexist. She did deserve to win. Of course she hated him for it. Why hadn't he seen that before?

He pointed to an area past the swings, which was near a huge rock outcropping kids were climbing all over. "There's a fence we can lean against."

The fence was out of the way, and it would be quieter there. "Sure." They walked over to the fence, which had a couple of bikes and a mini cooler beside it.

Stephen leaned against the top rail. "I figure this is far enough in that he won't be able to see us from the street."

"Good thinking." Whitney joined him at the fence, setting her paper bag of food and her purse between her feet but holding a sprig of grapes.

She plucked one grape and popped it into her mouth as she settled close to him—not inches away as she had in the cab. Granted, only their forearms were touching, but it was progress. He'd have a long way to go before winning her over for more than their shirts brushing up next to each other. Which he had every intention of doing.

"This is cool," she said, indicating the playground. "I would have died and gone to heaven with a place like this."

They couldn't see all of the equipment from their position, but not too far off stood what looked like a small concrete city, with at least three dome-like structures that had interconnecting bridges, slides, and even doorway-like openings to the caverns inside.

"That would have made the coolest fort for war games," Stephen said.

"I probably would have played house inside and used the bridges to go to tea or go shopping."

They sat eating quietly for several minutes. Whitney popped grapes into her mouth as Stephen took bites of the hearty rye bread, which was divine. "So after we eat, do you want to head back to the hotel? You're at Washington Square Hotel too, right?"

"Right," she said with a nod, and then her head came up as if a disturbing thought had just occurred to her. "Jeremy can't possibly know where we're staying, can he?"

Stephen lowered the bread and slowly swallowed a bite. "I doubt it. But even if he could find out which hotel, he can't get your room number."

"I'm getting paranoid." Whitney sighed. "After this meal—which is delicious, by the way—I'll be looking forward to a hot bath and resting in my hotel room until I fly out tomorrow."

Stephen nodded thoughtfully in agreement. The idea of being able to relax after a grueling week sounded great, but somehow he wanted to be with Whitney a bit longer.

He heard a ding, and Whitney touched her slacks pocket.

"Just a text," she said. "It can wait."

"What if it's Ellie?"

"You're right." Whitney groaned. "And I was just starting to enjoy this trip."

Stephen hid a grin at that. *Me too,* he thought, but didn't dare say.

She pulled her phone out with the other and checked it.

"Is it Ellie?" Stephen asked.

"No. I don't know the number." Her face drained of color.

A warning light went off in Stephen's head. "What does it say?" He moved closer to see it. She held out the phone with a shaky hand.

Enjoying your soup?

"It's—it's got to be Jeremy," she stammered, staring at the text. "How did he get my number?"

"And how in the hell does he know we went to the Soup Nazi?" Frustrated, Stephen squeezed the bread in his hand, ruining it. He tossed it into his paper sack and stood to look around the park, examining the area, searching for Jeremy.

"Maybe he's guessing where we are. He had to have heard us say how hungry we were." Whitney seemed to be scrambling to come up with a rational explanation.

Stephen shook his head and began pacing. "He didn't ask if we're enjoying our food or meal. He said soup."

"It's a cold day. Lucky guess?" But Whitney's voice belied the light tone of her words.

He shook his head adamantly. "The creep has got to be around here somewhere. I bet show security had to release him, and he followed us in another cab."

Whitney's phone buzzed again. "Another text." She looked up as Stephen stopped in his tracks. He hurried over, and they read it at the same time.

You deserve to die. Is the park nice today? See you in a second.

A surge of adrenaline shot though Stephen. "No way. Come here."

He took Whitney by the hand and dragged her across the grass and paused by the huge outcropping—could they hide on the other side of that? Maybe, but they'd be too easy to see climbing up it. He wouldn't take the chance. Quickly, he changed course and led Whitney to a retaining wall, which they hopped down, and then over to the nearest concrete dome.

He ducked low and ran inside, into the darkness.

Whitney followed suit. Two kids who looked to be about six years old gave them a funny look and scurried out. Now fully in shadow, Stephen and Whitney pressed their backs to the wall and tried to catch their breath. Whitney was nearly curled up next to him; he had his arms wrapped around her protectively. They waited in silence. But not for long.

In the distance Stephen spotted Jeremy's dirty jeans as he stalked around the playground.

"Whitney! Where are you? I know you're here." His heavy step sounded above them; Jeremy was walking over their dome. They both looked upward, listening. An outsider might have thought he was a father looking for his daughter—a scary father.

Stephen's heart still hammered against his ribcage; it hadn't gotten the message that he wasn't running anymore.

But I may have to fight or flee, he thought. *I have to protect her.* The thought began with the knowledge that it was simply the right thing to do, but inside, Stephen knew that wanting to protect Whitney went well beyond being a decent human being.

He refused to lose Whitney before he got to really know her, especially when he hoped that, given the chance, he could come to care for her even more. He swallowed back the emotion such thoughts brought with them. Waiting around for Jeremy was far harder than running from him; the latter had at least kept Stephen's mind occupied.

Jeremy appeared in front of the dome again. Whitney sucked in her breath and held Stephen's arm tightly. Jeremy was scanning the area, his face scrunched into a pissed-off expression as he stomped around.

He searched the swings, the trees—even the rocky outcropping. Whitney let out a shaky breath she'd been holding. "He didn't see us," she whispered, but didn't move.

Stephen turned to look at her. His face was awfully close to hers. She looked up at the same time, and their eyes locked. He braced himself for one of her jokes, but none came. They stayed in the same position, gazing into each other's eyes, for several seconds. They couldn't leave yet anyway; Jeremy could still be around.

Three inches, and I could be kissing her. His eyes sketched down to her lips—those red, beautiful lips—and back to her chocolate-brown eyes. They were the color of Peter's Burgundy, his favorite dark chocolate to work with.

The sound of Jeremy racing back toward the playground—kicking up gravel, crunching dried leaves—broke the moment. Whitney looked away and licked her lips—had she been thinking the same thing?

Probably not. She's barely past wanting to rip my arms out of their sockets.

Several yards ahead, Jeremy turned in a circle. He lifted his hands to each side of his mouth and yelled, "I'm coming for you! Don't think I won't find you!" He pulled his cell phone out of his pocket as if checking a text then ran off in the direction they'd entered the park.

Stephen leaned close to Whitney's ear to whisper; instead, he smelled her shampoo—fruity, with something else in it he couldn't quite place. Whatever it was, it almost made him want to stay right there and smell it for hours. But they had to get out of here. "I'll go grab your purse," he whispered.

"I didn't even realize I'd left it by the fence," Whitney said, bending to the side, checking to see if it was still there. It was, right next to the cooler and near the bikes.

Stephen went on. "When I return, we book it out of the

park, back to Central Park South. From there, we'll grab a taxi and go . . . somewhere."

She nodded. "Deal."

He mentally counted to three then scurried out of the dome and raced to the fence. He scooped up the purse and headed back to the dome. Whitney was already out of it and running in the direction he pointed. He caught up, and together they sprinted along one path and then another, dodging people and nearly tripping on a dog's leash. The whole way, Stephen prayed that Jeremy had kept going all the way back to the Soup Nazi and that he wouldn't see them when they reached the street.

The cold air burned Stephen's lungs as he ran. Whitney kept up, her arms pumping furiously. They returned to the street a block farther east from where they'd entered the park by Columbus Circle.

Stephen held out his arm to hail a cab. Miraculously, one stopped almost immediately. Stephen opened the back door, ushered Whitney inside, and was about to climb in himself when he spotted Jeremy at the traffic circle.

"Stop!" Jeremy screamed. He was running.

Stephen practically jumped into the car then slammed the door shut. He locked it and yelled, "Drive, fast. Please! And lock the doors!"

The cabbie nodded and pulled into traffic, the locks clicking shut right as Jeremy reached the cab and tried the front passenger door. He yelled obscenities as Stephen and Whitney blended in with the other yellow cabs on the streets of Manhattan and drove away.

Stephen handed over her purse. "That was close."

Whitney hadn't scooted to the other side of the bench. She sat right by him, no space at all between them. Stephen would have thought it felt good, except that a deep furrow creased her forehead, and her eyes were watery. He wasn't used to seeing this vulnerable side of Whitney. And he didn't like it.

Hesitantly, he lifted his arm and let it slowly settle around her shoulders. He held his breath, waiting for her reaction. *Please let it be good, not bad. I just want to help.*

Whitney shuddered as if with relief and sank into his arm, resting her head on his shoulder. "Thank you," she whispered.

"Of course." Stephen couldn't help himself. He turned his head and kissed the top of hers.

3

The cabbie cleared his throat to get their attention. "So where to?"

Without any hesitation, Stephen answered, "Battery Park."

Whitney had no idea where Battery Park was, but it sounded familiar, and she figured she ought to know where—or what—it was. She hoped it was a long drive away, maybe in another borough.

I'd be willing to pay a lot to sit with Stephen like this, in quiet closeness, for hours.

The thought stunned her. Since when did she want to not only be with Stephen, but be close to him? To touch him, to sit at his side, his arm around her, her head on his shoulder? And there was that delicious smell again. Not just cologne or aftershave. Something else was mixed in—his own masculine scent? Whatever it was, she would be happy to sit here all day, smelling it, knowing she was safe from Jeremy and with a man who seemed to take her well-being seriously.

She didn't remember the last time a man had really cared about her that way. Stephen had stepped in to confront a total stranger, defending a woman that he knew considered him to be her mortal enemy.

Maybe he doesn't see me as an enemy the way I've seen him. Maybe he's not as big a jerk as I thought. Maybe he's not a jerk at all. She hadn't ever interacted with him; she'd just seen him on stage, getting his awards and accolades—the ones she deserved.

She closed her eyes and breathed in his scent then realized she was practically snuggling with Stephen.

I've lost my mind. It's got to be the shock of dealing with Jeremy. Our emotions are already running wild. That's all this is—temporary insanity. That's all this is.

She pictured the two of them going back to Park City when all of this was over: working in the same city, knowing that they were rivals and that it was part of her professional duty to try to beat this guy in every way. The idea felt like chocolate that had been heated too high and had turned into an ugly, gritty, unsalvageable mess, and a total disappointment—scorched.

Deliberately, Whitney continued to breathe deeply, letting out as much stress and emotion as she could. This wasn't the time to think about what would happen after this crazy day was over and they went back to their own lives and kitchens. But with her eyes closed, she couldn't help imagining what it would be like to share a kitchen with Stephen.

Imagine what kind of amazing sculptures we could create together.

Stop that!

She forced her eyes open; closing them only helped her

fantasize about something ludicrous. Time to focus on reality and losing Jeremy altogether.

Another text came in. Stephen stiffened, apparently recognizing the chime. Mouth dry, Whitney clicked her phone open.

Heading back to Washington Square? I hear the hotel is really nice. Lobby's a bit pretentious, though.

"He knows." Whitney's voice sounded hollow to her ears. "How?"

Her mind spun. Maybe she could check out of the hotel a day early then head to the airport to wait for an earlier flight—during which time she'd make a point of not thinking about how Jeremy could very well meet her at the hotel when she got there or follow her to the airport. *Once I'm past security, he can't touch me.*

As much as she wanted to suggest going to the hotel, she knew it wouldn't be wise right now. Instead she said, "What's at Battery Park?"

"A lot of things," Stephen said. "I figure it'll give us options—and distance. It's at the bottom tip of the island, so he'll have a harder time finding us or getting there too, I'd think. From there, we can take the subway to—"

"No subway." Whitney lifted her head and shook it. "Not when I'm running. Maybe I've watched too many movies with subway fight scenes, but . . ." She shuddered.

"Okay, no subway. I'm good with that." Stephen smiled. It didn't escape her notice that he didn't even mention how expensive continuing cab fares might end up being—several times higher than subway fares.

"Thanks," she said, and lowered her head to his shoulder again. His arm pulled her close in a comforting squeeze. She wanted to enjoy the moment and melt into it, but she couldn't, not with Jeremy's texts staring at her.

Stephen cleared his throat. "Okay, so how about this: from Battery Park, we take the ferry to the Liberty Island—maybe see the Statue of Liberty—and then visit Ellis Island."

A ferry ride, two historic landmarks, and all of it far from any freaky Jeremy moments? "Sounds great."

"Plus, to get on the ferry, you have to go through a metal detector," Stephen added with a layer of significance in his voice.

Message received: Even if Jeremy figured out where they'd gone and tried to follow, he couldn't bring a weapon.

"No metal detector?" She smiled and tilted her head to look up to him. "Even better."

After a fifteen- or twenty-minute ride, the cabbie dropped them off near a grassy area with old trees. They got out, and Stephen paid the fare—Whitney made a mental note of how much it was so she could pay him back. Somehow she knew he wouldn't take the money right now. Not that she had much cash on her anyway.

The November nip in the air had her hugging herself and wishing she hadn't left her jacket at the booth. Stephen gestured at the grassy plot. "Battery Park."

"This is a park?" Whitney asked, looking around.

"It is by Manhattan standards—it's got grass and trees. But yeah, it's several times smaller than Central Park." Stephen jerked his head up the street. "The Twin Towers used to be there."

Whitney turned to take in the symmetrical glass structure. From where they stood, she couldn't see the memorial gardens or fountains. Maybe they'd have time to pay their respects later. She tried to picture the Twin Towers being there instead, of smoke billowing from them, of people running down the streets to get away from the debris and smoke after the towers came down. She'd been a kid then, but she still remembered how the news footage had looked like a lot of the movie scenes with people running down streets away from alien invaders.

She shivered and turned away to look out onto the water. "Which direction is the ferry?"

"Over here." Stephen led the way.

They reached the ticket booth and learned that they'd lucked out; the next ferry would leave in about five minutes. They went through the security checkpoint, boarded, and found seats below deck. Whitney would have loved to watch the water and Statue of Liberty approach, but it was too cold and windy without a jacket. Maybe the Ellis Island gift shop would have a hat or gloves or jacket or something.

As before, Stephen's arm rested around her shoulders. Whitney couldn't help but wonder if it was a habit now, or something he felt he could do, or maybe just a comfortable position for him. Certainly it didn't mean anything more than that.

When the ferry pulled away from the dock, Whitney breathed a sigh of relief.

Stephen noticed. "We did it. Jeremy's nowhere to be seen."

Even so, the levels of adrenaline shooting through her system were enough to make her want to cling to the one person who'd helped her shake Jeremy. Even if that person was her rival.

Not enemy. That's too harsh a word for someone willing to pay through the nose just to keep a colleague safe.

Even as the thought passed through her mind, she had to wonder if she was right. Why was Stephen helping her?

Being so . . . nice? And why had she never noticed that he had such awesomely defined arms? How many pastry chefs lifted weights? She'd known from her first glance at Stephen that he was handsome. But not until today did she know he was ripped—his white chef's jacket covered all of that up. She'd never again see his embroidered name on the front without smiling, knowing the physique hiding beneath the tent-like material. Having his arm around her, sitting this close, made her insides feel like the population of a beehive had taken flight in her middle.

They both leaned back and relaxed, Whitney with her head still on his arm. She found herself resting a hand on his thigh—a friendly gesture, right? But she really wanted to see if his biceps were a fluke. Maybe he carried cases of chocolate instead of using a dolly. But no, through his slacks she could feel a tight, toned muscle. The bees went crazy again, and she had to turn her face away so he wouldn't see her smile.

Now, thanks to their time in the concrete dome—had he been about to kiss her, and would she have let him?—she knew that his eyes were a dark golden brown, like honey. And that he had a cowlick, which made his hair curl on one side of his part and stick up sometimes. She wanted to reach over and tame it.

Neither of them talked for the first leg of the ride to Liberty Island, home of the Statue of Liberty. In theory, Whitney wanted to see the Statue of Liberty up close, but a greater desire had her wanting the ferry to get moving again so they could get off at Ellis Island.

When the ferry finally moved on for its last leg, she breathed another sigh of relief.

Stephen eyed her but then looked away. "So I've been meaning to ask you something. Out of curiosity . . ."

When his voice trailed off, she turned to him, her smile only partly under control, and raised her eyebrows in question. "Yeah?"

A pink flush came to his cheeks, making him look adorably vulnerable. Whitney smiled more broadly. Not arrogant at all.

"So I've gotten the impression that you sort of hate my guts." His eyes locked on hers for several seconds, which felt like an eternity—an awkward, horrible eternity.

She wished she could undo her behavior of the last few years, or at least convince him that she really was a nice person under the prickly competitive exterior. Whitney's cheeks were the ones heating up now. She swallowed and broke eye contact.

"Do you?" Stephen asked. "Hate my guts, I mean."

She looked over; his eyes seemed to plead with her.

What could Whitney say? Of course she hated his guts? That she used to, but had changed her mind in the last hour or so?

For that matter, did she hate him anymore? Today, she'd found herself drawn to him. But that was probably due to Stockholm syndrome or something.

Wait. If this were Stockholm syndrome, wouldn't I be attracted to Jeremy instead of Stephen?

Nothing changed the basic facts: they worked at rival resorts, and he beat her unfairly in competitions.

Is that a reason to hate his guts? Isn't that a bit like middle school?

The silence between them stretched on as Whitney tried to come up with an answer. How long was this ferry ride, anyway? She peered out a window in an attempt to see Ellis Island approaching.

"I see," Stephen said, and he withdrew his arm from around her shoulders.

Whitney wanted to grab it and put it back around her. "It's not like that."

Stephen leaned forward, resting his forearms on his legs. Dang, he looked good like that—somehow all the right muscles showed in all the right ways, and his cowlick was begging to be brushed back by her fingers. But the pained look on his face when he looked over made her focus.

She was about to try to explain, although nothing she could come up with sounded remotely decent.

Stephen spoke first. "Truth is, I've liked you from the moment we first met."

"You—wait, what?"

"Actually, since before we met. Your dragon sculpture for the contest in San Diego blew me away. Holy cow, was that amazing. I knew right then that I had to meet you. Every year, you make me up my game. I'm constantly trying to find ways to be as good a pastry chef as you are."

Whitney's mind spun in circles. "But . . . you always win."

He smiled a bit sheepishly at that. "It's felt good on the one hand, but who are we kidding? Your stuff blows mine out of the water. Honestly, I think the judges tend to be biased toward men. You deserve to win. I mean seriously, your castle this year—with the turrets and fairies—" He shook his head. "Brilliant. I have no idea how you did that."

"Thanks," Whitney said, smiling in spite of herself. Stephen admired her work? Always had? "I don't usually use so much glitter, but you sort of inspired me to, especially on the fairies."

"Really? Wow." Stephen seemed to take that in. "If

anything, every year I've sort of hoped that any award I got would . . ." He cleared his throat and flushed bright pink; his neck was redder than her favorite purse back home. "I sort of hoped you'd be impressed and want to get to know me." He shrugged. "But that hasn't happened, obviously, and instead, I somehow keep making the worst impression ever, and—"

"And you made me hate your guts," she finished.

He looked over; their eyes met, and he sat there staring at her. "So you do."

"No! I mean, I did. Not anymore." She leaned over and slipped her arm through his.

Mmm, that bicep. That Stephen smell.

Focus!

Stephen looked down at her hand, looked into her eyes, and then slowly, hesitantly, covered her hand with his own.

Sparks seemed to go off inside her. She gulped down a big piece of humble pie. "It's because of my pride. I've let it get the better of me, never letting myself see past the fact that our resorts were rivals and that you kept beating me. I thought we were sort of obligated to be rivals too, and it never occurred to me that maybe the guy behind the trophies and blue ribbons is actually a really cool guy. I should have seen that when you volunteered at our booth today. Who does that?"

Stephen smiled wryly. "Someone desperate for a chance to get to know you." He shrugged. "So I guess I can thank Jeremy for being a stalker, because this has given me a chance to spend a little time with you." He tilted his head one way and then the other. "Not under the most ideal circumstances, but still."

"It has been nice," Whitney said.

"Really?"

"Really." She leaned closer, resting her head on his shoulder in hopes of regaining the connection they'd had before. "Only a really good guy would help out a girl who hated his guts." Whitney chuckled, but he grimaced. "What?" she asked.

"Good guys always finish last."

"Not necessarily." Whitney gave in to what she'd wanted to do ever since the ferry had left the dock; she reached up and pressed her lips against his cheek.

In shock, Stephen turned toward her, which brought their lips only inches apart. He glanced to his side as if checking to see whether any of the passengers in the quarter-full room was watching before he moved closer. Whitney held her breath and crossed part of the distance, aching to feel his lips on hers.

But then, in her right hand, her phone dinged yet again with an incoming text. It was as if Jeremy knew exactly when to ruin a moment. She blinked, dissolving the chemistry between them. The text would almost certainly be from Jeremy.

Stephen rested his forehead against hers. "It's okay; check it."

She swiped the screen. Together, she and Stephen looked at Jeremy's text.

Enjoying the ferry ride? I'll meet you on the island. Be sure to look over your shoulder. I'll be there. Always.

4

"No way," Stephen said. "No freaking way."

Whitney gaped. "How in the . . ."

Had Jeremy followed them after all? That seemed farfetched. Following a cab in Manhattan was like trying to follow one person in a crowd. Not impossible, but awfully hard to do. Maybe someone was helping him track them? But if he knew they were on the ferry, why hadn't he boarded with them? Maybe he was trying to hide a gun or something before getting his ticket and didn't get through security in time.

Which meant he'd be on the next ferry, which would arrive fifteen or twenty minutes after they reached the island.

"Great," Stephen said. "Here I was thinking that we were going to get away from him and—"

"Instead, we're setting ourselves up to be trapped," Whitney finished. Her voice sounded surprisingly calm in her ears.

Stephen ran his fingers through his hair, seemingly

annoyed—at the text, or at the timing? If Jeremy had to text, couldn't it have been after he'd kissed her?

"What should we do?" Stephen asked.

She considered. "If we hadn't already docked at Liberty Island, I'd say we hide out there, but it's too late for that."

"We should probably get off Ellis Island as fast as possible. What do you say we stay on board and head back?"

"What if he's there waiting for us to get off at Battery Park?"

Stephen licked his lips as he concentrated on the problem. "You're right; there's no way to know for sure when he'll follow."

"I've never been to Ellis Island," Whitney said. "Do you think we could hide out there until after he's off the ferry and then somehow get back on it before it leaves without him seeing us?" The timid Whitney from the cab ride had been replaced by the one she recognized—the go-get-em professional who found a solution to any problem and attacked it with confidence. No more of this pathetic damsel in distress. She hoped Stephen liked this—real—side of her.

"There's nowhere decent to hide outside, at least, none I remember. But inside, there are a lot of small, interconnecting rooms. We'd want to avoid the restaurant and main-floor areas, I'd think. Then again, if we stay upstairs, we could end up even more trapped—the small rooms have displays that wind around, so there's really only one way in or out."

"We can do it. If we can get back on the ferry without him seeing us, he'll be stuck on the island until the next ferry. We'll have enough of a head start to get back to the hotel, pack up, and we'll be our way to the airport for an earlier flight, all before he gets back to Battery Park."

"'We,' huh?" he said with a smile.

"Oh, uh . . . I shouldn't have assumed that you'd—"

"No," he said, interrupting. "I like hearing it. And you're right; we'll finish this thing together."

After the ferry docked, they stepped onto the man-made island where millions of immigrants had passed through a century before on their way to what they hoped was a new life. Whitney sure hoped they'd have the same fortune as those who got through—and that maybe when this whole ordeal was over, she could find good fortune, maybe with Stephen at her side. But first things first.

He took Whitney's hand and led her under the red metal awning that led to the gorgeous old building. It had white stone arches along the front and almost looked like an old-time railroad station. In the center a square tower stood, with stripes of different colors of stone. She held Stephen's hand tightly and kept her pace close to his. Stephen strode purposefully, looking around as if searching for places to hide that would be easy to reach the ferry from, when the next one docked—after Jeremy got off it.

She did the same; they'd need a way to see him without being seen, and to board the ferry after he'd passed.

"I wonder if the gift shop has windows overlooking the ferry. I don't remember," Stephen said.

"No good place to hide outside," Whitney offered.

The best option was behind one of the concrete pillars below the red poles of the awning, but only one person could hide behind a pillar—and even that wasn't a sure bet for not being spotted. Whitney could probably hide behind one, but Stephen was probably too tall and would have to crouch down. Even then, they'd be hidden from only one angle. If Jeremy moved a couple of feet either direction, as he would walking into the building, they'd be noticed.

What were their other options?

"How long until the next ferry arrives?" Whitney asked, even though she had a general idea.

Stephen glanced at his watch but didn't seem to register the time. "Fifteen minutes, maybe? Not enough time."

Inside the building, they came to a display of old trunks and suitcases from the Ellis Island immigration period, stacked neatly together, with a placard explaining some of the history. Whitney normally liked reading museum signs, but today she didn't have the luxury. She looked over at Stephen, hoping he had an idea of what to do next. He was rubbing his neck with a pinched look on his face.

"You okay?"

He nodded and lowered his arm. "Just a headache. Probably from all the adrenaline of running from a psycho." He tried to smile, but it came off thin and didn't reach even an inch past his mouth.

"I've got some ibuprofen." She opened her purse, holding one handle out as she looked for the little white bottle she carried with her.

Stephen peered into her purse. "I thought you were an Android girl."

Whitney furrowed her brow. "I am." She pulled her cell phone out of her slacks pocket and waved it. "See?"

"Then what's this?" Stephen reached into her purse and pulled out an iPhone.

"Weird." Whitney cocked her head in surprise. "Maybe it belongs to someone who worked the booth, and it fell into my purse accidentally."

"Maybe," Stephen said, but his tone said he didn't think so. He turned it over, and Whitney, too, looked for anything that would indicate whose it was. Nothing. Not even in a protective case.

"Looks brand new," Whitney said.

"Yeah." Stephen clicked it on and swiped the arrow on the screen. It didn't even have a passcode. But instead of seeing the main screen, an app was running. It showed two pulsing dots, one blue, the other purple, on a map.

The map showed the blue dot on Ellis Island and the purple one on the water, halfway between Liberty Island and Ellis Island. Across the top of the screen read the words *Locate My Friends*.

"This is how he's been following us!" Stephen said. "Jeremy put this into your purse somehow, and he's using the GPS signal to track us."

His outburst garnered several stares, but Whitney didn't care. "How could he get it in there without me knowing it? He couldn't have gotten to it under the table."

Stephen squinted in thought. "But he did step into the booth briefly. Did you have your purse on you then?"

Whitney felt sick. "I did. He even leaned in and threatened me, but I was so distracted and creeped out that I didn't notice anything. He totally could have dropped it inside without me knowing it." Even more understanding dawned on her. "He'd probably watched me enough during the contest to know that I keep my phone in my pocket and that I wouldn't look in my purse when he texted me. How could I be so stupid?"

"Hey, I didn't realize what was happening either." Stephen began pacing back in forth in front of the luggage display. "We need to find security."

"Let's start there," Whitney said, pointing at a sign with an arrow that directed them to an information booth.

As they hurried that direction, Whitney checked her watch. The next ferry would be here in about eight minutes.

She pictured her Jeremy's purple dot on the app, getting closer and closer to their blue dot.

After getting directions from the woman at the information, they strode briskly down a corridor to security. A thought occurred to Whitney, and she stopped. "How come he didn't find us in Central Park?"

Stephen jerked his head in the direction they were going; Whitney continued walking. "GPS isn't 100% accurate," he said. "But obviously accurate enough that he's kept pretty darn close to us."

Outside the security office, Whitney stopped in her tracks and took Stephen's arm. "Why didn't he find us at the park? Sure, we were hiding but—"

Stephen grinned. "But you left your purse by the fence. It was by enough of other people's stuff that he probably thought it belonged to someone else. He knew we were in that area, but he didn't see the purse or us and had to rely on searching visually. No wonder he was so upset. The signal didn't make sense; he knew we were nearby."

"So glad this one's is boring old black; he would have recognized it if I'd brought my red one."

"No kidding."

Whitney nodded with excitement as the pieces fit together. "He picked up our trail again as soon as we moved the purse and headed for Battery Park."

"Let's destroy that phone," Stephen said, anger lacing his voice. "Throw it into the water. Or tie it to a bird and let it fly away . . ." Seeing Stephen get all worked up made Whitney want to throw her arms around him and hold him tight. He was upset for her.

But getting rid of the phone wouldn't be the solution. "He'll still find us eventually, maybe here on the island. But if not here, at home, and then what? No, we need to stop this. Besides, this phone could be evidence the police will need."

"So what do we do?" Stephen asked.

"I have an idea." Whitney walked into the security office, Jeremy's tracking phone in hand.

5

Whitney walked straight to the security officer sitting at the desk, an Officer Adams, judging from the name plate. He wore a green uniform, and his hat, resting on the desk, looked like it belonged to Smokey the Bear. He was a national park ranger? She supposed the island was a national landmark. But did this guy have the ability to help them?

He has to.

"Sir, someone is following us," Whitney said, abandoning all pleasantries; they didn't have time for any of that. "He's on the way here to hurt me."

"Whoa," Officer Adams said, raising his hands. "What makes you say all that?"

Whitney could now see a weapon at his side, and instantly felt better about getting his help. She pulled out her own phone and brought up Jeremy's text messages. She held out the screen so Adams could read them. "His name is Jeremy Stoddard. He's a recent culinary school graduate who lost a competition. I judged it, and he's mad at me personally about it. He's been chasing me and my colleague Stephen here for most of the afternoon, ever since we left the New York Chocolate Show around . . ." She checked her watch, trying to remember. What time had her shift ended? The day was blurring together.

"Noon," Stephen filled in. He nodded at Whitney's phone. "As you'll see there, he's sent threatening text messages, including one death threat. Plus, we found that he's been tracking us using the GPS on that other phone."

Whitney held it out and showed the dots on the app. "The blue dot shows this phone's location. The purple dot is him."

"Wow. That's . . ." Officer Adams shook his head. "That's messed up. And he's close."

Stephen nodded. "Exactly. Is this enough to arrest him? He's made a clear threat against Whitney's life."

"I don't think so," Adams said. "He could argue that it's a joke, or that someone else sent the messages. Now if you had eye witnesses to an actual threat . . ."

Whitney leaned forward, palms against the desk. "Get backup so we're ready for him. Stephen and I can be the bait. Let's get some witnesses."

For a few minutes, they debated the best location—somewhere with plenty of people, but less of a chance for Jeremy to destroy history. But also somewhere not too crowded, or he wouldn't make a clear threat.

They settled on a hallway leading to exhibit rooms in a side wing. On the way, they walked along the railing above the huge hall that was used for registering millions of immigrants, some getting their hopes dashed, others allowed through to America. She wanted to take a moment to really look at it, but they didn't have time.

Maybe with Stephen after next year's show.

The thought let her smile even though her insides were sour and her heart was jumpy.

"I'll be right inside that room," Officer Adams said, gesturing toward a door. "Backup should be here any second, but they'll wait out of sight until they're needed."

"Thanks." Whitney pulled out the iPhone and checked the dots. "He's approaching the building. Oh, I'm going to throw up."

"It'll be okay," Stephen said. He reached over and tapped to the voice memo app to start the recording. It would catch anything Jeremy said. Stephen slipped the phone back into her purse and put his arm around Whitney, which helped her take a few deep breaths.

Stephen managed a chuckle. "He'll be so pissed when he finds out that the very thing he used to track us will record the evidence we need to get rid of him."

Whitney nodded, but the reality of what they were doing began to hit her. What if Adams didn't come out fast enough? What if Jeremy acted normal in public and didn't make a threat? Where would she and Stephen go for help then? How would they get off the island safely?

She didn't have long to wait to find out.

"Whitney! I'm here!" Jeremy's voice boomed through the huge building, echoing off the old walls.

Her first reaction was to run. She forced herself to stay put, but she had to grip Stephen's arm with both hands to ground herself.

They waited a minute or two, but Jeremy didn't show up. Confused, Whitney pulled the iPhone from her purse and clicked back over to the GPS app. "He's over there somewhere," she said, pointing.

"I think the café's in that direction," Stephen said. "Odd."

"Never mind. He's heading back." Whitney bit back a whimper and slipped the phone into hiding. "Here we go."

They pretended to study pictures hung along the wall, but both of them were really keeping an ear and eye out for Jeremy. Sure enough, they heard his heavy tread.

"Whitney, where are you?"

His voice still sent shivers through her. She went through the plan—act scared, not friendly, so he'll continue to threaten her. That wouldn't be hard. She'd just show what she was really feeling.

"Go away, Jeremy," she called, knowing he'd hear her.

Crap. I shouldn't have done that.

And there he was, standing at the end of the corridor with the big registration hall behind, making him backlit. *Shoot. I can't see his face.*

Jeremy stepped forward, one step, two, three. The closer he drew, the more of his features Whitney could make out—including his disturbing grin. He still had crusted blood around his nose, which was swollen now.

"Please leave me alone," Whitney said, her voice trembling. She took a step back. Stephen did the same, staying with her. She'd told him not to get between her and Jeremy. This time, for the sake of getting a clear threat, it had to be just her and him. But she was glad Stephen remained close. His presence helped her stay calm when she wanted to scream and run.

Without answering, Jeremy pulled something out of his back pocket—a steak knife. It glinted under the lights.

"You got that at the café," she whispered.

"Very good," Jeremy said. His voice made her skin

crawl. "I needed a way of making my point, but I couldn't bring along my own tools." He moved the knife back and forth; Whitney stared at it, unable to take her eyes away, and swallowed hard.

"What are you going to do with that knife?"

Good job. You're making sure the important information is recorded.

"What do you think?" Another step forward.

She and Stephen each took another step back.

The few tourists from the hall had gasped and run into side rooms. The three of them were alone now—but they had witnesses to some of it. And they'd have more hard evidence soon.

"Maybe I should use this knife to make a sculpture out of you, the way you do with chocolate. You could be my masterpiece."

This time Stephen spoke up. "You're sick."

"Am I? Maybe so. But who's the one chasing whom? I'm also the one with all the power now. Let's see how you feel after I'm done with you."

He continued to ramble. At first, Whitney couldn't keep her eyes off the knife. Not until she realized that he was holding it like a chef would. Hand high on the handle, thumb to the side of the blade, fingers wrapped around the bolster. Of course he'd learned that hold in culinary school—a hold great for control in cutting onions or chopping chocolate.

But probably not so great for stabbing a person.

If she could stand to let him get a little closer . . .

She lifted her chin and whispered to Stephen. "Let go of me and take a step back. I'm going to try something."

At first Stephen stayed put. "You aren't going to try to be some superhero. Not on my watch."

The protectiveness in his voice warmed her. "I'll be okay."

"Love birds saying their goodbyes?" Jeremy tilted his head and held both hands out as if admiring something adorable. "Isn't that sweet?"

This was her chance, before he shifted positions. Whitney stepped forward, hands clasped in front of her so he'd keep his eye there. "Please, Jeremy," she said, getting close enough that he couldn't close his arms without stepping away.

"You really think that a simple please changes everything? I flunked out of culinary school. My girlfriend left me. My parents kicked me out of the house. And then you add the cherry on top by giving me the lowest score. No, please isn't enough. You're going to pay." He put his head back and laughed.

Whitney reached for the knife. She grabbed the dull side of the blade with her right hand. Her other took the wood end. In one fluid movement, she popped the knife out of his grip and stepped back. Now it was her turn to hold the knife, only she left culinary rules behind and held it in her fist, blade tip out.

"What the—" But when Jeremy saw the blade pointed at him, he didn't dare step forward. "You little . . ." His nostrils flared.

"Adams!" Whitney called. "Now!'

"Roger. Backup, now!" Adams appeared suddenly in the doorway. "Turn around and put your hands up."

Whitney held her breath, but the sound of feet pounding down the hall—and Adams snapping handcuffs onto Jeremy's wrists—sent a wave of relief through her. As he was led away, Jeremy threw expletives at Whitney and Stephen, but they were too glad to care.

The side rooms were quickly cleared of tourists, who were ushered to the security office to give statements. Several had seen something, and even more had heard everything. Whitney handed over both her phone and Jeremy's from her purse so the police would have all the evidence they needed from them.

Another officer approached Whitney and Stephen. "We've got most of this covered, especially with these phones. I'll still need you to stick around to give your statements, but I can see you're a bit rattled. You two take a break."

"Thanks," Whitney said. Post-adrenaline weakness overwhelmed her; she felt ready to collapse.

Stephen was there to hold her. "Maybe there's a chair in one of these rooms," he said and led her into the nearest one. It had video clips showing actual footage of immigrants, and tons of objects from the period, including signs in languages Whitney could only guess at.

But no chairs. The room was half lit and empty, creating pockets of shadow; the room was silent save for their own movements.

"It's over," Stephen said, holding Whitney.

"We outsmarted him." Whitney didn't pull away even though the danger was past. She still trembled, and she felt far safer in Stephen's arms than not. She could no longer imagine her life as it had been before, without him. Or, rather, with him as her enemy. Never again.

"You outsmarted him. And what was that ninja move you pulled?"

She grinned. "Just call me the Culinary Ninja."

The quiet of the room descended on them. With no one to see—except the faces of aged photographs on the walls—

Stephen leaned in, a question in his eyes. Whitney smiled and, in answer, drew closer and wrapped her arms around his neck. His lips hovered maddeningly close to hers; she could almost feel energy sparking between them.

"Know what? We make a good team," Stephen murmured, eyes seeming to take in her features—her lips, her nose, her eyes, which he then gazed into with an intensity that nearly unhinged her knees altogether. "Maybe we can work together?"

Was that all he wanted? She swallowed. "In a kitchen? I suppose..."

"Well, sure, that," he said. "But I'd like to give *us* a chance too."

His lips hovered over hers for a second until, finally, he leaned in, pressing his mouth to hers, soft and tender at first. With each movement of his lips, she gave an answering one. Her head grew dizzy, but she didn't want to stop kissing him.

Perhaps he'd been polite by starting slow, but Whitney's anticipation grew and grew, heating until she could hardly stand it. She ran her fingers through his hair and pulled him closer, deepening the kiss.

He paused for just a moment with a smile of surprise before returning to kiss her again and again, deeper. Whitney would have been happy to stay there forever in the semidarkness, kissing Stephen and feeling his strong arms around her, smelling the scent she now thought of as Stephen.

He finally pulled away, and they both caught their breath. "That was better than Vahlrona."

"And Amano. Combined."

ABOUT ANNETTE LYON

Annette Lyon is a Whitney Award winner, a two-time recipient of Utah's Best in State medal for fiction, plus the author of ten novels, a cookbook, and a grammar guide as well as over a hundred magazine articles. She's a senior editor at Precision Editing Group and a cum laude graduate from BYU with a degree in English. When she's not writing, editing, knitting, or eating chocolate, she can be found mothering and avoiding the spots on the kitchen floor. Find her online:

Website: http://annettelyon.com
Blog: http://blog.annettelyon.com
Twitter: @AnnetteLyon

More Timeless Romance Anthologies:

Visit Our Blog:

TimelessRomanceAnthologies.blogspot.com

www.ingramcontent.com/pod-product-compliance
Lightning Source LLC
LaVergne TN
LVHW021756060526
838201LV00058B/3117